"So just do it. Post th

"Suzy, I never meant for this to happen."

Her dad had never meant to leave her. Mama had never meant to die. To leave her this mess to deal with. She knew all about people letting her down. Why should Will be any different? "I know. Just put the sign up."

He walked to his car and returned with a bright yellow sign. Used a marker to date it and put her address on it. Then he taped it to the front door.

No entry.

He sighed as he placed the last piece of Scotch tape on the corner of the sign and stepped back. "Are you going to be okay?"

"Why do you care?"

He dropped his hands to his sides. "Because you matter. You mean more to me than some job."

"But the job came first today, didn't it?" Suzy shook her head. "Just forget it."

Dear Reader,

Welcome back to Lake Mildred! The grandmother that I named this fictional town after recently passed away, but before she did I was able to give her a copy of my first book and share with her how I used names in the family in my story. Her eyes lit up when I mentioned ones that were familiar to her. I've continued that tradition with using names of family and friends in this book, but the characters are not like their real counterparts. Well, not all of them anyways....

There are reasons for why we keep people from getting too close to us. It could be the fear of getting hurt, being rejected or left behind—to name a few. Some folks use things or rules to build barriers around themselves. Suzy and Will each grew up with parents who fell into these categories, and now they're struggling with the reality of trying not to follow in those footsteps. Ultimately, patterns can be broken and love found.

I hope you enjoy our return to Lake Mildred. I'd love to connect with you on Facebook (facebook.com/syndipowellauthor) or Twitter (@syndipowell).

Syndi Powell

HEARTWARMING

Syndi Powell
Risk of Falling

HARLEQUIN® HEARTWARMING™

Recycling programs
for this product may
not exist in your area.

ISBN-13: 978-0-373-36688-0

Risk of Falling

HARLEQUIN®
™ www.Harlequin.com

Printed in U.S.A.

SYNDI POWELL

started writing stories when she was young, eager to find out what happened after the happily-ever-after in her favorite books, and has made it a lifelong pursuit. She's been reading Harlequin romance novels since she was in her teens and is thrilled to join the Harlequin team. She lives near Detroit with her husband, stepson and a cat and dog who believe they run the household. She loves to connect with readers on Twitter, @syndipowell, or on her Facebook author page, www.facebook.com/syndipowellauthor.

Books by Syndi Powell

HARLEQUIN HEARTWARMING

THE RELUCTANT BACHELOR

This book is dedicated with much love to my husband, Jim, who encouraged me to send the first book in to Harlequin. You've believed in me, cleaned house and put up with fast food dinners while I was on deadline, and celebrated every step in this journey. There have been those who have doubted our love story, but the proof is in the partnership we've created. Each day we get closer to our dreams.

CHAPTER ONE

SUZY BYLIN PROPPED herself up on one elbow on the couch and registered the sun flooding through the top right corner of the living room window. Had she missed her alarm? She found her cell phone on the floor next to her and checked the time. Not even noon. She peered closer. It wasn't even in the double digits yet. What had woken her up?

The pounding on the front door continued.

Oh yes, that was it. She groaned as she rose to her feet, grabbed her jacket that she'd thrown over the recliner after work, pulled it on like a robe and stumbled to the front door. "All right, I'm coming."

With another pull on the jacket, she took a deep breath and peeked through the peephole. Ding dong. Who was the hottie on her front porch? Tall. Dark blond. Definitely handsome. Maybe she was still dreaming? She opened the door an inch or two and stepped into the crack in case he was a hot psycho. Well, a professional psycho if the gray suit and tie were any indication. "Yes?"

"Ms. Bylin?"

Suzy shook her head and felt the curls hit the sides of her face. Great. She must look a fright. She reached up a hand to calm the frenzied chaos atop her head. Maybe she should have brushed her hair before answering the door, especially if she was going to be confronted by such attractive strangers. And yet, there was something familiar about his eyes. "Did you go to Lake Mildred High? Football team, right?"

"Why? Were you a cheerleader?"

She had been, but that was maybe five years after he had graduated. "Are you looking for my mom?"

He frowned and glanced down at his notebook. "No, she's dead." He looked up and his cheeks colored. "I mean, I attended her funeral. I saw you there...I mean, you must be her daughter. I'm sorry for your loss."

With effort, Suzy gave him a smile. She longed to assure him it was okay. But losing her mom wasn't okay. Never would be. It had been six months, and she still woke up expecting her mom to be there. Still reached for her phone when on break at work to call

and check on her. A half year had passed, but
the hole in her chest hadn't healed. "Is there
something I can help you with?"

He seemed to take a moment, as if sum-
moning his strength. The steel in his spine
straightened him several inches. "I'm sure
you're aware of the problems your mom had
with the town."

Um, no. This was the first she'd heard.
But then Mama had liked to keep her secrets even after Suzy had moved in to care
for her in the last year. She frowned. "Problems such as…"

"Such as the neighbors' complaints about
all the clutter and trash on her property." He
marked something off in his notebook. "Or
the notices from the town that she needed
to get the yard cleaned up." Another check.
"And if she couldn't get it cleaned up, the
town would clean it for her at her expense
or evict her."

Suzy paled at each accusation. Okay. So
her mom hadn't been Mrs. Clean. Or Mrs.
Organized. But to threaten to take her home?
Things couldn't be that bad.

Could they?

She grimaced and tried to recall his name.
Rivers? Meadow? "Listen, Mr.—"

"Stone. Will Stone."

"Oh, that's right." She clutched her hands into fists at her sides. "My mom was sick for the last few years. She couldn't get out of bed for most of those, much less go outside and clean up her yard. And she never told me about any notices."

"My file says she received six."

Six? Crud. What had you been thinking, Mama? She glanced behind her and knew if Mr. Stone could see inside the living room and to the rest of the house, he'd have more of a problem than with the backyard. "Okay. Six notices. Well, I'm in charge now. And it will get taken care of."

"Miss Bylin, I knew of your mom's illness, so I didn't pursue any legal action. But time, just like my patience, has grown thin." He removed a yellow letter from his pocket. "You have two weeks. Or the town will bring its own crew to clear everything out. And we don't come cheap."

She nodded and accepted the letter. Opened it. Read it. Then clutched it in her hand, wrinkling the page. "Understood." She waited for him to leave, but he continued to stare down at her with those ice blue eyes of his. She glanced at her painted hot pink toe-nails. "Was there something else?"

"Are those scarecrows on your pants?"

Suzy grinned and pulled on the leg of the cotton scrubs she'd worn to work last night. "Aren't they a hoot? My seniors love them."

"I'm sure they do." He almost smiled, and it gave Suzy a glimpse of how more good looking he could be. The frown quickly returned, shattering her hopes. "I'm going to assess the backyard before I leave."

"Sure thing. Good night."

He looked at her as if she'd sprung a second head. "It's daytime. Are you always this flighty?"

She shut the door behind her and locked the bottom lock. Flighty? Okay, so maybe her life was upside down with working nights, but she was capable. Competent. And more than able to tidy up a backyard.

She yawned as she dropped the letter next to her car keys on the coffee table and returned to the couch to settle under the blankets. She'd deal with the notice later. But first, sleep.

Maybe even a dream about hot strangers showing up on her doorstep.

WILL FROWNED AT the closed door. Miss Bylin certainly resembled her mother in personality, but not looks. While Mrs. Bylin had been large and imposing, her daughter was tiny. Petite. Reddish blonde curls framing her face. And brown eyes that held laughter.

But he had a feeling that the sprite could sweet-talk him into giving her more time, exactly like her mother had on numerous occasions.

He walked around the house to the backyard and unlatched the wooden gate and went through. Nothing had changed, except he counted more trash bags that hadn't made it roadside for collection. Instead they leaned against the closest wall of the garage. He couldn't understand why such a simple thing was so hard to do. It wasn't difficult to remember trash day if you had a system. A way of remembering. He made a note in his book and moved on.

The abandoned car still took up space toward the back. The tires had long ago gone flat, and Will doubted that the engine would start. Two clothesline poles listed to the side. A rusted swing set missing the swings. A slide that a younger Miss Bylin may have played on, but now laid on its side, abandoned.

Elbow grease and some muscles. That's what Miss Bylin needed. That and a plan to conquer the yard methodically. Inch by inch. And he could scratch this eyesore off his to-do list.

Finally.

Maybe then he could prove to the town council they needed him. And his job would be off their chopping block.

He made some more notes in his book. Took a few pictures on his cell phone. Until it started ringing. "Will Stone."

"Will, it's Toby at the bank."

Why would his mom's boss be phoning him? "Is my mom okay?"

"That's why I'm calling. She passed out and fell. We can't wake her." He paused on the other end. "I've called an ambulance, and they're on their way. But you might want to get here too."

Oh, Ma. What is going on? "I'm on my way."

Any other business could wait. This was his mom.

WILL QUICKLY PARKED his pickup truck, turned off the engine and removed his keys. Got out and slammed the door shut. Winced at the ambulance with its lights flashing, waiting near the entrance.

He ran across the lot to the red brick building and pushed open the front door. Inside the lobby, the branch manager, Toby, waited for him. "She's back here in the break room."

Will followed him as the manager ushered him to where he found his mom sitting in a chair and hooked up to an oxygen tank. She looked up at him and removed the mask.

"I'm fine. Tell them."

He noted her pale appearance. The fine sheen of moisture at her hairline. The pain as well as the panic in her eyes. He knelt down beside her and put his hand on her knee. "What happened?"

His mom shrugged and frowned as the paramedic replaced the mask on her face. Will turned to the paramedic for answers. "Mrs. Stone passed out and was unresponsive when we arrived. Her pulse and breathing are abnormal. She's been given oxygen and chewable aspirin. We'd like to take her to the hospital for treatment."

They thought she'd had a heart attack? He

tried to remember what the doctor had said at his mom's last visit, but her heart hadn't been discussed. They'd discussed her cholesterol and how she could lose a few pounds. But nothing about her heart having problems. Still, it wouldn't hurt to get her checked out. Will nodded. "Good."

Ma removed her oxygen mask. "Not good. I'm not going."

"Oh, yes you are." Will turned to the paramedic. "I'll follow you guys to the hospital."

"I told you I'm not going. I got a little dizzy. That's all."

Will closed his eyes and looked to the heavens. "Ma."

"I'm fine, honey." She tried to stand, but was urged back down by the paramedic. She swatted at her hands. "I'm not an invalid."

"Not saying you are. But you need to go to the hospital." Will stood and removed the cell phone from his suit pocket. He needed reinforcements. "I'll call Tori and ask her to meet us there."

"Don't you dare."

Toby stepped forward and held up his hands in surrender. "I already did, Eva. Called her right after I called Will."

Thank goodness. Will appreciated the

manager's quick thinking even if his mom groaned and sat back down in the chair as if defeated.

The paramedic put the oxygen mask back over Eva's mouth and spoke into the walkie talkie attached to her shoulder. "Bring in the gurney, Pete."

Ma furiously shook her head while Will nodded. "You will get on that gurney if I have to strap you on it myself."

"And if he doesn't, I will." His sister Tori pushed forward and knelt by their mom's feet. He noticed that she'd lightened her dark blond hair to a platinum blond like his. Uh oh. Not a good sign. He'd deal with that later.

Tori patted their mom's knee. "We'll make sure you get the best care." She looked up at her brother for confirmation. "Right, Will?"

Of course they would. He nodded. "The very best."

The snap and squeak of the gurney's wheels drew their attention towards the door. They stepped out of the break room to let the paramedics do their jobs. Tori reached out her hand, and Will clasped it in his. They'd seen a similar scene with their father when they'd been just teens. They might be older now, but they weren't ready to lose their mother too. Not yet.

The paramedics wheeled the gurney out of the break room and down the hall through the bank lobby. Co-workers stopped conversations and turned to watch. Many stepped forward to check on Eva. She held up her hands as if parting the Red Sea. "I'm fine. They're overreacting. I won't be gone long. You'll see."

The paramedics pushed the gurney as if it was a barge carrying a queen in front of her subjects. She waved and offered assurances she was okay.

Will hoped she was right. Because by the looks of things, it didn't seem that way. One step at a time, he reminded himself. They only needed to find out what they were dealing with first.

Once the ambulance was off to the hospital, Will turned to Tori. "Why don't we take my truck over? I'll bring you back later for your car."

With their mom gone, Tori nodded but released the tears he knew she'd been holding back the entire time, just like their father had taught them. Will put his arm around her and led her to his ear. Helped her in. Found
truck

the box of tissues in the middle console and offered it to her. He ran around to the other side and started the truck before he'd shut his door and fastened his seat belt.

He turned the radio volume low and reached out to hold Tori's hand. She wiped her eyes with the tissue in her other hand. "It's spooky, you know? Just like when we lost dad."

Will kept his eyes on the road, but squeezed her hand. "Mom's tough."

"Dad was Marine tough."

Will winced. "With a bad heart."

"You think that's what this is? A heart attack?" Tori sniffled and wiped her eyes. "I didn't have enough time to ask Toby for details. I was volunteering at the boys' school when the call came."

"I don't know what this is. Honest." He hoped it was something simple. Maybe she'd forgotten to eat breakfast this morning, and her blood sugar was low. Maybe she had an inner ear infection that had thrown off her balance. Those were scenarios he could handle more than a heart attack. He took the turn off to the highway, accelerated and glanced behind him as he merged into traffic. "But I can guarantee we will get the best care."

"Did you call Carol or Joan?"

Their sisters. Who they hadn't heard from since Christmas, nine months ago. Will looked over at Tori. "Not until we have more answers. You know how they are."

"Think they'll come up to visit?"

He doubted it. After their dad died almost twenty years before, the family had splintered. His older sisters had gotten married and moved out of Lake Mildred as soon as they could, as if the small northern Michigan town couldn't keep them prisoner anymore. They had both moved out of state, Carol to Arizona, Joan to Georgia. It had been mom, Tori and him for all those years since. With the occasional phone call and even more rare visit. "I don't know."

"Mom's not going to want to slow down." She glanced at him. "She's still working. Still involved in the garden club. The library literacy club. She watches the boys for me after school at least twice a week." Fresh tears started at the thought. "What if this is my fault?"

"Before we go assigning blame, let's find out what we're dealing with. But no." He squeezed her hand again. "None of this is your fault."

He slowed down for their exit and breathed a sigh of relief when the hospital came into view. The sooner the doctors could examine his mom, the sooner they could find out what was wrong.

Then fix it.

CHAPTER TWO

SUZY'S ALARM SOUNDED from her cell phone. She sat up. Stretched. Rubbed her eyes. It had taken a while, but she'd finally fallen asleep. Good thing too. She had to work tonight at the nursing home.

She turned off the alarm and stood. Her eyes fell on the yellow notice. Oh, right. She'd forgotten about that. Two weeks to clean up the backyard shouldn't be hard, right? Just a matter of getting the trash bags to the curb on pick up day. Straighten a few things. No big deal.

After she made her afternoon cup of coffee and added plenty of cream and sugar, she pried open the sliding door that led to the deck. Stood and observed the yard. Tried to see what Mr. Stone had seen.

Yep, those trash bags were waiting by the garage. Had to be at least a dozen of them. But she worked on collection days, and by the time she got home, she wanted to sleep. Not haul trash to the curb. And that's if they hadn't already picked up her neighborhood. She could transport them herself to the dump, and probably would have to, but that meant more time taken out of her already busy, upside down schedule. Four twelve hour days left only three to catch up on everything, and that was if she was lucky enough to have those three days off instead of getting called in at the last minute to cover a shift at the nursing home. Not that she minded. It was easier to keep busy. Less time to think. To remember. To grieve.

Then there was the Camaro that had been parked in the backyard since Suzy had been eight or nine. Shortly before her dad had left her mother and her, he'd driven it there to work on the engine. But he never had. And so it sat, almost twenty years later. She wondered if she could even find the keys for it. Maybe in the glass bowl Mama had kept on her dresser.

She took her coffee with her and approached the rusted heap. It had been her dad's pride and joy once. The classic car he had wanted to restore. But he couldn't fix it any more than he could deal with the peo-

ple in his life. Instead, he'd left it behind for
them to deal with along with everything else.

She'd asked Mama why he hadn't stayed,
but answers had been rare. He'd never called,
never sent a gift for her birthday or Christmas. As if once he'd gone, they no longer
existed to him. Part of her wondered how
much of his absence was possibly due to her
mom keeping him away. Maybe he'd wanted
to see her, but Mama wouldn't let him. Or
maybe he just hadn't cared. Suzy had tried
finding him when Mama got sick, but it was
as if he'd disappeared completely that spring
morning when he'd said he was leaving for
work and never came home.

She shielded her eyes and peered into the
passenger side window. Noticed evidence
that some animal had made it a temporary
home. Shredded paper nested about a foot
wide. And, if the soft mewls were any indication, the resident had left her babies behind.

Suzy set the coffee mug on the roof of
the car and pulled on the handle to open the
door. With much effort, it wrenched free. She
popped her head in and wrinkled her nose
at the stench. She carefully kneeled on the
passenger seat and bent forward. Between

the driver's seat and the control pedals, three gray and white kittens huddled together. They couldn't have been more than a few days, maybe a week, old. Their eyes still closed. So tiny. So helpless.

Suzy glanced around the car for something to use to carry them inside. Nothing. Despite her mom's lackluster housecleaning skills, the interior of the car was empty. She'd have to go find something. "Okay, guys. I'll be right back. Don't go anywhere."

She unfolded herself from the car, slammed the door shut and grabbed her coffee mug from the car roof. She ran to the house and once inside, placed the mug in the sink before searching through piles of stuff until she found an old wicker Easter basket that still had plastic green grass inside. Figuring that the grass would act as a cushion, she placed a clean tea towel over the grass and sprinted back to the car.

The driver's side door took less effort to open. Probably because she'd found her mom sitting in the seat more than once over the years. She stooped down and carefully removed each kitten and placed it in the basket. Took her precious cargo into the house. Found a baby bottle in one of the boxes.

Washed the bottle since dust coated the surface and then filled it with milk. On the couch she took turns feeding each kitten and stroking its head.

As she did so, she wondered what had happened to their mom. They were orphans, abandoned just like her, and that connection made her heart break for them. "It's okay. I'll make sure that someone takes care of you. Promise."

They looked little more than skeletons covered in fur, and they would need more care than she could give. Propping the bottle on a pillow so that the last kitten could still eat, she dialed her best girlfriend Presley's number at the animal rescue. "Hey, Pres. I've got some little ones for you. Do you have room?"

A big sigh on the other end. "I'll find room. What have you got?"

"The cutest little kittens in the world." Suzy looked them over again and smiled as they rolled around each other trying to find a comfortable sleeping position. Almost as if they didn't want to be separated from each other for very long. "Well, they will be once they get some meat on their bones. And they probably need shots. I found them abandoned in Daddy's car."

"Any sign of the mother?"

Suzy shook her head and petted the two kittens who had fallen asleep after eating their fill. "Orphans. Just like me."

Funny how that word still hurt after six months. She kept the smile on her face. As if her best friend could see her through the phone. "I can bring them in before I go to work tonight."

"Yeah, okay." The line stayed silent. "Suze, are you all right?"

How many times had she been asked that question since her mom died? She gave the standard answer. Better that than admit she missed Mama so much it ached. "Perfect. Wait till you see these cuties." She smiled brighter. "They're going to break your heart."

"That's what I'm afraid of."

Once the last kitten had eaten and fallen asleep, Suzy took her shower then got ready for work. She had an hour or so before she needed to be at the nursing home, so she could stay at the animal rescue and help out with the animals. She knew Presley was swamped with strays, which meant less time to walk them and care for them. Suzy could volunteer to do that for her friend.

She nodded. That's what she'd do. And she'd deal with the backyard tomorrow.

SEVEN HOURS. WILL paced the waiting room of the hospital. They'd been there over seven hours with no word. No diagnosis. No solution.

Tori sat on a plastic chair, her head bent over a romance novel, but he could see that she'd been on the same page for the last thirty minutes. She was just as worried as he was.

"Where's the doctor? It shouldn't be taking this long." He stood in front of Tori and crossed his arms over his chest. Waiting for her to look at him.

Instead, she kept her eyes on the page. "Stop watching the clock and pacing, Will. It'll go faster." She looked up and patted the empty chair beside hers. "Now sit. Read a magazine. Or go get us some snacks. We haven't had lunch, and I'm starving."

He shook his head. "If I'm not here when the doctor comes in…."

"Then I'll talk to him. Not the end of the world." She put her bookmark in the book and laid it beside her. "Or how about I'll go get us some food. I need something." She stood and grabbed her purse from the floor. "Snickers bar? Mountain Dew? Doritos?"

"Fine. Whatever."

He took out his wallet and handed her a twenty which she waved away. "I've got this. And I'll call my neighbor Teresa and ask if she can pick up the boys from school." She checked her watch. "Hopefully I'll catch her before she leaves to get her son Noah."

She flipped her phone open and dialed as she walked out of the waiting room. Will watched her leave then took a seat in her abandoned chair. He noticed her romance novel and picked it up. Flipped through it. Read a particularly racy scene and raised his eyebrows. What was going on with his sister? First the dyed hair. Now the sexy book? Maybe she was finally over her ex.

About time.

When Tori returned with a bulging plastic bag from the gift shop, he held up the book to her. "You're reading this?"

She nodded and took the seat next to him, before handing him a wrapped sandwich and pop can. "Teresa recommended it. It's actually quite good."

He noted the bookmark was more than halfway through the book. "Obviously." He unwrapped the sandwich and toasted her with it. "Thanks."

"Anything for you." She popped the tab on her drink then took a sip. "Still no word?"

Will swallowed his bite and shook his head. "It's gotta be soon, right? I mean how long can they make us wait for answers?"

"Teresa said she'd keep the boys at her house as long as I need her to." She took a deep breath. "She's been a good friend. Especially since the divorce."

Will put one arm around her. "The hits keep coming, huh?"

She swiped her eyes with the back of her hand. "You don't know how hard it is being a single mom. There's no one around to give me a hand. To answer the nonstop questions. Or deal with the increasing emotions. To tell them no. And then there's the hormones." She shuddered as if a cold finger had run up her spine.

He bumped her shoulder. "Whenever you need me, just call."

"I know. But I've got to do this on my own. I can't depend on you all the time." She straightened in her seat. "Stones know how to get the job done."

She unwrapped her sandwich and took a bite. He did the same, and they sat in silence for a while. The only sounds were other families chatting while they waited for news and a talk show on the television in the corner.

After eating their late lunch, Will gathered the trash and threw it out in the receptacle. Tori returned to her book, so he checked his email on his phone and waited for word on his mom.

A doctor in blue-green scrubs entered the room. "Stone family?"

About time. Will and Tori stood and held hands as the doctor approached. "Why don't we step into the privacy room?"

Uh oh. That couldn't be good.

They followed her into the room. Tori sat on the bench while he remained standing. He could take whatever news it was. He could be strong. For his mom. For Tori.

For himself.

"I'm Dr. Westphal, and I've been supervising your mom's care since they brought her in." She consulted her tablet. "She arrived in the emergency room exhibiting pain and a possible bone fracture."

Will frowned. "She broke something? It's not her heart? I mean, we assumed…"

Dr. Westphal looked up at him. "The more persistent problem right now is her fractured hip. We need to get her into surgery."

"You bet. I'll sign whatever form you need me to."

"Mrs. Stone has already given her consent and will go into surgery to repair the fracture shortly after you see her." Dr. Westphal sighed. "But the problem is after surgery." She looked up from the tablet at first Will, then Tori. "She'll be in the hospital for a few days but then will need long term care. Physical therapy. Possibly a hip replacement. And when she's stronger, chemotherapy."

Will lost the strength of his legs and sat next to Tori. No. Not this. "Cancer then."

"We're still running tests, but it appears the cancer is attacking her bones. Making them brittle and fragile." Dr. Westphal took a seat in front of them. "A simple fall should not break bones, even in a woman your mother's age."

Tori started to cry softly beside him. He held her hand and squeezed. Their mom had cancer.

He closed his eyes to keep the panic from

invading his mind. When he opened them, he gave a short nod. "How bad is it? I mean, how long…"

The doctor shrugged. "We won't know any answers until more tests can be run. Let's focus on repairing the hip first."

Will nodded again. "We can see her?"

The doctor stood. "I'll take you to her."

As they followed the doctor down the white, sterile hallway, Will turned to Tori. "No tears in front of mom. She needs our strength right now."

Tori nodded and wiped her face. "I know the drill."

Dr. Westphal led them through a maze of hospital beds and curtained off areas. Eventually she pushed a curtain aside to reveal his mom hooked up to monitors and an IV. She looked tiny in the huge bed. Fragile. Lost. She opened her eyes and gave them a smile. "My babies."

The doctor left them, pulling the curtain closed behind her. Will moved to his mom's side and took her hand. His emotions were pressing on him, but he'd deal with them later. "Are you in any pain?"

Eva shook her head and pointed to the

IV. "They're giving me the good stuff." She pointed to the end of her bed. "Let's talk."

"They need to take you to surgery."

"They will." She pointed at the bed again. "I want to spend time with you before they take me away. Now sit."

Tori took a seat on one side of her. Afraid to jostle his mom and cause pain, Will stood beside her and held her hand. Besides, he could control himself standing. Be a good soldier like his dad and the Marines had trained him. He tensed his muscles, ready for whatever followed.

His mom's expression softened. "The doctor told you, didn't she? She asked if she could, and I said yes, but I'd hoped—"

"We'll fight this, Mom. I'll get the best doctors. Specialists." Emotion threatened to close his throat, and he swallowed it right away. "Stones don't go down without a fight."

His mom nodded. "Or they die trying."

Tori started crying, holding their mom's hand to her cheek. Will kept swallowing, unable to say anything. Unable to offer anything. Finally, his mom gave a soft smile. "Sorry. I didn't mean it like that."

Will cleared his throat. "It's okay, Mom."

A nurse pulled the curtain open. "They're ready for you, Mrs. Stone." She turned to Will. "I can escort you to the surgical waiting room."

Tori leaned over and kissed her mom on the cheek. "Lovey."

"Lovey."

Will kissed his mom and rested his forehead on hers. "Lovey."

"Lovey." She patted his cheek. "Everything is going to be fine. I promise."

Fine. Right.

A team of nurses surrounded his mom's hospital bed then wheeled her away. The first nurse led them to a different waiting room than before, but it looked much the same. "Surgery should be about two hours. Dr. Westphal will keep you updated."

Will sighed as he took a seat near the window. Tori fished in her purse for her cell phone. "I'll just call Teresa and tell her I'll be late."

She stepped away, leaving Will with his thoughts.

His mom had cancer. Life wasn't ever going to be the same after today. No matter what they needed to do to fight this, they'd do it. If she needed chemo, bone marrow transplant, whatever, she would get it. She had to get better because their family didn't work without her in it. She was their center.

He stood and resumed his pacing. How was he supposed to move on from this? Would they survive? He glanced at his phone. He should call Joanie and Carol. They had a right to know even if they didn't choose to be involved. He started to dial the first number.

SUZY PARKED HER bright yellow VW bug in front of the animal rescue shelter. She must have been a good girl that day to get such a prime parking spot. Despite her intention to arrive early, she would only have enough time to drop off the kittens and then hurry to work before she was late. Again.

She hooked her arm through the Easter basket and carried it with her to the front door. The receptionist Thoramae spotted her and rushed to open the door for her. "Hey, Suzy. More critters for us?" The older woman with tight permed curls peeked into the basket and smiled. "Aren't they the cutest fur balls?"

"They just need some TLC." Suzy squeezed past Thoramae. "Is Presley in her office?"

"You bet. Can't get her to leave." Thora-mae returned to her spot behind the reception desk. "She's been asking for you."

"Thanks." Suzy looked down into her basket. Two of the kittens slept while the third licked its paw. "You're gonna love Pres. She'll help you get big and strong."

Presley sat at her desk and looked up when Suzy walked in. "I'd ask if you always talk to yourself, but I know the answer to that one." She came around the desk and gave Suzy a hug. "How are you doing today?"

"Fine." Suzy avoided her friend's eyes and placed the basket on Presley's desk. "Tell me you can help these guys." Presley picked one of the kittens and held him up. "He's awfully scrawny. Good thing you found them when you did. Temperatures are supposed to fall over the weekend. They could have frozen out there." She held the kitten close to her chest and stroked his head. "With a little time and a lot of food, they should be fine."

Suzy wilted with relief into a chair. "Good. I can't deal with any more loss."

"Are you sure you're okay?" Presley put down the kitten and turned her attention to Suzy. Probed her with the same intensity she usually reserved for her animal patients. "We haven't hung out lately. Or talked much."

"Well, you know my work schedule. Midnight shifts don't help a social life." Suzy gave a forced chuckle. "I'm fine. Tired, maybe. They had me working six days last week." Her friend seemed to accept her words. At least for now. Suzy leaned in closer to Presley. "But I did meet a guy."

Presley clapped her hands and perched on the edge of her desk. "When? How? Details, details."

"Actually he showed up at my front door." Suzy let that sink in then laughed at Presley's expression. "He's some kind of code enforcement inspector who knew Mama. Told her she had to clean up the backyard."

"I can figure out how well that went over."

Suzy rolled her eyes. "No kidding. He's given me two weeks to clean it up. Or else."

"Or else what?"

Suzy shrugged. "They charge me to get someone else to clean it up, I guess." She thought about the mess. "It might be easier if they did. It's not like they'd take the house from me. Right?" She wished she sounded more confident.

"You can't afford that, Suze. Besides, I

can help you." Her friend crossed her legs at her ankles. For a moment, Suzy envied her long legs since she'd been born with short ones. Pres leaned back on her desk. "Anytime. Just ask."

"But your job here…"

Presley laughed and shook her head. "Despite what Thoramae says, I do take time off from here occasionally." She bit her lip and watched Suzy. "I notice you talked about what he did. But not what he looks like. That good, huh?"

Suzy fanned herself. "Hotter than hot. In an uptight, straitlaced kind of way." She thought back to Mr. Stone. "He kind of reminds me of that guy who plays James Bond now."

Presley smiled wider. "Yummy."

"No kidding." Suzy stood and hitched her purse higher on her shoulder. She glanced at the clock behind Presley's desk and sighed. "I've got to get going, but…" She glanced at the kittens one more time. "You'll keep me updated?"

"Absolutely." Presley hugged her again.

"And I mean it. I'll help you. You don't have to do this on your own, Suze."

"I know." That's what she said, but she didn't quite believe it.

CHAPTER THREE

THIS WAS THE longest two hours in history. Had to be. Maybe time had stopped. Will glanced at his watch then held it up to his ear. Nope. Watch still ticked. Hands still moved. Seconds. Minutes. Hours.

He slammed the magazine he'd been reading on to the plastic chair next to him and stretched. Moments later, he walked to the wall of windows that overlooked the parking lot and put his palm against the cool glass. He watched as a woman hurried into the hospital. Did she have a loved one here fighting for their life too? Maybe her daughter had had a baby. Or a friend needed a ride home from work.

He shook his head, scattering the thoughts like wind blowing dried leaves. If he didn't get out of here soon, he'd be writing poetry about hospital visiting hours or penning that mystery novel he'd always dreamed of. He turned from the window and found that Tori had nodded off, her head back, mouth open. He took his cell phone from his pocket and snapped a quick picture. She'd kill him if he posted it on Facebook, but it might be fun.

Tori stirred, then squeezed her eyes shut before opening them and finding him watching her. She rubbed her face. "Did I miss the surgeon?"

He shook his head. "How late did you tell Teresa you'd be? It's close to seven already."

"It's okay. She said she'd feed the hooligans dinner." She took out her cell phone and started texting. "But I'll let them know I'm still here."

"I can't believe you got them cell phones. They're only fourteen." He took the seat next to her.

Tori finished typing and frowned at him. "Fourteen and involved in so many activities that I feel more like a chauffeur than a mom some days. They need to be able to get a hold of me at all times."

"We didn't have phones when we were their age."

"Well, Dad wasn't exactly generous, was he? No, he lived by the rules of shoulds and should nots." Tori stopped texting. "Don't get me wrong. I loved him, but I don't think he had any clue about how kids should be raised."

"He was a Marine captain. He had to know how to lead his men into battle, not raise kids." Will couldn't let it go. "So are you overcompensating for Dad's strictness or Shawn's absence?"

Tori's head snapped up, her eyes blazing. She'd be breathing fire if she could. "Don't tell me how to bring up my sons because that's an argument you won't win. You're as clueless as Dad was."

He bit back his retort mostly because she was right. He didn't have the first clue about raising kids. He marveled at how well Tori was doing on her own.

They sat in silence for a while. Then Will reached over and grabbed his sister's hand. "You're a good mom."

Tori squeezed his hand. "Thanks." She rested her head on his shoulder. "Maybe I do indulge them more than I would if Shawn was still around, but they're missing out on so much."

"Shawn's the one missing out." He kissed the top of her head.

She sighed then got to her feet. "I'm going

to get some coffee or something. You want anything?"

"Coffee sounds perfect." He picked up the magazine he'd discarded. "Think I'll take this quiz and see what kind of girlfriend I am."

Tori rolled her eyes, but laughed. He watched her leave then started flipping pages. Where was that quiz?

SUZY PULLED INTO the parking lot of the nursing home and finished singing with an edgy rock song before grabbing her work bag and heading inside. Still humming, she opened the door for a couple leaving. As she passed the front desk, her shift supervisor Rita glanced from Suzy to the clock on the wall. Five minutes early. Whew.

Suzy walked to the employee lounge and put her work bag in the locker. The frozen dinner and bottle of water she'd dug out first, she put in the staff fridge. She'd chosen her flashiest scrubs for today: bright purple top with neon yellow bottoms and yellow crocs. The seniors seemed to like the bright colors. Those who could still see anyway.

She checked the schedule posted on the bulletin board and flexed her shoulders. She enjoyed the seven at night to seven in the morning shift. More patients, less families. Too much family only reminded her of what she didn't have.

She bumped the door with her hip and entered the hallway, slinging her stethoscope around her shoulders. She checked in at the west nurse's station where she found Carly signing off on her tablet. "How's it been today?"

Carly shrugged. "Fine. A bit too quiet, so you might find yourself with some night crawlers later."

Suzy nodded. It seemed that her seniors loved to save their drama for her shift. "They do keep life interesting." She turned on her tablet and brought up the charts. "Any new residents?"

"Not today. But you might want to keep an eye on Mrs. Henderson in sixteen." Carly leaned in closer. "Her daughter was here this afternoon. The doctors aren't optimistic about the new treatment, and she's taken it pretty hard."

Mrs. Henderson had once been crowned Miss Pickle at the Pickle Festival back in the 1920s. Or so she said. She also claimed that she'd been screen tested for the role of Scarlett O'Hara but lost out at the last minute to Vivien Leigh. With an Alzheimer's diagnosis, Suzy was never sure which stories were true and which ones weren't, but they were all entertaining. "I'll be sure to make her my first stop. Thanks, Carly."

The other nurse patted Suzy on the shoulder before leaving the station. "Good luck. You're going to need it."

Suzy read over the notes from the day then checked the monitors. Dinner had already been served, and televisions in the rooms as well as in the community room blared with strains of the music from "Jeopardy". It was also Tuesday and that meant Yatzhee night in the dining room. She'd better make her rounds then check back to make sure no fights had broken out. Those seniors were serious about their games.

Mrs. Henderson's room was first. She poked her head in and found the older woman sitting in a chair looking out her window at the garden. Leaves swirled as the wind blew and more fell on to the lawn. Suzy sighed. "Pretty time of year, isn't it? I love it when the leaves shed their green summer wardrobe and put on their reds and golds and oranges."

Mrs. Henderson didn't say anything. Suzy

went farther into the room and went to stand next to her chair. Suzy put a hand on her shoulder. "Don't you wish you could paint this scene?"

"Did I ever tell you about the time Vivien Leigh stole my part in a movie?" The older woman looked up at Suzy, but her eyes didn't focus.

Suzy crouched next to the chair. "No, I don't think you did. Why don't you tell me?"

BY THE TIME Dr. Westphal entered the waiting room, Will's stomach threatened to eat itself if he didn't find something else first. But thoughts of food fled when their name was called.

Tori and Will followed the doctor into a private room off the hallway. A surgeon in clean scrubs joined them. "The surgery was more complicated than expected. Although your mother is in recovery now."

Will nodded. "The fracture?"

"It's been repaired. But the cancer appears more advanced than we first thought."

Tori grabbed his hand. "What does that mean? She's going to die?"

The doctor looked at them both over her eyeglasses. "It means things get complicated. The fracture needs to heal before Dr. Lewis can discuss treatment options, but it also means your mother needs to stay in long term care to prevent any more bones from breaking."

Long term care. That meant money, and lots of it. Will's mind started calculating his mom's insurance coverage, amount of savings, and saw a lot of dollars flying out of both. "So a nursing home."

"Lake Mildred's is not only close, but one of the best." She handed him a few pamphlets, the one advertising their hometown's option on top. "I'd recommend that you check it out sooner rather than later. We need to have a plan in place before she's released from here."

Tori covered her face. He put a hand on her shoulder, hoping to… What? Convince her things weren't bad? Because it sounded like they were moving from bad to worse. Still he gave her a reassuring squeeze on the shoulder. "Are we talking days? A week?"

"Like I said, the sooner, the better." She opened the door. "Would you like to see your mother?"

He nodded and helped his sister to her feet. In the recovery room, he stood at the bedside of his mom who seemed to still be sleeping. Tori stood on the other side of the bed, holding their mom's hand. Will looked across at his sister. "What are we going to do, Tori?"

She looked up at him, the surprise written on her face. "I thought you would know."

"I don't have a clue." He shook his head and closed his eyes. He'd been a teen when his father died. His only involvement had been visiting the hospital with his sisters, hoping and praying that he would get better. His mom had made the decisions. Had faced the tough choices. Now she needed him to do the same for her.

And he didn't know what to do.

He opened his eyes and saw Tori staring at him. "Are you okay, Will?"

No. Not at all.

But he nodded, knowing that's what she needed. "We'll figure things out."

Their mom stirred, opened her eyes, but then faded into unconsciousness again. "She's not going to want to go to a nursing home. And with my job and yours, plus the kids…"

"We do have two more sisters."

He wanted to laugh. They'd be no help, but he'd give them a chance to step up. To see if they wanted to be involved or, as he suspected, would leave things up to him and Tori. "They still haven't returned my first two calls, but we'll see."

"I've heard a lot of good things about the seniors' home in Lake Mildred." Tori stroked their mom's arm, but her eyes stayed on him. "It would be close to both of us so we could visit often."

He nodded. It would be the easy choice, but was it the right one? He'd always been good at fixing things. But to make decisions for his mom? What if he made the wrong one? In the Marines, he'd learned how to succeed, how to repair a situation. But he felt out of depth here for the first time. He needed to do some recon, he realized, to make the informed choice. "If I can set up a visit tomorrow, would you be able to go?"

She looked down at their mom. Reached out to move a curl that had fallen on her face. "I'll make sure I can."

At least he wouldn't be alone. At least he had Tori.

IN THEORY, SUZY finished her shift at seven a.m.

By nine-thirty that morning, she admitted

things weren't going according to plan. She still had paperwork to complete after the ambulance left with her patient who had been complaining of chest pains. Mr. Wyckoff loved to complain, but those kinds of complaints weren't meant to be played around with.

She yawned and stretched before continuing her report on Mr. Wyckoff, noting his earlier symptoms. Rita passed by the desk with a man and woman, probably showing the facility to potential clients. She stopped the tour at the nurses' station. "And this is one of our favorite nurses, Suzy Bylin."

She stood and held out a hand to the woman first. "Checking us out for your parent?" She turned to face the man and paused. "Mr. Stone."

He looked tired compared to yesterday. Worry had etched lines next to his ice blue eyes and left bags below them. He frowned at her. "I didn't realize you worked here, Ms. Bylin."

"I didn't know you kept tabs on me." She flipped over her tablet to keep the details of her report confidential. She didn't need this; didn't need to see the man who could make her life miserable at home and now here at work. "But I think you'll find that we take good care of our patients. We provide not only nursing care, but activities designed to keep up their spirits while they rehabilitate."

"You sound like the brochure."

Mr. Stone's frown deepened, and she felt her smile widen. He wasn't going to bring her down. Nope, he wouldn't ruin her day. "I only speak the truth."

The woman next to him nudged him in the side. "I apologize for Will. He's not usually this grumpy, but we're worried about our mom. She fell and fractured her hip, so now we need somewhere for her to recover."

She was his sister then. Why that thought made her feel better, Suzy didn't want to explore. So she focused on their visit, and reached out and touched her hand. "I'm so sorry. But I can promise that your mom will get the best care here. I'll see to it personally."

The sister smiled and covered Suzy's hand with her own. "That means a lot. Thank you." Again, she nudged her brother. "Right, Will?"

He looked at his sister then at Suzy. Blinked several times. In those ice blue eyes, she could see he was out of his depth. That what was happening was not easy for him. And that made him approachable. Relatable. Her heart softened to him. Finally he gave a curt nod. "Yes."

Suzy continued to look at him. Wanting to soothe the wrinkles in his forehead. Remove the fear and doubt shining out of his eyes. "If there are any questions you have or anything you need…"

An alarm went off, and Suzy focused on the monitors. Room thirteen, Mr. Taber. She left them and ran down the hall. Mr. Taber was lying on his bed, eyes closed. She leaned over him to check his vitals. Still breathing. Good. She noticed that his heartbeat was weak and irregular, the numbers said forty beats per minute. Without a thought, she began hands-on CPR. Rita joined her in the room and glanced at the monitors. "I paged the doctor."

"Good. I think it's a drug interaction. We just switched his meds last night." She continued her compressions. She looked up from her task and saw Will watching them. "Mr. Stone, we'll have to finish the tour later. You need to go back to the nurses' station."

He nodded and walked away. After a minute or so, the doctor on call arrived and took over the situation. With the group's effort, they were able to resuscitate Mr. Taber and stabilize his condition. Suzy went back to the nurses' station to make notes on Mr. Taber's condition and found Will and his sister still standing there. She pasted a smile on her face again. "Sorry about your tour getting cut short."

"Does that happen a lot?" he asked.

"Define a lot." She shrugged. "It happens enough. But I can guarantee we will do our best to care for your mom and her needs."

He gave a short nod, and his sister offered to shake hands again, and they did. "Nice to meet you, Miss Bylin."

"Likewise." And she meant it. She could sense a kindred spirit in this woman. Something about how she smiled or her concern for her mom made something inside Suzy warm towards the woman.

Mr. Stone shook her hand also but didn't say a word before they moved down the hall with Rita, continuing their tour.

Suzy watched them leave and then got out her tablet. She needed to finish her report and go home to sleep before she did something crazy like hug Mr. Stone just because he didn't know how to take care of his mom.

AFTER THE TOUR of Lake Mildred's Seniors' Home, Will drove them to the hospital to check on their mom. He kept his eyes on the road as Tori gushed about their tour. "It's so nice there. And everyone is so friendly. Especially that one nurse, Miss Bylin." She paused and glanced over at him. "Do you know her from somewhere? I think she went to high school with us."

Knew her and her mother. "I know her a little."

"She's so cute and bubbly. I love her already." Tori rested her chin on her fist. "I think Mom would like it there."

"It's going to be a hard sell no matter where we decide to leave her."

"You talk as if we're sending her away forever." She shook her head. "I'm as clueless as you, but I have a good feeling about that place. Can we afford it?"

That was the big question. After leaving the hospital the night before, he had gone through his mom's records to find the insurance papers that spelled out how much of the convalescent care would be covered, as well as their bank statements that showed how much they could pay for. Hopefully, it would be just enough. "Dad made sure Mom would be looked after. He might not have been a warm man, but he made arrangements so we'd be taken care of."

"Good, then it's settled. We'll tell her today about our plan."

"I'm warning you that she's not going to like it no matter what we say." He knew his mom. Knew her independent spirit. She wouldn't be agreeing to this so easily. "She won't want to go."

Tori nodded and sighed. "She can be stubborn."

"Luckily she has two kids who inherited that from her." He gave a smile, his first since the call yesterday. Had it really only been a day since their world had shifted? It had started as a normal day but had changed in a moment with a phone call. Nothing would be the same again. He nodded. "But I agree. That's where I'd like her to go, too."

The exit for the hospital arrived, and Will took the exit ramp. As they got closer to the hospital, he made a vow that he'd take care of his mom. No matter what.

But that meant convincing his stubborn mother that he was right.

She folded her arms across her chest and refused to look at him. Much like a four-year-old would. He moved so that he'd be in her line of sight. "Ma, this is not up for discussion. You can't go home right now."

"Yes I can. I'm a grown woman who can make her own decisions." She looked to Tori. She gave her daughter a large grin. "Baby, you think I can do it, right?"

Uh oh. Ma was dragging out the cutesy nicknames. Stay strong, Tori. Will watched his sister, willed her to hear his thoughts. They had to remain united to convince her that their plan would work.

Tori paled and shrugged. "It's not what I think, Ma. This is what the doctors say."

Will let out a puff of air. He'd hoped they'd be on the same page here, but when his mom pulled out the baby card… He nodded at Tori, letting her know she was on the right track. They were only doing what was right for Ma.

"Doctors." Their mom shook her head. "What do they know?"

Will sat on the bed next to his mom. "They know that you need to recover from this surgery. And they know you can't do it at home on your own."

"I'll be fine."

Tori sat next to Will. "No you won't. You'll be out in the garden when you shouldn't be. You'll be going back to work too soon. And that's why you're going to the seniors' home."

"I promise I'll be good."

Yep, a four-year-old. He took his mom's hand in his. "It's not forever. Just for now."

His mom shook her head and took her hand away from his. "I can't believe you're doing this to me. That you're sending me to a home and forgetting me there."

Tori pleaded, "I'll visit you every day, Ma."

"You just want to get rid of me." She covered her face. "You don't love me."

Tori put her arms around their mom. "Don't say that. Of course we love you." His mom and sister burst into tears, hugging.

Frustrated, Will got up from the bed. He had to take control of this situation before they agreed to do anything his mom asked. She might be good at manipulation, but he'd learned from the best. He summoned the spirit of his father, and let the steel surrounding his heart tighten…because it was for his mother's own good.

"That's enough."

Startled, his mother and sister let each other go and stared up at him. Good. He had their attention. "You're sick, Ma. Dying even."

Tori gasped. "Will—"

"Unless you're willing to fight to get better." He crouched in front of his mom. "So do you want to go home and die? Because that's what will happen." He used the most serious tone he could. "Or do you want to go to the seniors' home and fight this? Be around for your kids and grandkids? Live to see your first great grandchild?"

His mom narrowed her eyes at him. Let her be angry at him. It might give her the strength she needed to beat this.

He didn't let up on her. He clenched his fists. "You will be going into that home. You will have chemo once you're recovered. And when the doctors clear you, you can finally go home." He stood. "Am I clear?"

There was a pause and then Ma sighed. "You sound just like your father."

And by that, he knew he'd won this round.

CHAPTER FOUR

Suzy took her afternoon coffee on to the deck and surveyed the backyard. Two days had passed, and she hadn't started the clean up. Twelve days remained. She still had trash bags to drive to the dump. Old equipment to throw out. And Daddy's car to be donated or sold.

She leaned against the railing and winced. She needed more time. She needed at least another eight hours a day for the next week to get all of this done. And if she didn't finish in time, she'd pay a hefty fine and might lose Mama's house.

She'd lose everything.

She walked back into the house and surveyed the cluttered kitchen and dining room. She couldn't remember what the kitchen table looked like anymore. It had been years since she'd seen it cleared off. She might have done her homework there during her high school days, but that was before Mama covered it with plastic bags, boxes and the various stuff she'd collected.

Now that Mama was gone, it was Suzy's problem to deal with.

She put her mug in the kitchen sink and rinsed it out. Placed it face down in the wooden dish rack, a purchase she'd made after moving back in with Mama. Just one thing she'd had to do out of a million last year after her mother called for help. Her mother had put off getting medical attention until it was too late, meaning the cancer would win. And all Mama wanted was Suzy.

Her cell phone rang from the living room. She carefully moved past the stacked bundles of old newspapers and squeezed between the refrigerator and numerous boxes filled with china.

She checked the caller ID. Presley. "Hey, girl."

"You working tonight?"

Suzy wrinkled her nose. "Don't remind me. It's my sixth day, and I'm ready for a day off. But Candice is on vacation, so…"

"When are we going to have a girls' night out?"

"Soon." She mentally reviewed her calendar. "Sunday night?"

Presley groaned. "I've got an early Monday. When's your next day off?"

"Tuesday. As long as nothing else comes up." Suzy loved her job. Usually. But these crazy hours robbed her of a social life. "And we don't have to go crazy. Even a pizza in front of the TV sounds fabulous."

"Pizza and TV. You got it." Presley covered the phone, muting her conversation on the other end. Then her voice came back. "Gotta go. Vet emergency. I'll call you."

Then she was gone.

Suzy sat on the couch and rested her head. Okay. Time to get organized. Make some lists. She looked around the living room. Mama had to have a notebook and pen around here somewhere, right?

After searching several boxes and piles, she gave up. She'd get those from the drugstore in town. A walk would do her good. Get her out. Clear her mind. Give her a moment to collect herself. And then she could come up with a plan.

She didn't bother locking the front door. Just grabbed her wristlet purse and left. The town hadn't had a problem with crime in years. Plus, if they wanted to rob Mama's house, it might make things easier on her in the end.

She took a can of cat food from her jacket pocket and used the ring to pull back the top. It was easy to find the empty dish at the end of Mr. Fletcher's deck—where it always was—and she emptied the food on to it. She called out to Snowflake, but didn't hear an answering meow. Maybe the cat was napping in the house and would eat later. She then left her neighbor's yard and walked down the driveway and on towards town.

The walk took less than ten minutes, but it felt good to be outside with the sun on her back. To be free from the house and its issues. To leave her grief behind for just a moment.

She passed by the elementary school where kids played on the swings and chased each other. One of the playground monitors waved to Suzy then approached her. "I've been meaning to stop by and see how you're doing."

Mrs. Drayton had been a friend of Mama's for as long as Suzy could remember. She shrugged. "I'm okay." Mrs. Drayton peered at her, and Suzy was tempted to squirm a little. Okay, a lot. "Really. I'm fine."

"When I lost my mother, I stayed in bed for weeks."

Suzy hadn't been given that choice. "It's been six months."

Mrs. Drayton nodded. "Call me if you need anything, sweetie. Anything."

"I appreciate that."

A scream from the slide got Mrs. Drayton's attention, and she excused herself to take care of a crying child.

Suzy could appreciate the concern that people had for her, but she was okay. Usually. She'd discovered how strong she was after spending months bathing and feeding Mama. Doing things for her that no daughter should be expected to. But she'd done it with a smile because that's what Mama had needed. And being needed had felt good.

Suzy continued towards Main Street, passing the town hall before reaching the drug store. Inside, she found Mr. Stone talking to the cashier. Ducking behind one of the shelves, she snuck back to the office supplies and grabbed a notebook and pack of pens. She popped her head up to see if he had left. Whew. It was clear. She took her purchases to the cashier and added some bubble gum.

Chewing her gum, she stepped outside

and started for home. She had just gone beyond the town hall steps when she heard her
name being called. She turned and spotted
Mr. Stone coming towards her.

Crud.

She pasted a smile on her face. "Mr. Stone,
what a surprise."

He stopped a couple feet from her. "I
wanted to check in to see how things are
going at your mother's house."

Double crud. "Fine." Her cheeks hurt from
keeping the smile on her face. She held up
her shopping bag. "Bought some supplies
so I can make a game plan for the clean up."

He frowned at the bag. "Make a plan? You
haven't started? You only have…"

"Twelve days, I know." She shifted her
weight to the other foot. Wanted to leave, but
it would probably be considered rude. "You
don't have to worry."

"Still I think I'll check in on you early
next week."

She shook her head. She didn't need to be
checked on like a child. She could do this.
She was capable. Strong. "You don't have
to do that."

His frown deepened. "Something tells me

that I should." He looked her up and down. "I won't keep you."

"So I can go home and work on the backyard? How kind of you." She blew a bubble and let it pop. "Have a splendid day, Mr. Stone."

"Likewise, Miss Bylin."

WILL NOTICED TORI'S car outside the hospital when he arrived after work. He locked his car and walked up to the entrance. The coffee stand in the lobby called his name, but he'd need to sleep later. Not that he'd had much luck the past three nights.

Tori stood at the door of their mom's room, leaning on the wall. Head down, arms crossed. Will went up to her and put his arm around her shoulder. "Everything okay?"

Tori looked up at him, the skin below her eyes puffy and dark. She looked tired. Lost. And a little scared. "The doctor is giving her an exam now. I think they'll be moving her to the nursing home soon."

"Already?"

"They've done all that they can do here. She needs to recuperate in a home."

Will nodded. He'd expected this. With the plans in place to send her to Lake Mildred

Seniors' Home, it wasn't a matter of if but when they moved her there. In his mind, the sooner, the better. Then they could all move forward. "Good."

Tori shrugged. "I guess."

"It's a positive sign. Shows that she's improving." He rubbed her arm. "It's going to be okay."

"You can't guarantee that. Her hip is repairing, but she still has cancer." She held her hands to her face. "She could die. And then where would I be?"

"She's too stubborn to die." But did he really believe it? Yes, his mom was one tough cookie. But cancer had a way of making the strongest person frail and helpless.

He couldn't think like that. Had to stay positive. Had to focus on the mission: getting his mom into the home and healed so she could start chemo. That was the plan. That was the goal.

Tori looked up at him. "I haven't heard from our sisters. Have you?"

Will shrugged. "Are you really surprised by that? They've made it clear they don't want anything to do with Ma or us." He shook his head. "When's the last time they were here for Christmas? Or even called."

"Carol calls Ma every month."

"To ask for money." He hit his fist against his thigh. "I don't get it, Tori. Ma didn't do anything to deserve this. What did she ever do to them?"

"She didn't protect them from Dad." She frowned. "Sometimes it wasn't the belt that hurt most. It was the names."

He could still hear his dad's voice after all these years. Loser. Worthless. Useless. Good for nothing.

"That wasn't Ma's fault."

There was surprise etched on her face. "You're defending her? That's a switch."

"I'm not that harsh."

"Except when you want her to do what you want."

He knew that would come back and bite him in the end. He took a long, deep breath. "She has to go to the home. She can't live on her own and expect to get better. You know it as well as I do."

"Sure, but you were so…" She seemed to be searching her brain for the right word. "Cruel."

Had he been? Is that how they'd seen him? "Tough love isn't cruel. It's necessary."

"And I'm sure Dad would have said the

same thing." She pushed off the wall. "I need some air."

She started to walk down the hall. Will called after her. "Am I really like Dad?"

His sister stopped and turned. "Sometimes," she said, and then she turned back and kept on walking.

WHEN SUZY DROVE UP to the seniors' home, she noticed the ambulance near the entrance. The lights weren't flashing, so that was a good sign. Maybe a new patient arriving? Or an old one leaving? She checked the ambulance but noted no one was inside.

In the break room, Suzy punched in and checked the assignment sheet before arriving at her usual station. As she walked, she pulled her hair back into a ponytail and secured it with a rubber band. There was activity down the hall. Two medics were pushing an empty gurney and she waved at them as they left.

A new patient then.

Which meant she'd be spending most of her evening monitoring the room and answering the tons of questions her new patient would have. She smiled. She loved meeting people.

Carly came up to her at the station. "Is it almost seven already? No wonder I'm tired."

"We get new blood?"

Carly glanced down the hall and nodded. "You'll like her. She's feisty. Right up your alley."

Suzy nodded. "The family?"

"Worried, of course." Carly leaned in. "The son is a real looker, FYI."

They shared a giggle then squelched it as the person in question strode out of the patient's room. Mr. Stone. Suzy's giggle died in her throat. Couldn't she get away from the man?

He approached the nurses' station. "Miss Bylin, thank God you're here."

She frowned. That wasn't the reaction she'd been expecting. "What can I do for you, Mr. Stone?"

"My mother is being…" He sighed. "Difficult. Could you give me a hand?"

Carly looked between Suzy and Mr. Stone, questions written on her face. She nudged Suzy who nodded. "Of course. Let me just get my things, and I'll meet you in her room."

After he left, Carly spoke, but dropped her voice. "You know that guy?"

"A little." She shrugged and grabbed her

tablet. Turned it on. Wound her stethoscope around her neck. "If you need to take off before I'm finished, I'll just read over your notes later."

"You go ahead. Let me know what happens." Carly winked at her.

Suzy shook her head as she walked down the hall to room twenty-three. Inside, Mr. Stone and his sister glared at the older woman in the bed. She took a deep breath and rushed in. "Am I in luck or what? A new friend in my wing."

The woman merely stared at her, her upper lip clenched behind her lower. This was going to be a tough one.

Suzy clicked on the room information, but obviously Mrs. Stone hadn't been there long enough for her files to get uploaded. She placed her tablet on the side table and moved around the bed instead. Noticed the stiff way her patient rested, favoring her right side. "They give you a new hip?"

Mrs. Stone turned to look at her children. Her son shook his head. "Repaired a fracture."

"Those aren't any fun, are they?" Suzy fussed with the pillows behind Mrs. Stone's head though they looked fine. She observed how her new patient stayed quiet. Sullen. She warmed the stethoscope on her hand then placed it on Mrs. Stone's chest. Moving into a facility could cause anxiety, and she wanted to check her heart. She paused a moment, listening. Sounded normal. "At least you'll belong to me while you get better."

Mr. Stone cleared his throat. "That was my request."

She jerked her head up and stared at him. Interesting. Maybe he didn't think she was so hopeless after all. "Well, thank you. I'm thrilled to care for your mom." She tugged at the blanket and smoothed it out. Then she checked the leads for the monitors to make sure everything had been hooked up right. "Can I get you something, Mrs. Stone? Glass of water? Piece of pie?"

"You can get me out of here."

Suzy laughed as if that was the first time she'd heard that. "Absolutely. Once the doctor gives you the all clear, I'll be glad to wheel you out to your car."

Mrs. Stone turned her face away from them. "Until then, get out. Leave me alone."

"Can't do that, I'm afraid. You're my new best friend." She addressed the family. "Is there anything I can get you two? The chef makes strawberry pie on Thursdays. I can go snag a couple of pieces."

The sister nodded. "Ma loves strawberries." She smiled at her mother. "Doesn't pie sound good?"

"I want to go home."

Mr. Stone shook his head again. His voice came out low and sounded almost dangerous. "Ma, we've been over this."

"You've been over this. You're the ones imprisoning me here." Their mom looked out the window.

"Does that make me your warden, Mrs. Stone?" Suzy made a face. "I've been called a lot of things, but not that. Mr. Stone called me flighty the other day."

Mrs. Stone looked her up and down. "My son is usually right."

Suzy considered this and agreed. "You're probably right. But once we get to know each other better, you can let me know what you think yourself." She winked at the older woman who again turned away.

"So about that pie. Who's up for it?" She pulled out an imaginary order pad and pen. "I can bring some coffee to go with."

The sister grinned. "I think we could all use some. Right, Ma?"

Mrs. Stone rolled her eyes. "You do what you want. Obviously, it doesn't matter what I think anymore."

Yep, a difficult one. Suzy looked at Mr. Stone. "Think I'll grab your son to give me a hand. We'll be right back."

He followed her out of the room and down the hall towards the main entrance and the kitchen. "I'm sorry about my mother."

She stopped to look at him, noticing the bags under his eyes. Here was a man who loved his mom. It made him less forbidding. More...attractive. She shrugged. "You don't have to apologize. I'm used to that."

"She's not usually that nasty."

"She's just had her life turned upside down. Anger is normal. Almost expected." She opened the door and let him pass in front of her. "She needs a few days to adjust, then she'll be back to almost normal."

He looked at her. "Almost?"

"Mr. Stone, her life will never be the same even after she leaves here." She went to the refrigerator and pulled out three pieces of pie and thrust them at him. "She has to learn a new normal."

He nodded as he juggled the plates. "This

is why I requested your section. I saw the way you handled the trauma the other day."

"Just doing my job." She grabbed a tray from below the coffee station, poured three Styrofoam cups of coffee, and added packets of cream and sugar to the tray.

"She needs some sunshine too, and I thought of you."

She smiled at him. "I like that. Sunshine. Much better than warden." She looked at him right in the eye. "Or flighty."

"Miss Bylin, I—"

"Suzy, please. If I'm going to take care of your mother, you might as well call me by my first name."

He nodded. "Suzy, I apologize for calling you that."

She'd heard worse, especially from some of her angrier patients. "Like I said, I've been called a lot of things." She arranged the tray and took the dessert plates from him. Added forks and napkins beside them. "Now this looks fabulous."

He followed her back to room twenty-three. Suzy placed the tray on the bedside table with some flair. "Your dessert, madam."

Mrs. Stone glanced at it then shook her head. "I'm not hungry."

"We'll leave it for later in case you change your mind." Suzy passed a plate of pie to the sister along with a fork. "If you need anything else, I'll be your waitress tonight."

Will took a fork from her. "Thank you, Suzy."

Mr. Stone attempted a smile, but it didn't quite work. She had a feeling he wasn't used to it. She grinned instead. "You betcha. Enjoy."

She whistled as she waltzed out of the room. Mrs. Stone might prove to be an interesting case.

And seeing Mr. Stone again might not be so bad either.

As long as they didn't discuss Mama's house.

AFTER AN HOUR of short answers and cold silence, Will sighed and rose to his feet. His backside was getting numb from all this sitting anyway. He turned to his mom. "Visiting hours are ending, Ma. Do you need us to bring anything from home?"

Silence.

Tori approached the bed and put her hand

on their mom's, who snapped it away. His sister gestured at Will, probably hoping he could fix this. Just like he fixed everything else. But remembering Miss Bylin's…Suzy's advice, he overlooked the slight. "Well, if you think of anything, you have both of our cell phone numbers."

He kissed his mother's cheek then waited as Tori did the same. He then put his arm around his sister. "We'll stop by tomorrow."

"Don't bother."

Tori gasped, but Will nodded. "Lovey."

"Lovey," Tori echoed.

Nothing back. He pulled his sister from the room.

Tori began crying as their mother's door shut behind them. He tugged her down the hall and stopped at the nurses' station. Suzy popped her head up at their approach and smiled. "How's my new friend?"

He winced. "The same. Angry. You'll check on her?"

"It's my job, Mr. Stone. But I'll peek in her room a couple extra times." She came around and gave his sister a tissue, then a hug. "I know this is hard, but it will get easier." She handed them each a Post-It note with a handwritten phone number and smiley face. "This is my cell phone number. Call me anytime. Seriously."

Tori hugged Suzy. "You're an angel."

"You and your family calling me names. Trust me, I'm no angel." She looked up at Will. "Mr. Stone knows that all too well."

Tori seemed confused, a question in her eyes. He thrust his hand out at Suzy. "Please call me Will. It's only fair after putting up with my mother."

She waved it off. "I took an oath to be there for all my patients. But I especially look out for the new ones." She eyed the clock. "I'd better go check on your mom. She probably misses you already."

Tori looked back at the room. "Maybe I should go talk to her. Maybe she'll listen to me."

Suzy looked at her. "What's your name?"

"Tori."

Suzy put her arm around the woman's shoulders. "Tori, you've done all you can do today. Going back in there right now will only make all of you feel worse. I mean it when I say give her a chance to miss you, to look forward to seeing you again."

Will nodded. "We'll be back tomorrow."

"Perfect." Suzy peered into Tori's face.

"This isn't a sprint, but a marathon. You're going to need all the rest you can get, so enjoy your evening. Go home. Watch some TV. Read a book. Go to bed early. And don't worry about your mom. She's in good hands."

Tori turned into Suzy and hugged her again. "Thanks."

Will took Tori from Suzy's arms and helped his sister leave the nursing home. She took a few steps and looked back. Walked a few more, and glanced behind her a second time. When they reached his truck, she opened the passenger side door but stared back at the home. "Are we doing the right thing?"

"You heard Suzy. And I don't think she would steer us wrong."

Tori climbed into the pickup truck and fastened her seat belt. "I know you're right. But I hate leaving her like this."

"We'll be back tomorrow. And the next day. And the next." He started the engine then turned to her. "Suzy said her attitude will improve in a few days."

"Suzy, huh?" Tori wiped the corners of her eyes, then blew her nose. "You two seemed awfully cozy."

"We talked when we got the pie and coffee." He shrugged. "I wouldn't exactly call it cozy. But she did help explain things."

"Well, I like her." She grabbed a new tissue. "She seems so nice."

She did. And not like the flighty woman he'd met only days ago. "She's good at her job. And you can see that she's good with people."

"I feel better knowing that she's watching out for mom."

"I do too." Despite her house and the disaster in the yard, she appeared competent. Friendly. And he wouldn't have to worry about his mom.

At least not about the nursing care she was receiving.

CHAPTER FIVE

"I TOLD YOU I wanted eggs over easy." The breakfast tray clattered to the floor as Mrs. Stone swept it off the bedside table with her arm.

It had been a quiet night, Mrs. Stone falling asleep soon after her children had left. She was obviously making up for lost time. Suzy sighed and squatted to collect the pieces of broken china mixed with scrambled eggs and toast. She loaded the mess on to the tray and took it to the cart by the nurses' station. She picked up the phone and ordered a replacement breakfast for Mrs. Stone: eggs over easy with wheat toast. Orange juice. Coffee.

The woman had ordered scrambled eggs, but Suzy gave her the benefit of the doubt. Maybe she hadn't heard right.

But she knew she had.

She returned to Mrs. Stone's room. "I ordered you a new breakfast. Eggs over easy, just like you like them."

"I'm hungry now."

"It will only be a few moments." Suzy checked the woman's vitals and made note of them on her tablet. Her blood pressure teetered on the high side, but considering her mood, it wasn't a surprise. "I'm going to deliver the rest of the breakfast trays and return with yours." She started to walk out of the room.

"I'm sorry."

It was so soft, she almost didn't hear it. Suzy nodded. "I'm sorry too."

By the time she'd finished her rounds and made notes on all her patients, Carly had arrived for the day. "How's the new patient?"

"We're waiting on a new breakfast tray after she threw the other one on the floor. I already put in a call to housekeeping." Suzy shrugged. "I get it. She's angry, but she doesn't have to take it out on me or my clean floors."

Carly put her arm around Suzy. "Don't take it personal."

Suzy shook her head and gave a wide smile. "Never do." She brought up the main menu of her tablet. "Nothing new to go over. Besides Mrs. Stone's temper tantrum. I spoke with her family, and they'll be back later today to see how she's doing."

Carly nodded. "I get the feeling we'll be seeing a lot of them."

Suzy agreed. She had plenty of patients who saw their children once a week or once a month. Some who never had visitors. But Mrs. Stone would probably have more than her share of time with her kids. "I also had a call from Mrs. Stone's supervisor at work asking if he could visit. He might be by at lunch."

Carly made notes. "Any plans for today?"

"Besides sleeping?" She dismissed the niggling feeling that she should be cleaning the backyard. She still had time. Nine days. Plenty of time to get it all done, right? "I should probably do some laundry. A little grocery shopping." She groaned. "Three more days, and I get a day off. I can't wait."

"Well, go get some well-deserved rest. I'll hold down the fort until you get back."

In the break room, Suzy punched out and retrieved her purse and coat. It was late September, so mornings started chilly. As she walked out the main entrance, she almost bumped into Will. "Wow, you're early this morning."

"Thought I'd check on her before work." He seemed to note her appearance. "You're just leaving for home?"

"Only a half hour past my usual time too. Let's write the day on the calendar." She crossed her arms. "You might want to tread lightly around your mom, she's had a rough morning."

"She's never been a morning person. At least not until after two cups of coffee when the caffeine kicks in."

"Thanks for the tip." She stood while he watched her intently. She glanced behind her then touched her cheeks. "Do I have something on my face?"

"Pardon?"

"Was there something else you needed, Mr. Stone?"

"It's Will. Remember?" He glanced at his watch then at her again. "Do you have time for coffee?"

She peered down at her scrubs. "I'm not actually dressed for going out."

"I don't care what you're wearing. I was hoping we could talk. Even for a moment."

She bit her lip and considered it. On one

hand, it had been a long night and she could use the sleep. On the other, when was the last time an attractive man had taken her out for anything, even coffee? "Fine, but it has to be quick. I have a yard to clean up."

He gave her a smile then led her to his truck. Once he started the engine, he glanced at her. "I really appreciate this, Suzy."

"Sure." She turned and looked out the window as he drove into town and to the diner. He helped her out of the truck then walked beside her into the restaurant. They could only find two open spots at the counter. "They're busy this morning."

"It's blueberry pancake day." He motioned to the waitress for two cups of coffee. "Would you like a stack?"

"I'm not much for breakfast in the morning." She thanked the waitress who poured her coffee then added double cream and triple sugar. "But coffee? Now you're talking my language."

Will gave her an almost smile and stirred one sugar packet into his coffee. "I was hoping we could discuss how to help my mom."

"Bring her some familiar things from home that will offer her comfort. Remember that she's in an unfamiliar place, so that will help her find some peace."

"Things like what?"

"Pictures. Favorite book. If she likes to do crosswords…" Suzy shrugged. "You know, things she enjoys."

Will brought out a small notebook and made notes. "Puzzles, ok. What else?"

"Be patient with her. She needs that more now than ever." She ticked the items off on her fingers. "Call or visit her often. Include her in what is going on with your life so she doesn't feel so isolated. And above all, just love her."

Will looked up from his notebook. "I already do that."

"She needs to know it more now."

He added that to his notes and then put the book down. "When my dad was sick, I was only a teen. So I didn't have to do much. But this is different."

Suzy placed her hand on his. "It's going to be overwhelming at times, but you'll get through this."

He stared down at their hands, and she snatched hers away. They finished their coffee in silence and Will paid the check. He walked her out to his truck. He took a deep breath, and she waited for him to say something. Before he could, he swallowed hard. "I can't tell you how much it means to me that you did this."

"It was only coffee and some advice."

"You gave me reassurance when I felt lost." He looked into her eyes and reached toward her.

She felt a warmth spread over her chest as she glanced at his mouth. But then all he did was open her door and help her into the truck.

THE GROCERY STORE bustled with shoppers who stopped in on their way home from work. Will grabbed a basket from the stack at the front and headed for the produce section. With his mom in the hospital, meals had been catch it when you can, and he grew tired of fast food and carryout. He wanted some fresh food. Even a salad sounded great.

He must be losing it.

The pyramid of oranges called to him, so he walked in that direction and pulled a plastic bag from the roll. He was quick to find four nice size oranges that felt and smelled juicy, which he put in the bag and tied it shut at the top; turned and noticed Councilman Barry watching him from the bakery aisle.

He wasn't going to let him get to him today. He had to focus on buying food and then getting to the hospital to check on his mom. He had already dealt with several phone calls from the town council members about his job. Had justified six times over why they needed him in office to keep the town safe. He didn't need to explain it a seventh time.

Bad enough he was one man doing a job that required a staff. What were they going to do if they did eliminate it? Give the responsibility to an already overworked colleague? He shook his head. It was starting to feel personal.

"Fancy seeing you here, Will."

Will forced a pleasant expression on his face. At least he hoped it was pleasant. "Councilman Barry."

The man glanced into Will's basket. "I'm a big fan of oranges myself."

"Can I help you with something?" Will didn't have time to talk about the benefits of citrus.

Councilman Barry huffed, and his eyebrows slammed together. "The budget meeting is coming up next month. You realize, of course, that your job is on the line."

"Yes, you all have been telling me that for months now." This was hardly news. Will had slept with it, worked with it and eaten with the knowledge that his job could disappear. He'd taken the post after his predecessor had a heart attack on the job. He'd only been the man's assistant at the time, but he'd accepted the position and done a great job. Why didn't anyone else see that? "I'm hoping to have your support."

"That depends on you, son." Councilman Barry folded his large arms across his chest. "We pride ourselves on getting results and reward those who do the same."

"My track record speaks for itself."

"And the Bylin house? What does that say?"

Will tried not to grimace. He had to bring up Suzy, hadn't he? "The resident has been given a deadline of a week from now. I'm sure we will see a positive outcome."

"Rose Bylin had years to get the yard cleaned up, but we can see how well that was enforced." Mr. Barry shook his head. "The last code inspector was too soft. I'm not saying you are too, but we want results.

Success. And the Bylin situation has to be dealt with."

The man was determined to rub Will the wrong way. But he wasn't about to react. Not today. This was just a job, not his life. His life was his family. And he needed to finish here and get back to that life. "I appreciate your concern, but we are dealing with it."

"Results, Will. Not excuses. And then maybe you can keep your job." Councilman Barry returned to the bakery counter on that pronouncement.

Will closed his eyes. The council wanted results. Well, so did he. And they'd get them.

He checked his grocery list again, but the rest of the items on it now held little interest. In fact, the oranges no longer appealed to him. He considered putting them back and leaving the store. He could shop tomorrow. But then this would be a waste. And if there was anything he hated more than clutter, it was wasted time.

He scanned his list again and walked to the deli department and took a number. He browsed the case while he waited for his turn. The turkey looked good, but he'd had a craving for ham lately.

"I'd recommend the salami."

Will looked up and found Suzy smiling at him. "Miss Bylin…Suzy, what are you doing here?"

"Choosing a little something for my dinner later." She perused the prepared salads and pointed at the macaroni. "That would do."

"You should be working on your yard."

Suzy glanced down at her scrubs under her jean jacket. "And miss seeing your mother? Not on your life."

Will closed his eyes and willed the headache away. "You only have…"

"Over a week. Yes, I know." She examined a package of rolls then replaced them on the shelf. She glanced up at him. "Worried I won't make my deadline?"

"Your mother never did."

"She didn't believe in ultimatums either. Trust me. I know better than you."

The deli clerk called out a number, and Suzy held up her slip. "I'll take a half pound of the macaroni salad."

The clerk left to package up Suzy's order, and she turned back to Will. "You'll get your results. Don't worry."

"But I do. This is my job we're talking about."

She patted his arm, then removed her hand quickly, obviously as surprised as he was that she'd touched him again. She accepted the plastic container from the deli clerk and thanked her before addressing Will. "Speaking of jobs, I need to get going. Don't want to keep my patients waiting. I'll see you later?"

"Yes." He opened his mouth to say more. To encourage her. To make sure that she met the deadline. But she was already gone. The deli clerk called his number. "I'll take a pound of the boiled ham."

SUZY HUMMED AS she walked into the animal rescue building and then greeted the receptionist. "Is Pres in?"

"Of course she is. In her office." The older woman scoffed. "She didn't leave until almost midnight last night and was back before I got here at eight."

"I'll talk to her." Suzy headed for Pres's office and popped her head in. "You need a day off."

Pres looked up from her files and took off her glasses. "You talked to Thoramae." She groaned. "I swear she's worse than a mother."

"Why were you here until midnight last night?"

"Stray dog hit by a pickup. I wasn't going to let him die."

Suzy tensed. She wished motorists would pay more attention when they were driving. "Did he?"

"Nope. I stayed until I knew he was going to make it."

"Well, thank goodness." Suzy came into the office and glanced around before taking a seat on the sofa near the wall of windows. "How are my little furry friends?"

"Why don't you go see for yourself?"

Pres led her out of the office and down the hall into a large room with several cages and gated areas. Suzy saw three familiar gray balls of fur sleeping in a corner of one cage. She peeked in and poked her finger through the bars to pet one. "They're still tiny."

"But getting better." Pres opened the cage and took one out and handed it to Suzy. "They didn't like the food I gave them at the beginning, but I finally found the right blend. They've been eating more since then."

Suzy buried her nose into the side of the kitten and breathed in its warm scent. "They should bottle this scent. This and that of puppies."

"You're biased." Pres took out another kitten and gave it to Suzy. "After a month or so, they should be ready to come home. Interested?"

Was she? Oh yeah. She juggled the two kittens as Pres handed her the third. "I've got to get the house thing under control before I can. But yes. Let me know when, and I'll be sure to make a space for them."

Pres smiled. "Good. I'm sure I could find families for them, but I figured you need them as much as they need you. They'll keep you company and give you something to love. You won't be so lonely."

"You think I'm lonely?" Pres looked her over until Suzy confessed. "Okay, maybe a little. But are you a vet or a therapist?" Suzy rubbed one kitten on her cheek. "I told you I'm doing fine."

"And the house?"

Suzy groaned. "Don't remind me. It seems impossible. I don't know what I'm going to do."

"So let me help." Pres put her hand on Suzy's shoulder. "That's what friends do, you know? They reach out and give a helping hand. All you have to do is ask."

"Not exactly my strong suit." Suzy laughed then glanced at her watch. Crud. "I gotta go. Duty calls." She handed the kittens back to Pres. "We're still on for pizza and TV on Tuesday at your place?"

"I wouldn't miss it for the world."

AT THE NURSING HOME, Suzy found Wendy, the physical therapist, working with Mrs. Stone. "I want you to push with your foot against my hand."

"Why?"

"You need to build your strength back up."

"I don't see how kicking your hand is going to do a thing." But she pushed her foot against the therapist's hand.

Suzy smiled extra hard. "So, it seems like things are going well in here." Wendy gave her a look as if she didn't believe a word Suzy said and neither did Mrs. Stone. "At least you two are doing something instead of fighting."

"Can you be with Mrs. Stone tonight while she's doing bicycles lying on her back?"

Suzy nodded. "I'll make her do whatever you want."

"Fat chance." Mrs. Stone glared at them both. "I do what I want, when I want."

"Then do it so you can go home."

She opened her mouth to answer Suzy, then shook her head and looked away.

Suzy put a hand on Mrs. Stone's shoulder. "I'll let you finish up with Wendy and check on you later."

She gave the physical therapist an encouraging smile and returned to the nurses' station. She could get through to Mrs. Stone. She knew she could.

A STREAK OF green tried to rush past Will as he walked towards his mom's room later that evening. He held out his hands and captured his nephew. "Conner, where's your mom?"

"Talking to grandma." He stopped and slouched his shoulders forward "Suzy said that they have ice cream tonight in the dining room."

"I'm sure she meant for the seniors." He continued down the hall and put his arm around his nephew. "Getting a little cooped up in grandma's room?"

"Just a little." He shrugged off Will's arm. Right. Teenage boys didn't like being touched. "It's so boring." A little chirp sounded from his jean's pocket. He pulled out his cell phone. "It's Ashley."

And just like that, his teenage nephew disappeared into his own world. Will steered the boy into the room as he texted on his phone, fingers flying faster than Will had seen anyone else do. When he entered the room, he saw Tori with her head over Brady's school book. She looked up at him and smiled. "Good. You're here. This algebra thing has me stumped."

He went over and kissed his mom's cheek. "Hey, Ma. Lovey."

She blinked at him and shifted her gaze back to the iPad she held, probably belonging to one of the twins. Will joined Brady by the window ledge and took the book from Tori. "All right, let's see if we can get this figured out."

After a few minutes, Will got Brady on the right track. He motioned with his head to Ma and asked Tori, "Has she said anything?"

His sister glanced at their mother who kept her gaze on the tablet's screen. "She's still not talking to us. Though she did say plenty to the boys."

"So we're still on her list."

"Where you're going to stay until you get

me out of this place." Ma glared at him, but it had little effect now. When he'd been Brady and Conner's age, it might have made him straighten up. But he was almost thirty-five now and wasn't about to…

He flinched. "Aw, Ma. You know this place will be good for you." He took a seat at the end of her bed. "Why won't you give it a chance?"

"I want to go home."

"Yes, you've made that clear. Many times." Will rubbed his forehead. "I love you to death, Ma, but you're giving me headaches."

"Why don't you ask that nurse for some aspirin then? She seems to think she knows what's good for everyone." She turned back to the iPad and shut him out.

Fine. He didn't have to be treated like this. He stood and walked over to Tori. Kissed his sister on the cheek and ruffled Brady's hair first then Conner's. "I think I might as well leave."

"And none too soon," Ma mumbled from her bed.

"You just got here," Tori said. "Don't leave yet."

Ma turned the volume up on the iPad while Will did his best not to lose his temper. "Sorry, sis. But this evening is going from bad to worse." He turned to their mom. "Good to see you, Ma."

Conner and Brady both stood. "Take us with you, Uncle Will. We're starving."

Tori laughed. "They're always hungry." She grabbed her purse and opened it, finding a few bills. She stuffed them into Brady's hand. "All right. If you'll take them and get some dinner, Ma and I will have a little girl time."

Their mom scoffed at the suggestion. "Don't need any girl time. What are we gonna do? Paint our nails?"

"And maybe fix our hair too. Who knows?" Tori motioned to the door. "Go on now. It's an estrogen party, and no boys allowed."

Will appreciated his sister's offer, grateful to leave with an excuse and no guilt. "I promise to feed them a healthy dinner."

The boys groaned. Will winked at them. "Pizza hits all four food groups, right?" He ushered them out the door as they gave each other high fives. "Maybe we'll try that new place off Main."

On the way out, Will glanced at the nurses' station and saw a familiar face. He gave her a quick nod as they left. But it must not have been quick enough to miss his nephew's notice. "Who's the chick, Uncle Will?" Brady asked as they got into his truck.

"First of all, Nurse Suzy is not a chick."

Conner laughed. "She definitely doesn't look like a dude to me."

"She's a woman who deserves our respect." When the twins fell into peals of laughter, Will shrugged. "What did I say?"

"You like her."

Weren't teenage boys supposed to be clueless? Especially about the opposite sex. "She's a nurse who's taking care of Grandma, so of course I like her."

"No, you like *like* her." Conner laughed again and pounded on his twin's shoulder "Oh man, wait till Mom hears about this."

"Your mom doesn't need to hear about this because there's nothing to tell." Will wondered why he'd agreed to feed these horrible children. "And I have respect for Suzy but I don't have any other feelings for her."

"So it's Suzy now, huh?"

He was just making it worse for himself. He pulled out of the parking lot and concentrated on the road. Maybe if he ignored the teasing, they would stop.

After an hour of listening to the twins, however, Will knew he was in trouble. And all the more for liking their teasing about the pretty nurse.

Wait. Pretty? He thought of Suzy's perky nose. Expressive brown eyes. And those strawberry blonde curls. Oh, yes. Definitely pretty.

"He's thinking about her." Brady nudged his brother. "Look at his goo goo eyes."

"My eyes do not goo." He glanced at their plates with several half eaten pizza crusts, then the empty pitcher of pop. "But my belly could definitely use a cookie from the Sweetheart. You guys game?"

The twins stood, almost as if they were racing to see who could get to the bakery first. Will left a generous tip then put his arms around both of their necks and pulled them outside. "If you want a cookie, then no more talk about gooey eyes."

Because Will was afraid they might be right. He just might like *like* Nurse Suzy.

SUZY CHECKED ON Mrs. Henderson then heard the television blaring from Room 23. At the open doorway of Mrs. Stone's room, Suzy asked, "Can't sleep?"

The older woman chastized her. "You don't have to hover over me."

"Not hovering. Merely checking on you." Suzy entered the room and scanned the monitors. Everything seemed normal. "Warm milk usually helps me sleep."

"I sleep just fine." She turned the television off. "At least I do in my own home." She punched the pillows behind her. "There's too much going on here for me to relax."

"I understand that. What would help?"

"Besides getting me out of here, you mean?" Mrs. Stone chuckled. "I don't know. When I was home, I'd have a cup of tea before bed and read the newspaper. It was... comforting."

Suzy got the need for rituals. "Give me five minutes. Let me see what I can do." She left Mrs. Stone's room and walked down to the main office. She found the day's paper and took it with her to the nurses' station. She heated some water in a mug then carried that, plus a tea bag, with the paper. Mrs. Stone looked up when Suzy returned to the room. "I don't know if you like herbal or green tea, but I found a tea bag and the paper."

Mrs. Stone looked shocked, then reached

out and ran her hand over the top of the newspaper. She glanced up at Suzy. "Why are you being nice to me after the horrible way I treated you?"

"It's my job."

Mrs. Stone shook her head. "Nope. Don't buy it. This is going above and beyond. So why are you being nice to a cranky old lady?"

"Being nice doesn't cost me anything. And you look like someone who could use some nice."

She narrowed her eyes at Suzy. "Did my son put you up to this?"

"He loves you."

"If he loved me, he'd let me go home."

Suzy countered, "It's because he loves you that he wants you to stay here and get better. He and Tori both want you to be around for a long time."

Mrs. Stone looked at her then sighed. "Maybe."

"Definitely."

Long moments went by as they stared at each other. Eventually, Mrs. Stone accepted the newspaper and searched the front page. Suzy backed away and took her leave. But before she did so, she heard another soft "Thank you."

Suzy kept her eyes on the door. "You're welcome." And then she left.

It wasn't quite a breakthrough in their relationship, but something had changed with Mrs. Stone. She only hoped it could continue.

SUZY STRUGGLED WITH the third bag of trash and groaned at the thought of dragging nine more to the curb. There had to be a better way to do this, right? She set the bag next to the mailbox post and expelled a deep breath. Stretched and twisted. She might not need to do her workout if she kept up this physical labor.

A sky blue pickup truck honked at her as it pulled into her driveway. The town's mayor, Rick Allyn, gave a wave then hopped out. What was he doing here? Sure, he'd been a friend of her family for years. Her mom had been his dad's assistant for twenty-two years before he died then she'd retired when Rick's brother Dan had taken over the company. She'd seen Rick at company parties and picnics, and of course, at school. He'd been five grades or so ahead of her, but she knew about him. The whole town did.

He surveyed the bags of trash. "Need help?"

Suzy looked around. "How did you know?"

"That you needed help? A little bird might have told me."

"More like a big bird by the name of Will Stone, right?"

"He might have mentioned it during soft-ball practice the other night."

She should have known that man wouldn't leave her alone. He was determined to in-terfere with her work. But then if he'd sent his boss to help, she wasn't going to refuse. "Yes, I could use a hand."

Rick rubbed his hands together and fol-lowed Suzy to the backyard. He gave a low whistle as she opened the gate and went to the garage for the remaining bags of trash. "Wow. I didn't realize there was this much stuff. You know who you need to call? My Lizzie. She'd get this place organized in no time. And all with a clipboard in her hand." He gave her a goofy smile that she knew meant he truly loved his fiancé.

Her eyes swept over the cluttered space. It

looked the same as it had since she'd grown up there. "Mama liked to hang on to things."

"The whole family was sorry to hear about your mom. She was a staple at the pickle factory for years."

"Thanks."

Rick pointed at the Camaro and ran a hand along the rusted hood. "Nice. A collector could do something special with this."

"My dad had planned to restore it, but he left before he had the chance." She motioned to the other bags of trash. "I've got to get these out before the truck comes."

Together, they were able to shift all of the trash to the curb. Rick waved at the sanitation workers as they arrived and loaded the bags into the garbage truck. He shook their hands before they left. Suzy had always marveled how Rick could talk to anyone. But then as mayor, he probably had to.

Suzy thought about inviting him inside for coffee, but she'd been up almost twenty-four hours and needed at least four hours sleep before she returned to work. She rubbed her arms. The temperature had been dropping steadily all week. Their first frost couldn't be too far away. She gave a smile to Rick. "Thanks for the help."

"There's a lot more to do."

"I know. And I still have a week left."

Rick frowned. "Do you think you'll have it ready in time?"

"Sure. If I don't sleep between shifts at the home." She chuckled a little. "Sleep is way overrated as it is."

Rick surveyed the yard. She wondered briefly if he saw the disaster that Will seemed to or the neglect that she did. "I don't want you to lose the house because of lack of time. Maybe I can get Will to give you an extension."

"It would only delay the inevitable. I'll be fine. But I appreciate your help today."

He nodded and bit his lip. "What if I could do more? Maybe come back and give you a hand with some of this? My Lizzie would love to step in and do the same if you gave her the chance."

Everyone was always offering to help. Even when Mama had been alive, people had offered but her mom had insisted they could do this just with the two of them. As if she didn't trust anyone else with her secrets. Only Suzy. It got a little tiresome at times when she had to do it all. She closed her eyes and fell into old habits of relying on no one but herself. Mama had always told her you couldn't trust anyone. And after a while, Suzy went along with it because it was easier than arguing. "No, you've got the diner. Running the town. It's too much. Besides, I've got the weekend off and can get a lot done then."

He snapped his fingers. "Great idea. I'll bring a crew with me on Saturday morning. Some of my softball team maybe. Lizzie, of course. Say nine o'clock?"

A crew? Here where all Mama's secrets would be exposed? "I can't let you do that."

"Why not? Neighbors help each other out. And we could have it in tip top shape by lunchtime."

Tears sprung to her eyes. "Why would you help me?"

He put his hand on her shoulder. "Because I didn't help your mom out more when she was alive. If I'd known how sick she was…"

"She didn't let anyone know." She had only let Suzy know when it got so bad that she couldn't take care of herself anymore and called her, begging her to move in and nurse her. Why couldn't Mama have told anyone else? What had driven her to keep all these secrets? Daddy leaving had been

hard on them both, but she had survived.
Why couldn't Mama?

"So let me make it up to you. Let me and
my team help you."

Suzy looked down at her hands. They
seemed so small and incapable of doing what
needed to be done. Maybe it was time to let
the past go in more ways than one, to rely
on someone else when she needed them. Finally, she relented. "All right. And I'll provide donuts and coffee."

Rick held out his hand, and they shook
on it. He left soon after, and Suzy grinned
at him as he backed out of the driveway and
drove away. She walked back into the house
and studied the state of the living room. It
wouldn't take her long to clear out the whole
house if she had a few extra bodies.

But Mama never allowed people inside.
And Suzy couldn't either.

THE NEXT EVENING, Will and Tori checked in
on their mother and found Ma had calmed
overnight. She was less angry, more re-
signed. It was almost a relief.

Will left Tori in the room saying he needed
to make some phone calls. He took his cell

from his pocket and fiddled with it, trying to find the courage to make these calls.

One. Two. Three. Will gripped the phone and counted the rings. Four. Five.

And then the answering machine clicked on. He waited while the message played then the beep. "Hey, Joanie. It's Will. Again. Listen, I know things between you and Ma haven't been the greatest. But you need to come and see her. Don't wait until it's too late."

He ended the call and thought about his message. Getting the answering machine made things easier. He wouldn't have to argue with either sister. Just state his case and hang up. He took a deep breath and dialed the next number. One. Two.

"'lo?"

Oh, great. "Hi, Carol. It's Will."

"Yeah, I know. Caller ID."

Obviously, she wasn't going to make this easy for him. "Right."

"If this is about Ma, you're wasting your breath."

Which is why he'd hoped to get her answering machine. "She's getting worse. The cancer…"

"Not my problem."

"She's your mother."

"She didn't exactly shower us with love, did she? No, she let him hurt us and kept her distance."

Always the same arguments. Didn't matter how he tried to explain things. "She took enough from him too. Did the best she could to get him to change his ways, treat us with kindness."

Silence on the other end. Then her voice came back, quieter and sounding a little more watery. "Whatever makes you sleep better at night. I gotta go."

"She's dying, Carol."

"Then call me for the funeral."

The dial tone rang in his ear, and Will stared at his phone. Not exactly how he'd hoped that would go. In fact, it opened old scars. Made him itch and sweat.

Tori came around the corner, and he held up his hand. "Left a message with Joan, but I got ahold of Carol."

"I can tell." She put a hand on his shoulder and rubbed it back and forth. "Don't let her get to you. She's a bitter, angry woman."

"So why aren't you? We grew up in the

same house. Got yelled at, called names by the same father. Why aren't you like her?"

"What would it change?" Tori held out her hands, palms up. "It's not worth my time or effort to dwell on it, so I don't. Why get upset over something that I can't change or fix? I'd rather focus on the good in my life. The boys. Ma. Even you."

He gave her a grin. "Good to know I'm in the positive column."

"Don't push it." She glanced behind him and nodded at the nurse's station. "I don't see the cute nurse."

"Suzy has the day off."

Tori snapped her fingers. "I knew you had a crush on her. You can't deny it now. I didn't say who I was talking about, but you knew her name."

"Oh, stop."

"I'm just saying." She linked her arm through his and they returned to Ma's room.

SUZY SETTLED BACK into the sofa pillows and groaned as she clutched her belly. Thank goodness she'd worn her yoga pants that night. "Don't let me eat another piece. I'm stuffed."

Pres nodded and changed the channel on the remote control. "We have all night. In the mood for a chick flick? Or something scary?" She waggled her eyebrows.

"Chick flick. You know me and scary movies." Suzy shuddered. The last one they'd watched, she'd ended up sleeping with a butcher knife next to the sofa.

"You can spend the night if you get scared."

Suzy shook her head and took a sip of her soda. "Something light. And fun. Where I don't have to think too much."

Pres changed the channel and found a movie on the Lifetime channel about a woman who met a psycho online. They considered it a compromise. Romance with a dash of thriller. On the second commercial break, Pres turned to Suzy. "What don't you want to think about?"

"Want a list?" She picked at a loose thread on her sweater. She could write a book on the things she'd rather avoid. "I've got to deal with the backyard but would rather be doing anything else. I'm still paying bills from when Mama was sick. And don't even ask where I'm going to find the money. On top of all that, I think I'm working too much."

She looked up at Pres and gave her a grin. "I dream that I'm working when I'm not there. I should be getting paid for that time too, right? Maybe even time and a half."

Her friend smiled. "You and me both. We haven't had a chance to hang out together for a while because of our schedules." She lowered the volume when the movie returned. "Are you doing okay? And don't tell me you're fine."

To be honest, Suzy didn't know how she was doing. She avoided her feelings even more than dealing with her problems. Feelings were messy, Mama had always told her. And talking about them certainly didn't solve anything. But she knew Pres wouldn't have asked the question if she didn't want an answer. Her friend cared, and that meant a lot to a woman who was alone. She shrugged. "Is everything perfect? No. But I'm dealing with it."

"Are you?"

Okay, so it was a tiny lie. She was planning on dealing with things when she had more time to do so. Unfortunately time seemed to be running out. Suzy nodded. "Yes. Once the backyard is finished, I have some things I want to clear out of Mama's house. Get it straightened up."

"So you're deciding to keep the place then?"

"You're the one who told me not to make any major decisions for the first year after Mama died. So I'm trying to figure out what I want."

Pres leaned forward. "What do you want, Suzy?"

That was the big question, wasn't it? She'd been doing what she was supposed to for years. What was expected. She'd put her own wishes aside to become a nurse because Mama had insisted she would never be without a job. Not that she didn't like nursing, but it hadn't been her first choice. And now she had the freedom to choose. To explore.

If only she had the time.

She could sell the house and go back to school. Or she could keep doing what she was doing—working with people she loved. Maybe she could move somewhere warm that had tropical drinks named after it and live on a beach. Mama's death had opened her future wide.

But the house and all the stuff inside it was

an anchor around her neck. Until she could get rid of them, she was stuck.

She couldn't escape. Couldn't move forward.

CHAPTER SIX

SUZY SET UP a card table that she'd found behind a pile of boxes then wiped it down with a damp rag to rid it of the cobwebs and dust that covered it. Maybe after the day was over, she'd pitch it in the dumpster she'd rented. She covered the table with one of her mother's linen tablecloths then arranged the boxes of doughnuts, cups and napkins on it. She ran an electrical cord from the outlet next to the front door and plugged in the percolator she'd cleaned up and filled with fresh water. Within a few moments, coffee percolated and sent a welcoming aroma through the neighborhood.

Suzy expected Rick to be the first to arrive, but he was soon followed by a familiar silver pickup truck. Apparently, Will had volunteered too. Probably more to oversee the work and make sure she did it right. She resisted the urge to roll her eyes, and instead plastered a smile on her face. Lizzie Maier

got out of the passenger seat of Rick's jeep
and joined Suzy by the breakfast table. She
held out her hand. "Hi, Suzy. I'm—"

"Lizzie. I know." The women shook hands
and sized each other up. "Rick talked non-
stop about you the other day." Suzy glanced
at the woman's left hand and smiled at the
ring. "And I see Rick still has good taste."

Lizzie looked down at her hand and
blushed. "I told him simple." She fingered
the diamond solitaire ring and smiled. "I just
didn't expect perfect."

Suzy liked what she'd heard about the
young woman. But then anyone who loved
Rick as much as everyone else in town had
to be special. Even more so when she pro-
duced a clipboard and pen. She had a list of
names of those who'd volunteered. "Let's see
the backyard so we can make a plan. Sound
good?"

They left the rest of the volunteers to fill
themselves up on sugar and caffeine and
walked to the back of the house. Lizzie didn't
judge as she made notes on her clipboard
while Suzy gave a tour and listed what Will
said he'd wanted removed. When they had
made the entire circle, they returned to the
deck. Lizzie nodded as she reviewed her

notes. "No problem. We can get this done by one, then descend on Rick's diner for lunch." She looked up at Suzy. "Okay?"

Suzy choked down the tears that threatened to spill. She couldn't talk without crying, so she gave a simple nod. Why were people being so nice to her? Why would they help her out? She hadn't done anything for them to be so generous.

Rick joined them on the deck. He put an arm around Lizzie's neck and laughed at the clipboard. "You couldn't resist, could you?" He kissed the tip of her nose. "I bet you've got one for the wedding plans too?"

"More than one."

Rick turned to Suzy. "You're coming, right? It's only…" He took a deep breath and gazed at his bride. "One more month, and then you're all mine."

Suzy shifted her weight, and her gaze drifted to Will who directed some guys to the garage. With effort, they lifted the door. One of the guys groaned at the sight of the confusion of boxes and trash bags that filled the space. Suzy had no clue what was in there, if there was anything to be kept or not. It might be better to load it all into the dumpster. What she didn't know wouldn't hurt her, right?

But what if there was something important buried under the trash? A memory she'd need one day.

Suzy glanced over to Lizzie and Rick. Try not to think about it. Try not to. "Wait!" She ran to the garage and peered inside then turned to Will. "What were you planning on doing in here?"

Will pointed to a stack of boxes on the left side. "Taking those to the dumpster." Trash bags impeded their progress into the garage. "After we get those cleared out first."

"You can't."

He raised an eyebrow at her. "Come again?"

"I haven't had a chance to go through anything in here. You can't just throw it all away." She stood in front of the garage and spread her arms. "I won't let you in here."

Will took a deep breath then lifted her and set her to the side. "This is not only a fire hazard, but it attracts critters."

"Critters?"

"Mice. Rats. Snakes."

Suzy shivered and peered inside. "I

haven't been inside here since I graduated high school."

"All the more reason to let it go." He crossed his arms over his chest. "You have to start letting things go, Suzy, or we'll never get anything accomplished. And you will lose."

She looked inside at the boxes that held something. Maybe nothing. She hadn't needed anything out here ever. Mama probably hadn't known what was there. Maybe she could let it go. She gave a short nod. "Fine. Take it all away."

"I promise if I find anything important, we will set it aside."

"Thanks." She took one last look then headed towards Lizzie who was giving out orders to the rest of the volunteers. She pointed to Suzy then to the fence line. "You're on trash detail with me."

With this many workers, they'd be finished in no time.

THEY WERE NEVER going to finish with the yard.

Suzy sighed and lifted another trash bag over the edge of the dumpster. Liking the squishy sound it made when it made contact with the others. She dusted her hands off and walked back to the yard. And sighed again.

They'd been hard at it for almost two hours but had only made a dent in what needed to be done. The old mowers hadn't started so they were in the dumpster along with the other trash bags. The walls of the shed had rotted so a few of the guys had dismantled it and thrown them out as well. But the old car still waited to be moved. The flat and worn tires made moving it difficult, so Will had let them postpone that job while they worked on clearing the rest of the space.

Jeffy, a young man with Down's syndrome who played on Rick's softball team, passed by her with two full trash bags. Right. She was supposed to be helping him. She grabbed one bag then groaned as it opened and spilled the contents among the weeds. Why did this always happen to her?

She found a new bag and started stuffing trash inside. "Problems?"

She looked up and had to shield her eyes. Will stood in front of where the sun shone, but it still required her to squint. "I guess the bag was too full."

"Or too old." He swept the yard with a

glance then focused on her. "Would you mind if I used your bathroom?"

A familiar panic hit her stomach. No one went in her house. Ever. She could almost hear her mom telling her that no one would understand how they lived. But when nature called, how could she refuse. "Umm…"

"Is that a problem?"

Big time. She hadn't cleaned the bathroom that week. She tried to remember the last time it had been done. Maybe on her day off the week before? It wasn't a pig sty by any means, but letting him into the house to use her bathroom meant he'd have to tunnel down the hallway to get to it. It meant letting him see the rest of the house, her mother's awful secret. If Mr. Town Code Inspector didn't like how her backyard looked, he certainly wouldn't appreciate Mama's organization inside the home. "I told Rick that I've been having plumbing issues, so my neighbor agreed to let us use his bathroom." She pointed to the brick house on her right. "Mr. Fletcher has the back door open. It's just off the kitchen."

Will frowned as he looked at her. Probably trying to figure out what she wasn't saying. What she couldn't say. "I'm pretty good

with my hands. I can take a look at it. Fix
your plumbing."

"That's sweet of you, but it's fine."

"If it's fine, then I can use your bathroom?"

Crud. He'd caught her. Think, Suzy, think.
He can't go in. He just can't. "Well, I haven't
had much time to clean lately."

He shrugged. "I think I can handle it. I'm
a guy."

Like that would excuse it. She was running out of excuses. If she gave any more,
he'd know that she was hiding something.
That is, if he didn't already. "Sure. Go in the
side door though. It's past the kitchen and
down the hall. First right."

Will nodded. And Suzy tried to ignore the
growing panic. She hadn't had company inside her house since before her mom got sick
two years ago. And even then, it had been
Presley and only for five minutes.

She closed her eyes. What had she just
done?

WILL COULDN'T get INSIDE the house on his
first try and had to brace his shoulder against
the door and push. He had to squeeze through
the slight opening between the frame and

door, and could only take two steps into the room before he stopped.

Mostly because he could only take those few steps before he had to avoid something.

His jaw dropped as he took in the piles of stuff that lined both sides of the kitchen. Some boxes were labeled in black marker. Most were not. Mom's dishes. Baking tins. Tupperware. Silver tea set. Lace linens.

Will took a deep breath and found a small path between the boxes that led to the hallway. He popped his head into the living room and groaned. More boxes. And appliances. Junk. Even clothes with price tags still attached. The sofa was at least cleared off and held two pillows and a blanket. A clear path led to it between the clutter, and he assumed that Suzy slept there. Sighing, he took the notebook from his back pocket and started writing.

He walked down the hallway, careful not to disturb the line of chairs and an end table that had a ton of books stacked on top of it. The bathroom at least was clean. But still crowded. He found plants in the shower stall. A pile of paper towels and toilet paper still in plastic sleeves next to the toilet. He was a big guy and had difficulty moving around the tight space.

How did she live like this?

After doing what he had come in to do, he took his time and poked his head into the bedrooms on the lower floor. Crammed with stuff, he knew his assumption about Suzy sleeping on the sofa was correct. Where did she find the room to stretch out?

He sniffed the air. A faint moldy smell but nothing rotting. At least there was that.

He replaced the notebook in his pocket then reviewed the mess. He should have known that the condition of the backyard was an indicator of what was inside the house. In the kitchen he tried to get a glimpse into the backyard through the window above the sink. Unfortunately, the stacked dishes partially blocked his view. He could see Suzy working with Jeffy, gathering up trash. With the crew that Rick had commandeered, they would finish with the backyard that morning. If only he could get them to help with the house too.

Problem was, by letting on that he knew about the house, progress on the yard would slow if not stop. He couldn't set her back just yet.

He could wait.

Once outside, he took a deep breath. While inside the home, he'd felt trapped and closed in. Out here, freedom.

In the backyard, he found Suzy watching him, chewing on her bottom lip. She had to know what he'd seen. Had to realize what he needed to do. He gave what he hoped was a reassuring smile. She returned the smile then went to the Camaro where she emptied the items from the trunk into her garbage bag. Jeffy asked Suzy something, and she bent her head closer to hear what he had to say. She nodded, and they both started coming towards him. He stopped their progress.

"What are you two doing?"

Suzy pointed to Jeffy. "He needs to use the bathroom, so I was going to show him the way."

"Not a good idea."

She looked at him and paled. Yep, Miss Suzy, I know your secret. He shrugged. "The plumbing issue was a little more complicated than I thought." He put his arm around Jeffy. "But I can take him over to Mr. Fletcher's. Sound good, buddy?"

They started walking to the neighbor's. Will glanced back and saw Suzy watching them go, biting her lip, then turning to look at her house.

Yep, he could wait. But not much longer.

A LITTLE AFTER NOON, Will shaded his eyes from the sun as Suzy threw the last bag of trash into the dumpster. She dusted off her hands then turned and saw him watching her. She gave him a thumbs up then walked past him back into the yard. He followed her. "I need to talk to you."

She shushed him. "Rick is speaking."

His softball coach was indeed speaking. "I wanted to thank all of you for your hard work today. It's nice to see us come together and do some good for one of our neighbors."

"Are you campaigning for re-election already?" someone called.

After a couple of chuckles, Rick held up his hands for silence. "All I'm saying is thank you. And that lunch is on me. Let's go to the diner."

The team seemed to like that idea and soon paired off and left in the cars they'd brought that morning. Suzy went up to Rick and offered her hand. "Thank you again, Rick. I don't know how long it would have taken me to do this on my own."

"You can always ask for help, Suzy."

She gave a short nod, then turned to Will. "Well, Mr. Inspector, I believe the yard is now up to code. And with two days to spare."

He nodded. "Yes, but there's something we need to discuss." He extended his hand to Rick. "Thanks, coach. We'll see you at the diner. I need to talk to Miss Bylin for a moment privately."

Rick put his arm around Lizzie, and the couple left the yard. Will turned back to Suzy who bit her lip. "You sound serious."

"It is serious."

She sighed. "I know you saw inside the house. You saw it all."

"Miss Bylin…"

"Suzy, please."

"The condition of your home…" He frowned, shaking his head. "It's a hazard to your health and your safety. You need to get it cleared out." She had to know how serious the situation was. She could get sick from the hoard. Hurt if something fell on her. Didn't she get it? "Public health matters aren't a laughing matter." He brought his notebook back up and ticked off items. "No clear pathways. That's a fire code violation. Papers and boxes near an appliance with an open flame." He looked up at her. "Another violation." Back down at his notebook. "No defined sleeping space."

"That's not a violation."

"No, but a concern." He stepped closer and dropped his voice. "Miss Bylin, Suzy, how do you sleep? Prepare your meals? How can you live in that squalor?"

Suzy backed away as if he'd slapped her, which he had in a way, even if it had been with his words. "I live just fine. I've been trying to take care of things since Mama died, but you don't know what that's been like. To have to deal with what's been left behind on top of everything else." She seemed as if she wanted to say more, but she hesitated and took a deep breath instead. "I'm fine."

"As code inspector, I have no choice but to give you notice."

"So another two weeks?"

As if two weeks would solve her problems. And his. "You'll need more time to take care of this." He watched her while she probably prayed for six months. Finally, he told her, "You have thirty days to clean it up."

Her shoulders sagged but he didn't know if it was from relief or defeat. "Or what? You'll do it for me? Because that's sounding pretty good right now."

"Or the town will confiscate your home."

He winced at the expression on her face. This part of his job always made him feel like the bad guy.

CHAPTER SEVEN

SUZY ARRIVED A minute early before she was scheduled to clock in at the nursing home. Which considering her state of mind was a miracle in and of itself.

Thirty days, and she'd be homeless. What was she going to do? Where would she go?

Before she could let those thoughts overwhelm her, she dumped her purse and things in her locker and checked the schedule on the bulletin board. Good. An easy night.

At the nurses' station, she found Rita lounging there. "Mark the calendar, you're on time today."

Suzy attempted a smile but knew it missed its mark by the way her boss looked at her. Rita put her arm around her shoulders. "You okay, Suzy Q?"

Suzy nodded and walked down the hall towards her first patient. She paused outside for a moment and tried to conjure up her smile. It had never been a problem in the past. Even when her mother lay dying and after she was gone, Suzy had been able to smile and bring comfort to those who needed it. If she could cheer Mama from her darkest doldrums, then she could do that for her patients.

Problem was, she'd smiled for everyone else but needed someone to smile for her now.

She entered Mrs. Stone's room. Again the television played in the background, but the older woman didn't pay attention to it. As Suzy walked around the bed, Mrs. Stone closed her eyes and pretended to sleep.

Suzy could use the quiet so she didn't say anything. Checked the monitors. Noted vitals on her tablet. Glanced at the dinner tray that had been delivered but not touched.

She had her hand on the doorknob to leave when Mrs. Stone asked, "Dearie, what's wrong?"

Suzy turned back to find the older woman propped up on one elbow and watching her. "I thought you were sleeping."

"No you didn't." She patted the side of her bed. "You look like you need to talk to someone. Tell me what's going on."

Suzy shrugged. "Nothing. I'll check on

you later. And you might want to eat something before I do."

"Come on. You can tell me." Again she patted the empty space beside her.

Suzy was tempted to sit and spill, like a daughter to a mother, but there was protocol for a reason. Instead, she evaded. "Did your family come to see you today?"

Mrs. Stone sighed. "Tori was here with the twins. Then my son stopped by this afternoon." She adjusted the pictures on the nightstand. "Doesn't matter whether they visit. I want to go home."

Suzy consulted the woman's chart. "The doctor doesn't think you're ready just yet."

"I'd heal faster at home."

"I know it's hard to accept help, but we have the best therapy program for you here."

Mrs. Stone cleared her throat. "It's because none of my children will help me. If they loved me, they would take care of me and not put me in a home."

Suzy sat on the bed next to Mrs. Stone and took her hand in hers. "They do love you. But there are times when they can't do what we nurses and doctors can. Let us do our jobs and help you heal." She pulled the table with the food tray closer to them and removed the lid covering Mrs. Stone's dinner. "But you have to do your part too. And that means eating your meals."

"Your cook can't make meatloaf that comes close to mine." She peered closer to the plate and sniffed. "The potatoes are lumpy. And I can't stand gelatin with fruit cocktail."

Suzy made notes. "Okay, I'll let the kitchen staff know." She looked back up at Mrs. Stone. "But you still have to eat. If I can get you something else, what would you like?"

The older woman shrugged. "Doesn't matter."

Suzy stood and nodded. "Okay. Liver and onions it is." She started to walk out of the room again.

"Wait."

Suzy smiled and turned back. "You gotta give me something."

The older woman huffed. "Fine. I could go for some pie."

Suzy grinned. "Dessert first? My kind of woman." She grabbed the food tray. "I'll be right back."

"Wait." Mrs. Stone reached for the tray. "I could probably force myself to eat the meatloaf and potatoes. But after my pie."

"You got it, Mrs. Stone." Suzy placed the tray back on the table and left the room. In the cafeteria, she found the staff washing dishes and prepping the meals for the next day. "Hey, Al. Any pie left?"

He brought a piece of coconut cream out of the cooler. "Anything for you, Miss Suzy."

"Can you make a note that 23 has a picky eater? She's got a sweet tooth though."

"She's sent back full trays the last two days." Al noted on the white board. "But she must like pie."

"Especially yours. Thanks."

When Suzy returned to the room, she found Mrs. Stone sitting up and waiting for her. With a flourish, Suzy placed the piece of pie in front of her. "I hope you like coconut cream."

"Adore it." Mrs. Stone picked up the fork and started to shovel the dessert into her mouth. "This is good."

"It's Al's best." Suzy placed a napkin under Mrs. Stone's chin. "If he sends you more, will you eat it?"

The older woman nodded between bites.

At least one woman's blues could be saved by pie.

AFTER WORK THE following Monday, Will stopped by his mother's house. She'd complained on his last visit that she needed something to read. Knowing her, she had a bunch of books on the nightstand by her bed. He figured he'd run in, feed the cats again, grab the books and get home at a decent time.

The house smelled as if it hadn't been opened in a while, so he left the door open to let in some fresh air. He also opened a few windows.

In Ma's bedroom there were several books on the nightstand so he got those then searched the room for a bag to place them in. Finding none, he went into his dad's office, which hadn't changed in years. Maybe Ma had kept his dad's book bag that had gone to libraries around the world.

He sat in the chair behind the desk and opened the lower left desk drawer. Files neatly labeled, but no book bag.

He shut the drawer and tried the other side of the desk. He spotted the leather book bag, pulled it out and snapped it open before adding the books. Good thing he knew Ma better than she probably did herself.

He stood and planned on leaving but glanced at the lower left desk drawer again. Files. He sat back down and opened the drawer. Flipped through the files until he found the one he wanted. Ma's will.

After his father died, Will had been afraid of what would happen to them if something had happened to her as well. After a lot of arguments, he'd convinced Ma to visit the lawyer and update the will. He opened the file and perused the document. From the looks of things, not much had changed. Everything split between the four kids. And donations to several charities that Ma supported.

He heard the screen door open and slam shut from the living room. "Will?"

He looked up and stuffed the will back into the file. Tori wouldn't understand his need to make sure things were ready. Just in case the worst happened. Instead, she'd think he'd given up.

He knew he wasn't ready for that.

He followed the sound of her voice to their mom's bedroom where she had a suitcase open on the bed. Will held up the book bag.

"Ma said she was getting bored with television."

Tori nodded and opened a dresser drawer. She pulled out several nightgowns, T-shirts and jogging pants. "She told me she misses her own clothes."

"Ma's subtle way of telling us to do stuff without coming out and asking us directly." He sighed and looked around the room. Ever since he could remember, their mother had kept the house immaculate. Probably because of his father's insistence that everything had a place and detested clutter. Said it distracted them from what was important. Whatever the reason, his mom had obviously kept it the same. "Do you ever remember the house being messy growing up?"

Tori frowned and stopped pulling socks from the dresser drawer. "No, I don't. Why?"

"If we had grown up with clutter, would that be our normal?"

"You're asking some weird questions."

"In a weird mood, I guess." He paused then took a seat on the bed. "I keep my house clean."

"You mean sterile."

"But that's what feels normal to me. A bunch of boxes and a stack of newspapers dated from years ago doesn't." He waved off her questions. "Never mind. Just thinking of someone I know. She grew up with a messy house."

Tori's face broke into a grin. "I knew it must be a woman that had you acting so strangely. Maybe that nurse Suzy?"

"It's not what you think."

"Uh huh. You think she's pretty."

He thought she was beautiful. "That doesn't matter. She's in trouble, and I don't know how to help her."

Tori paused and looked him over. "You mean fix her."

"Same thing."

"Helping means that you work together towards a solution." She wagged her finger at him while she folded their mother's clothes and put them in the suitcase. "You, dear brother, prefer to step in and take over by fixing it yourself."

"Do I do that with you too?"

She checked the items in the suitcase before shutting it and zipping the lid closed. "And Ma. We're used to it. Is Suzy your friend?"

"I don't know if we're friends. More

like…" He coughed then stood. "Acquaintances. And barely that."

"But you want to be more."

"I want to help her out because she needs me." He felt his cheeks warm. "I mean, she needs help. Whatever."

Tori laughed and put her arm around him. "Oh my. You must have it bad."

"I don't have anything." He shook her arm off him affectionately. "And speaking of fixing, what's with the new hair color?"

Tori reached up and touched the blond ends. "You don't like it?"

"It's fine. Just wondering what prompted the change." He bumped her hip with his. "A new friend?"

"I wish." She heaved the suitcase on to the floor. "Think you can carry this to your truck?"

He lifted it easily and followed her down the hallway then out to his pickup. With the suitcase in the back, he could swing by the home before going to his own townhouse. Maybe sneak a peek at his favorite nurse.

"You're doing it again."

"I'm not doing anything."

"You're thinking of Suzy who's just a friend." She used her fingers to put quotes around the word. "You get this look on your face when you do."

He reached up and touched his cheeks. "I do?"

"Yep. Like I said, you've got it bad all right."

An image of Suzy filled his head, and he tried to clear it before his face gave away anymore. "Never mind. So why the new haircut? And don't think I didn't notice that you're wearing new clothes too."

She reached out and touched the hem of her shirt. "I get a discount since I work at Roxy's so I thought I'd take advantage of it."

"Is that all there is?"

"I'm lonely, okay?" She ran her fingers through her hair. "This is my desperate attempt at trying to attract a guy."

"Any particular guy?"

"If you're asking if there's someone I'm interested in, no. Sadly. Seems that every one I meet gets compared to Shawn. That should make it easy since he turned out to be a jerk. But…" She hesitated and pulled her hair off her neck then let it go. "I've loved him since I was fifteen, Will. More than half my life. I can't just forget that."

Will put his arm around his sister and let her gain her composure. He knew that there had been a reason behind these changes. Had suspected it was his ex-brother-in-law, but his sister had the same strength they had been taught. She could get over him. Find a new life. Right? "It will get better."

"When? Because I'm tired of being alone. Raising twin teenage boys is a challenge, and to do it alone is impossible at times." She shook her head. "They're starting to ask questions about girls and sex and...I'm clueless. I've loved only one man my whole life. What do I know about dating anymore?"

"I can talk to them."

She gave a short, bitter laugh. "No offense, but you haven't exactly been burning up the dating scene. When was your last one?"

He paused and tried to think. "I date."

"Trish was three years ago. And she was no catch."

"It hasn't been that long." Had it? He tried to remember when he'd shared a meal with a female that he wasn't related to or worked with. "Okay, so I'm no expert, but I am a guy and I remember what it was like being a teenage boy. I'll talk to them."

She finally nodded. "Fine. Thanks." She looked up at him. "You done trying to fix me?"

He smiled. "Only offering my help." He glanced at the darkening sky. "I think I'll lock up the house then swing by and deliver this to Ma. Interested?"

"I've got to pick the boys up from soccer practice then try to find something to feed them. I swear, they're turning into walking stomachs with hormones." She hugged him around the waist. "Thanks."

Will hugged her back. "Lovey."

A KNOCK ON the front door startled Suzy. Was Will back to remind her that she had less than four weeks? Would he recognize that she'd begun in the living room? Four bags of trash waited by the garage to be taken to the curb for collection, but it didn't look like she'd made much progress.

Another knock. Suzy peered through the peephole. She sighed. Presley.

She opened the door but only slightly. "Hey, what's up?"

"You're not answering your cell." Presley tried to look beyond Suzy. "You going to let me in?"

Suzy glanced behind her then opened the door wider. "Sure."

Presley walked past her and entered the living room. Then she turned to face her. "Why didn't you tell me, Suze? I thought we were best friends. That we shared everything."

Suzy frowned and scanned her brain for what she'd kept from her. "About Will?"

"About the big notice on the front of your house."

Oh that. Will had stopped by two days before and taped it to the front window. Notice of eviction if the premises didn't pass inspection. And the end date. "It's no big deal."

"You're losing your mom's house, and it's no big deal?" Pres shook her head. "Why can't you ask for help? Especially when you need it the most."

"Because this is my problem. Not anyone else's." She swept her hand around the room. "If I don't know what to do with this, how can I ask anyone else?" She pointed at the boxes. "You don't understand what it was like growing up like this. No one does."

"So tell me."

Suzy covered her eyes with one hand. "There was always…stuff. Everywhere." She looked up at Pres. "And it didn't matter if I cleaned things up or threw things out, she'd just get more. It was never enough. Never."

"You don't have to deal with it alone." Pres put her arm around Suzy's shoulders. "I want to help. There're other people who do too. Please let us."

"I can't."

"Why?"

"Because Mama said we couldn't let anyone see this. Our secret she called it." Suzy picked at one of her nails, avoiding her friend's piercing gaze. "Mama wouldn't let me—she was depressed and wouldn't let anyone in. Sometimes not even me. And definitely not anyone outside of the family. She had a few friends, but they never came over. We've been friends since college, and you've been in my house how many times? Twice. And only so far. Because I couldn't let you see. Couldn't let you know what it was like in here."

"Well, I'm here now. So show me."

Suzy sighed. "You're pretty much seeing it. It's like this in every room. Still feel like helping?"

"You're my best friend, so yes. Of course I'll help." Pres left Suzy in the living room

and went towards the bathroom and bedrooms. She paused as she saw the path that
Suzy had made after moving in with her
mom to take care of her. "Oh, Suze."

"Don't say it." Suzy walked past her and
led her to the bathroom and opened the
door. "It took me almost a month after moving in to get the bathroom cleaned and be
able to use it." She motioned towards her
mom's bedroom. "Mama stayed in there her
last days. I couldn't move her around so I
had to make these paths to get to her." She
opened the door to her childhood bedroom.
"I haven't slept in there since I left for college. Mama seemed to fill it with stuff once
I was gone, and I haven't been able to get in
there since."

"Why didn't you say anything?"

"What am I supposed to say? My mom
can't throw anything away? She shops for
things she doesn't need, doesn't even want?"
Suzy felt the tears coming. "If I told you
what it was like here, would you have believed me?"

"I couldn't imagine this." Pres pushed on
the door to Suzy's old room and peered inside. Clothes in bags. Boxes of books. Not
one, but two full sets of dishes stacked

against the wall. "It's like she needed to fill the space you once held."

That was exactly what Mama had done. Suzy had finished her first semester at college and come home for the holidays to find her bedroom brimming with stuff. She'd been forced to sleep in Mama's bed with her because there hadn't been any room. And it wasn't just her room. It was in the living room where the loveseat got covered so they had to sit on the couch next to each other. And at the dining room table, so they ate meals at the counter sitting on stools pushed together. The stuff crowded them in, until soon, Mama filled so much space that there wasn't room for Suzy anymore. "Will gave me thirty days, Pres. Thirty. I've been working on this since before Mama died. How in the world am I going to get it all taken care of in time?"

"We can do it." Pres looked at her then back at the bedroom. "Because we have to. You can't lose the house."

"It's all I have left."

Pres shook her head. "That's not true, Suze. You have me. And I promise to be there for you."

Right. Because people had never left her.

Suzy tried hard to clear away those negative thoughts. Presley wasn't like her dad or mom. If she said she'd be there, she would be.

Suzy nodded. "Thanks."

PAYDAY, AND THE living was good. Will made a beeline for the bank. At the desk, he took his check out of his back pocket and tore the stub off that listed how much of his check had gone to taxes and insurance. He tried not to look at the gross amount. It would only depress him. He endorsed the top then completed a deposit slip and double checked his math.

There wasn't much of a line, only one person waiting ahead of him so he was at the teller window pretty quickly. He handed his check and deposit slip to the teller. "Hey, Sandy. How're things going?"

"Pretty good, Will. How's your mom?" She glanced around then leaned forward. "We really miss her around here. When is she coming back?"

If she was coming back was a better question. "It might be a while."

Sandy reached out and touched his hand with hers. "Tell her we miss her and love her. And to get better so she can get her butt back here quick."

Will chuckled. "I will. But you might want to stop in and see her. I'm sure she'd get a kick out of a visit."

He felt a hand on his shoulder and turned to find Toby standing there. The man gave him a short nod. "Would you mind stopping in my office before you leave?"

Sandy handed Will his receipt and counted his out cash. "We'll see you soon."

He nodded then walked back to the branch manager's office and knocked on the door before entering. Toby looked up from the papers he'd been reading and motioned to the chairs in front of his desk. "Thanks for stopping in. How's your mom?"

"Hates being at the seniors' home. I'm sure she'd appreciate a visit."

Toby winced. "I stopped in there soon after she was moved." He pushed the papers toward Will. "According to our records, you are your mother's power of attorney."

"Only in the case that she can't make a decision for herself."

Toby pushed the papers closer to the edge of the desk. "Your mother needs to read these and sign them."

Will quickly scanned them. "You want her to quit?"

The manager colored and cleared his throat. "We…I want her to take a medical leave for an indefinite period."

"In other words, quit." Will stood and tossed the papers back on to Toby's desk. "By law, my mother is allowed six weeks of leave. And your company policy extends that another six."

"Do you think she's coming back? Really?" Toby lumbered to his feet and walked around the desk. "I can only keep her position open for the twelve weeks. After that, I can't promise to keep her here. They'll find her a teller position in another branch."

Will shook his head. "I gotta go see my mother. Assure her that everything is okay." He opened the door then paused with his hand on the knob. "She always told me that you were a jerk, but I chalked it up to you being her boss."

"My hands are tied, Will. I can't keep going short a teller."

"So find a temp to fill her spot until she returns from her leave."

"Can't. I need Eva, or I need a permanent replacement."

Will glared at the man. "Good to know you care about my mom."

He left the office and walked through the bank lobby. An older man stopped him. "How's Eva doing, Will?"

He glanced towards Toby's office. "On the mend. You should stop in at the seniors' home and see her."

The older man shook his head. "Those places depress me. Probably because I know I'll be there myself one day."

"Give me a break, Walt. You'll be living forever in your cottage." Will pounded the guy's back. "I'll tell Ma you say hello."

"She's a heck of a woman."

Will nodded. "The best."

FROM THE BANK, Will drove home to his townhouse. When he pulled up to the curb, he noticed a familiar yellow Volkswagen parked not far from him. He walked over, but this car was missing the smiley face bumper sticker. Not Suzy's car then. The thought of her reminded him that he missed her. He wondered what she was up to. Not the clean-up, though he hoped she was busy with that. But if she was okay.

When he let himself into his townhouse,

he flipped on the lights and put the truck keys on a hook near the front door. His stomach growled, reminding him that lunch had been hours ago. He went through to the kitchen and opened the fridge. He peered inside at the scant supplies. Since Ma had been in the hospital, he hadn't had much time for domestic chores, particularly cooking. He claimed an old apple and washed it before biting into it.

He took his dinner out into the living room and flopped on to the sofa. Will glanced around the room. No pictures. No knick knacks. Nothing that proved who lived there. The walls painted white. The carpet a light beige. Little color.

Little life.

He didn't have to walk through the rest of his home to know that he'd find more of the same. The only thing that held any meaning was the picture of him and Ma at his graduation from Parris Island that he kept on his nightstand. One of the proudest days of his life. How he'd missed his dad that day he graduated from boot camp. Even if it was only to prove to him that he was a man.

He thought of the difference between his house and Suzy's. While his was clean and neat, hers teemed with too much stuff. But it showed a life lived.

Restless, he stood and walked room to room. His house needed something that he couldn't give it. It was merely a place to sleep for him. He could sell it tomorrow without a second thought.

Shouldn't a home mean something more?

SUZY WANTED TO shake off the blues that had edged her mood after Pres had left. They'd worked for an hour on her old room, and five more trash bags had joined the ones already by the garage. She'd also filled the back of her car with donations to take to the charity center. Maybe other families could use the clothes and dishes.

Now at the nursing home, she pasted a smile on her face and ventured out on her first rounds. She made Mrs. Stone's room the last on her stops. She noticed that she had been eating more lately, especially desserts. Not exactly the most nutritious, but it was better than nothing. She breezed into the room and stopped at the sight of Will sitting in the chair next to his mom's bed. "I can come back later."

He stood. "I was about to leave anyway."

He leaned over and kissed his mom's cheek. "Lovey. I'll see you tomorrow."

He glanced at her before leaving then walked past her, leaving a chill in the air. Mrs. Stone looked at her son's departure then to Suzy. "What was that about?"

"Nothing. Why do you all say lovey when you leave?"

"You're changing the subject. That was not nothing." She narrowed her eyes. "Did something happen between you two?"

"Not what you think."

"We say lovey because it's something my grandmother and my mother always told me, so I passed that on to my kids." Mrs. Stone peered at her closely. "Did you two have a fight?"

Suzy warmed the stethoscope then placed it on the older woman's chest. "Your heart sounds good."

"And how does yours sound?"

Suzy straightened and looked at her. "We're not discussing my heart. Did you see the therapist today?"

"What does my chart say?"

"It says that she wants you to start getting up and putting weight on that hip." Suzy placed the walker at the side of the bed, then moved the bedside table out of the way and left the tablet on top of it. "Want to try?"

Mrs. Stone shook her head and pulled the covers tighter around her. "No, I think I'll wait until tomorrow."

"You're hurting my feelings. Don't think I can handle you?"

"I don't think I want to fall."

Suzy gave her a smile that hopefully reassured the other woman. "I won't let you fall. I'll be right here the entire time."

The woman inventoried her from head to toe. "You can't possibly lift me. You're tiny."

"So are you." Suzy helped Mrs. Stone swing her legs around to the side of the bed then got her to shift forward. She pressed the button on the bed to lower it so that the older woman could put her feet on the ground. "We'll do a count of three."

"Make it five. My husband always counted to five." She adjusted her nightgown over her legs then put her arms around Suzy's neck. "One. Two."

"Five." Suzy brought her up and out of the bed and hung on to the older woman until she could get adjusted to being on her feet again. "How does that feel?"

"It hurts."

"It will until your body completely heals. And walking will help that process." Suzy reached around and pulled the walker closer. "I'd like you to meet your new friend. You'll be spending a lot of time together."

Mrs. Stone made a disgusted noise. "How did I get this old? What happened?"

"You're only as old as you feel."

"Well, I feel a hundred at least. Maybe two."

Mrs. Stone inhaled a deep breath then took one hand off of Suzy's shoulder and placed it on the walker. Then she moved her other hand, while Suzy hung on to her until she could take the weight of standing and knew that she wouldn't fall. "Good. Now try a step."

"Can I get used to standing for a minute?"

"The longer you wait, the harder it gets." And didn't she know that lesson. Suzy stood back and scrutinized her patient. "If you can make it to the door, I'll tell you what happened with your son."

Mrs. Stone gave a faint smile. "You know what buttons to push, don't you?" She pressed the walker forward a few inches then took one step.

"It got you to walk, didn't it?" Suzy stayed

close just in case but watched her slowly walk towards the door.

When they reached it, the older woman sighed. "I know I made it here, but I don't know how I'm going to make it back." She glanced at the bed then Suzy. "It looks a million miles away."

"It's only three feet."

With Suzy's help, Mrs. Stone moved the walker around to face the bed. But before she'd take a step, she looked at her. "I made it to the door, so you have to give me something for my efforts."

Suzy bit her lip then shrugged. "Your son was at my house last weekend. Helping me clean my yard."

"And?"

"You'll get the rest of the story once you walk back to the bed."

Muttering about hard bargains, Mrs. Stone took her time getting back to the bed. Once there, she shoved the walker away and Suzy helped the older woman get into bed. "There. That wasn't so hard."

"Says the younger woman with two good hips." She adjusted the blankets around her again. "Are you dating my son?"

"Not even close." Suzy updated her tablet

about Mrs. Stone's progress with the walker. "He's kicking me out of my home."

"What? I'm sure you're exaggerating." Mrs. Stone thought about it for a moment then gave a short nod. "My son doesn't do anything without weighing all sides. And driving a woman out of her own home is not something he would do on a whim."

"Well, he is."

"He must have a reason."

"He doesn't have much use for mercy, does he?" Suzy didn't wait for a response. "Never mind. He's your son, so you'll defend him no matter what I say. But he's a hard man."

"Made in his father's image, dearie." Mrs. Stone patted the side of her bed, inviting Suzy to take a seat. When she did, the expression on the older woman became serious. "Will was raised to be tough. To ignore emotion and focus on the facts. My husband made sure that Will would never be vulnerable. Unfortunately, it made him hard too."

"Seems I was raised to give up the things I wanted in favor of everyone else. Especially my mom." Suzy glanced out the window to the courtyard. "I loved her. Still do. But when she was depressed, it wasn't easy."

"None of us have ideal family lives, Suzy. We might like to pretend otherwise, but it's simply not the case." She squeezed her hand. "Will needs someone like you to bring balance to his life. To add the light to the darkness. Joy to the difficult."

"He doesn't need me, Mrs. Stone. He's just doing his job."

"We'll see." The older woman peered into her face. "Do you like my son?"

Suzy slid off the bed then used the controls to raise it to its previous height. "I've got some more patients to see. Will you be okay? I'll peek in on you later but use the call button if you need me before then."

"What are you going to do about Will?"

"What I have to." She would do what she had to do to get the house cleaned up. If that meant getting rid of the things that were holding her back, then she would have to do it. She'd lost her mom. She wouldn't lose her house too.

WILL LEFT THE office early so that he could meet with his mom's doctor who'd called both he and Tori for a consultation. The drive to the seniors' home was becoming way too familiar. It's like the truck knew how to get there even if his eyes were closed.

He parked in the lot next to his sister's car. He entered the building and walked down the hall to his mother's room, found Tori brushing Ma's hair while they waited for the doctor to arrive. "What do you think he's going to say?"

Ma looked up with a wide grin. "That I'm going home. Has to be, right?"

Will knew that his mom could barely make it down the hall using a walker. They wouldn't be releasing her already, would they? "Ma, you can't go home yet. How would you get around the house?"

"Suzy seems to think I'm doing great." She watched him as she said the nurse's name, and he wanted to escape under such scrutiny. "Didn't she tell you herself?"

"Nurse Bylin doesn't discuss your care with me much."

"What does she talk about with you?"

Tori's head popped up and she gave a short laugh. "I think he likes her, Ma. Look at his eyes. They're all gooey."

"My eyes are fine." He frowned at them. "What are you two doing?"

His mom smiled. "Trying to match you up with the nurse. Is it working?"

"Thank you for your concern, but things between Suzy and I are…strained." He stared at them both as they shared smiles and knowing looks. Well, what they thought were knowing looks but they didn't know anything. They didn't know that he was going to have to force Suzy from her place. That he would be responsible for her being homeless.

That he longed to scoop her up in his arms and protect her from the harsh realities of her situation. That he wanted to save her. Be her superhero.

"The two of you can stop that right now." He pointed at his mother and then his sister. "I'm not getting involved with Suzy."

"Oh, not at all." Tori bit back a grin. "Just the mention of her name makes you get all flustered, but there's nothing going on."

"Right." He was grateful that the doctor had appeared. "Thank God you're here. Are you sending my mom home?"

The doctor removed his glasses and sucked on the end. "Not yet. I'm concerned that your mother isn't more mobile by now. She's been up and walking for a few days and should be able to make it farther than she has."

He whipped off the covers and started to feel along Eva's hips and thighs. His mom tried not to cry out, but bit her lip. "I'd like to order some tests. See what we're up against."

Tori grimaced. "More tests? Does that mean you're expecting bad news?"

The doctor replaced the sheet over his mother's legs. "It means I want to know what we're dealing with. Your mother should be further along in her recovery, but something is keeping her back." He glanced at Eva. "Are you doing the most you can to get out of this bed?"

"Maybe."

The doctor eyed her as Will glanced at his sister. What was going on? She shrugged back at him and concentrated on the doctor. "Ma, are you following the doctor's orders?"

"Of course, I am. What else do I have to do in this place?" She turned on Will. "You've left me here to rot, so I do what I have to do in order to get out of here. I want to go home." She turned to the doctor. "Tell me what I have to do to get out of here."

For the next twenty minutes, the doctor laid out what he wanted her to do. To get out of bed and walk more. To eat the meals he prescribed to build her strength. To get enough rest. But it also meant pushing herself more. Listening to her physical therapist rather than fighting against her. And above all, to find the strength to fight. "You do that, and I'll sign you out to go home in two weeks."

Ma looked worriedly at each of her children. "I'll try."

Will scrutinized his mother. She always did more than just try. There had to be something else going on. Some fear maybe? He put his hand on her shoulder, as if he could give her his strength to fight this.

They thanked the doctor, and he left them alone. Tori glanced at her watch and grabbed her purse. "I've got to run and get the boys." She kissed her mother on the cheek then reached up on tiptoe for Will. "Lovey."

Then she was gone.

Will pulled up the chair next to his mother's bedside. "What's going on, Ma?"

She picked at the sheet. "Don't know what you're talking about."

"You don't trust the doctor. Fine, I get that. You want to protect Tori. Okay." He leaned forward. "What didn't you say earlier?"

Eva sighed and closed her eyes. "You're so much like your father. Couldn't keep anything from him either." She opened her eyes and gazed into his. "It hurts to walk, and it's not the trying to heal kind of ache. It's all the way to the middle of my bone kind of ache like I was feeling before I fell."

"They fixed your hip but not the cancer, Ma. We haven't even started to deal with that." Will reached out and took her small bony hand in his. "Is that what's scaring you?"

"I almost wish it was my heart, and I'd die quickly. Instead I have to linger."

"Not just linger, but recover. I mean, isn't that your goal? To beat this?"

"Oh sure, sure." She waved him off, but then paused. "But what if I can't?"

He didn't want to think of that. Couldn't think of her dying. "You have children and grandchildren who need you."

"No one needs me. You've all got your own lives." She gave him a weak smile. "So tell me about you and the nurse."

"Why? So you can feel needed?" He shook his head. He'd do anything for his mom, but even he couldn't lie to her to make her feel better. "I told you. There's nothing to tell. She hates me."

"I wouldn't say that exactly."

He glanced at her. She'd said that as if she knew more than what she was letting on. Could Suzy have confided in his mother? In a way, it was nice to know she felt comfortable with his mom to do that. On the other hand, it might be perceived as manipulation. Get to his mom first so that she could persuade him to take it easy on Suzy.

Nah. Didn't sound like his favorite nurse.

He had to say something. "I might have to take her home away from her."

"So don't."

As if it were that easy. "It's not up to me, Ma. There's rules. Policies. When you don't follow them, there are consequences."

She took his hand in hers. "But wouldn't it be nice to show some mercy instead? She's a good person and works really hard."

He wasn't sure he'd know what to do with mercy if he had the chance. "I do that, and I could lose my job. It's about results. Not about looking the other way."

"Then give her a hand."

"She doesn't want help. Especially from me."

"Have you asked her?"

A nurse opened the door, dragging a cart behind her. "Ready for dinner, Mrs. Stone?"

"You bet she is." He stood and kissed his mom on her cheek. "Lovey. I'll see you tomorrow."

DEATH IN A nursing home was expected, but it still shocked and saddened the patients as well as the staff. Suzy signed the paperwork to release Mrs. Duff's body to the funeral home then handed the documents to the paramedic. "I was hoping she'd make it."

"You and me both. But at least she's at peace now."

"See you, Suze." The paramedic motioned to his partner who pushed the gurney with Mrs. Duff's body to the ambulance at the front entrance.

Suzy called up Mrs. Duff's medical file and made notes of how they'd try to resuscitate her for fifteen minutes before the doctor on duty had pronounced her dead. At least her daughter had been here for a visit when that happened. Shanna might not see it now, but one day she'd appreciate being able to say goodbye in the moment.

At least Suzy did. She'd been holding Mama's hand, telling her it was okay to go.

That she'd remember her but survive without her. And she'd watched her mother take that final breath.

Loud voices from the community room startled Suzy from her reverie. She saved her notes then left the tablet on the desk to go referee. Tonight was euchre night which tended to spark more fights than usual. She found Mrs. Henderson and Mrs. Stone glaring at each other across the card table. "You're cheating." Mrs. Stone tried to stand but her hip must still be bothering her since she sat down quickly.

Mrs. Henderson shook her head. "I am not. I simply asked about Myra's ring."

"You were talking about diamonds. Letting your partner know what you had in your hand." Mrs. Stone slapped her cards on the table, and they slid off and on to the floor.

"Well now you've ruined the game." Mrs. Henderson stood as Suzy approached the table. "I don't want to play anymore."

"Ladies, is there something I can help with?"

"You can tell her not to cheat." Mrs. Stone scowled at the other woman. "Or maybe that's why Vivien got the role and not you."

Mrs. Henderson's mouth gaped open as

Suzy put her hand on Mrs. Stone's shoulder. "I'm sure this is just a misunderstanding."

The games at the other tables quieted as the residents turned to see what was going on. Suzy was growing impatient. She didn't need this. Not right now while she was trying to deal with Mrs. Duff and everything else that followed a death. "Listen, everyone, I have some news. About Louise."

The residents focused on her. Mrs. Henderson nodded. "We already know. Thomas came down to tell us."

"She was one of your friends here, right?"

Mrs. Henderson shrugged. "We shared a table in the dining room. On the days she could make it there anyway."

"Well, if you or anyone else needs to talk, I'm available." She glanced around the room. "One of us leaving is always hard."

"She didn't leave to go home. She died." Mrs. Stone dragged her walker over and struggled to get herself situated before standing. "Let's not sugarcoat it."

Suzy watched her fight with the walker. "Want me to help you to your room?"

Mrs. Stone shook her head. "If I can't walk to my room on my own then maybe I need to leave like Louise did."

She slowly shuffled out of the room, and Suzy turned to the other residents. "Death isn't something that we like to talk about, but talking can help."

Mrs. Henderson nodded again but didn't say anything. Everyone else stayed in their seats and eventually returned to their card games. Suzy waited. If they'd been told of Mrs. Duff, she was surprised that there hadn't been more than one fight over cards. She'd keep an ear out because there would likely be more. Easier to fight over games than talk about the real issue. The grief. The fear.

She left the community room and headed for the nurses' station. She noticed that Mrs. Stone still ambled down the hallway. Something about her made Suzy follow her into her room. "Would you like some help getting back into bed?"

"No."

Suzy stayed and monitored the older woman as she carefully turned a circle so that she was able to back up onto the bed. She pushed the walker out of the way then swiveled to get under the covers. She turned to Suzy and scowled. "I told you I was fine."

"Just making sure."

"You don't need to hover."

"Didn't think that's what I was doing. Since this is my job." Suzy stayed where she was, just in case. "Are you okay?"

"Fine." Mrs. Stone pulled the covers higher to her chin and settled back into the pillow. She closed her eyes. "I can't believe Louise is gone."

Suzy took two steps inside the room. "You knew her?"

"We were in the garden club together. You should have seen her hydrangeas." Mrs. Stone shook her head. "No one could get them to grow like she could. Large blossoms in deep blues and purples. Beautiful. She knew a secret for growing them, but now it's probably died along with her."

Suzy walked to the bed and put her hand on Mrs. Stone's shoulder. "I'm sorry for your friend."

"We were hardly friends. More like..." Mrs. Stone bit her lip. "I think you youngsters say frenemy?"

"Rivals then."

"Definitely that." Mrs. Stone expelled a long breath. "Don't they say deaths come in threes?"

"Not here at the seniors' home. So you

don't have to worry." Suzy rubbed her shoulder. It wasn't exactly the truth, but better to hold on to hope and thus life instead.

"I wasn't thinking of me. But that Mrs. Henderson says she's got weeks. And Thomas isn't doing much better."

The older woman could say what she wanted, but Suzy knew that everyone wondered about their own mortality after a death. Instead of pointing that out, though, she nodded. "If you don't need me, I have paperwork to finish. Can I get you anything?"

Mrs. Stone looked as if she was about to say no, but then paused. "I'd love a cup of hot tea with honey. Might take the chill off. The weather is definitely getting cooler."

"You've got it." Suzy left the room and returned to the nurses' station where she kept a stash of tea bags and honey packets. She'd learned to have them ready rather than making the trip to the cafeteria. She used the microwave to heat up a mug of water then took everything into Mrs. Stone's room.

And found that she'd fallen asleep holding a picture of her grandsons.

Suzy set the tea and honey on the bedside table then gently pushed Mrs. Stone's bangs away from her face. Most residents found their way into her heart, but then there were a certain few who took up space and never left.

She had a feeling that Mrs. Stone was one of those.

Suzy left Mrs. Stone's room and went back to the nurses' station. She found Tori waiting for her there. "Do you have a minute, Suzy?"

"I've got all evening." She leaned against the counter. "What's going on? I thought you left over an hour ago."

"I heard about Mrs. Duff and I thought…" Tori swallowed hard and closed her eyes. "I know she's not Ma, but it got me thinking, you know? What if that happens to Ma? What if she doesn't beat the cancer?" The tears spilled down her cheeks, her shoulders shaking slightly.

"Death is hard to face, whatever the circumstances. Something like cancer certainly doesn't make things any easier, if that's even possible. It robs you of the person and leaves only a shell."

"Oh."

"But it can be beat." Suzy put a hand on Tori's shoulder, trying to send comfort through her touch. "Your mother is tough.

Trust her to fight this, and be there for her when she doesn't think she can."

"How did you get to know so much?"

"I watched my mother die from this horrible disease. But she gave up, didn't even try to fight and so didn't have a chance. Your mom does."

Tori wiped at her eyes. "Are you sure? I can't bury her. I just can't. I need her too much."

"So let her know. Give her a reason to fight."

"Thanks." Tori gave a tentative smile. "I understand why Will likes you so much."

"More like tolerates me." Suzy rubbed Tori's arm a second time. "You going to be okay?"

"Better now that I've talked to you."

CHAPTER EIGHT

SUZY TOOK A deep breath then opened the door to her mother's bedroom. The last time she'd been in this room had been the day after her mother had died. She'd chosen her mother's outfit for the burial then shut the door with no intention of entering again.

And yet here she was, standing at the threshold and trying to take that first step inside.

She had to start cleaning out these rooms if she was going to meet Will's thirty day deadline that had now dwindled to twenty-one. And that meant going into this room and dealing with Mama's closet.

Suzy walked past the bed, but avoided any glance towards it. Seven months, and she still expected to see her mom lying there, fighting the cancer that robbed her of her health. Still thought she'd find the rows of bottles and ointments on the dresser. The medical equipment she'd bought and borrowed to try to extend her mom's life. Instead, she'd cleared it away that last day and disposed of it, hoping to never see it again.

Suzy opened a trash bag and decided to tackle the pile of books and papers that had spilled from the nightstand by the bed. She picked up a few paperbacks, glanced at the contents then stuffed them in the bag. Utility statements from three years ago. Receipts from purchases before her mom had gotten sick.

A photo album. Suzy picked it up and took it with her to sit on the bed. She opened the album. Sighed. Empty, of course. Mama bought it but didn't have the time to put the pictures in it.

Suzy worked through the rest of the pile and found an envelope of pictures. She dumped them on the mattress and started to tear up. Here were her memories. But neglect and age had left them yellow and aged. Ruined. She couldn't make out the faces thanks to the splotches of water on them.

She couldn't get mad at Mama, right? Her mom had a problem. A disease. Depression had pressed down on her until she could barely keep her head up. Ever since her dad had left, Mama had never been the same.

He'd taken her spirit, her joy. And Suzy had been left with her shell.

But still...

Suzy left the pile of books and papers and decided to organize the closet instead. Carefully squeezing between the bed and dresser, she reached to open the closet door. Her knees almost buckled from the trapped rose scent that still lingered on her mom's clothes.

I miss you, Mama. Every hour. Every day.

Suzy tried to push hangers along the pole but they wouldn't budge since they overlapped each other. So many clothes crammed in there, at least half still had tags attached. Pretty ironic considering her mom had lived in the same pair of jeans and a handful of sweatshirts most of the year. Suzy opened another of the trash bags. A friend at Goodwill had told Suzy she could drop off the clothes anytime. Good thing too. There would be plenty.

Suzy yanked out a red sweatshirt near the front. One of Mama's favorites with puppies tumbling across the chest. She brought it to her face and inhaled deeply. She could definitely still smell the scent of roses.

Unable to hold herself up anymore, Suzy

crouched on the floor, crying and rock-
ing as she held the sweatshirt to her chest.
She couldn't give it up. Couldn't throw it
away. That would be like throwing away her
mother.

She surveyed the crowded room. Every
item had belonged to her mother, some to her
grandmother. Though they wouldn't bring a
good price, each one had value because they
had meaning. Especially now that Mama was
gone.

She rested her head against the bed. How
in the world could she do this? She got to
her feet and left the room without clearing
a single item.

It was only the first room. There was
her bedroom down the hall that had to be
cleaned and the attic. Not to mention the living room. The kitchen. Dining room.

Suzy groaned. She couldn't do this. Not
alone.

She flipped open her cell phone. It was
time to get help.

Suzy waited on the porch until Pres drove
up in her car. She got out and walked to the
house. Put her hand on Suzy's shoulder.
"What do you need me to do?"

"I can't do this." She rocked back and forth, clutching her stomach. "It's too hard."

"Cleaning out the house?"

"Getting rid of Mama." Suzy looked up at her friend. "I need help, Pres. And I don't know who to go to."

Pres took a seat next to her on the concrete porch. "I might." She got her cell phone out and punched in a few numbers, waited then asked for Dr. Layher. "Hey, Page. Do you have time to see a friend of mine?"

Pres made an appointment for the following day then put the phone back in her pocket. She slipped her arms around Suzy and pulled her head down on to her shoulder. "We'll help you. I promise."

WILL MET TORI at their mom's house before they'd visit her for the day. He needed to talk to his sister without their mother listening to their every word. "The doctor said Ma could be released as early as two weeks. What are we going to do?"

"So she'll come home. What's the big deal?"

Will scanned the living room. "Look around you, Tori. She can't live alone like this. She needs to be with someone who can take care of her."

Tori nodded, but didn't offer any solutions. She groaned. "You're right. She can't live on her own anymore. But she's going to fight you on this. She won't want a live-in nurse. Or worse, one of us."

"And that leaves us where?" He ran a hand through his hair. "Our sisters haven't called since Ma got hurt, so I doubt they'll step up and offer a hand. What about you? Do you think you could take care of her?"

"Oh, Will. You know I love Ma, but I'm barely hanging on as it is." She collapsed on to the sofa and crossed her legs. "At least we have the next two weeks or so to figure this out. Longer, if the surgeon decides to go forward with another surgery."

"And my townhouse has stairs, so that's out too." He sighed. "I want a solution now. But I don't know what it is."

Tori got up and gave her brother an affectionate nudge. "I know. But we have time." She looked around the room. "You could move in with Ma here. No stairs. She'd be at home with her stuff."

"And my job? Am I supposed to quit and take care of her?"

"Hey, I'm trying to help here."

"No, you're pushing it on me rather than doing it yourself." He rubbed his face and shut his eyes. "I don't have any answers, Tori. Not a single one." He held his arms out. "I'm clueless."

Tori looked him over, surprise etched on her face. "But you always know what to do. That's why we all look to you. You're supposed to have the answers."

How he wished he did in this case. He didn't like not knowing what to do. He liked being in control and having all the solutions at the tips of his fingers. Annoyance warmed his chest. "Not this time. So back off." Tori's brow furrowed, and he winced. He hadn't meant to get so angry. Not at Tori, especially. They were in this together. "Sorry. This frustrates me."

"Well, it frustrates me too. I don't know what I'm doing either because I've never had to deal with something like this."

"That makes two of us. Although I'd rather be dealing with this than the alternative."

Tori gave a solemn nod. "So do we have it settled?"

"No." Will tried to smile but found the effort too difficult. "We have to be united on things. You can't side with her because it's easy. You and me, we're a team."

"And Ma?"

"She'll have to go with what we say."

"And you really think she'll do that." She patted his shoulder. "Must be nice to live in your fantasy world." She glanced at the clock. "I'll meet you at the home. The doctor said five, right?"

Will nodded. "I hope he has good news."

THE DOCTOR'S FACE indicated this would not be a pleasant conversation. The fact that he'd had more chairs brought into Ma's room so that they could all be comfortable seemed to show that this was going to be bad.

Will took the chair closest to the bed and reached up to hold his mom's hand. She looked down at him and tried to smile. But it was as if even she knew this wasn't going to be easy.

Dr. Lewis cleared his throat and kept his focus on Ma. "We got the test results I ordered. And I'm not happy with these numbers."

He laid out a chart with a bunch of lines and numbers that made no sense to anyone but him. He pointed to one section. "Your white blood cell count is low, which we expected. The leukemia is attacking your bones and that drives those numbers down. But when I compare them with the tests run earlier…" He glanced at them all. "We know the reason you aren't progressing as much as I'd like is the cancer. The bones that are trying to heal are fighting off an attack, and they aren't winning."

Silent tears streamed down his sister's face, and Will reached out across the gap to take her hand in his. He hated that it seemed like he couldn't breathe. "So what do we do to fight this?"

"I'd hoped to let the hip heal before chemo began, but I think we're beyond that. We need to attack the cancer before it gains any more ground. I'd suggest chemotherapy now. Aggressive enough, it could turn this around." He looked at Ma. "But Mrs. Stone, it's up to you. What do you want to do?"

She took a deep breath then stared at them both. Will longed to tell her that the doctor was wrong. That she was getting better. Finally, she said, "Could I have a moment with my children alone?"

The doctor stood and left the room. Ma turned to them. "You need to let me go."

Tori was the first to respond. "What? You're not going to fight this? Ma, it's cancer but you can beat this."

"I don't think I have the strength to fight. I know this is difficult to hear, but it's my choice. I want to be comfortable but I don't want anything aggressive."

Will refused to accept what his mother was saying. "No. We're Stones. We fight. We don't give up. And you're going to do exactly what the doctor tells you to."

"But it's my body, not yours."

Will gestured to Tori. "You tell her to fight. You make her do this."

"Since when have I ever been able to tell Ma to do something?" Tori brought out her phone and pulled up a picture of the twins. "If you won't fight for yourself, do it for them. They need you."

"For what? To give them presents and money? No one needs me."

Unbelievable. This whole conversation was impossible to believe. "I can't talk any more about this." He stormed out of the room and down the hallway to the main door. He threw it open and took in deep breaths. Placed a hand on one of the pillars and closed his eyes. Breathe in. Breathe out.

He stood for several moments like that, trying to tame his heartbeat, then he felt a hand on his arm and noticed Suzy looking up at him. "You okay?" He opened his mouth to say something but couldn't find the words. He shook his head. Suzy rubbed his arm and nodded. "I know the feeling. Bad news turns your world upside down, right?"

"How did you know it was bad news?"

"Because I've been where you are. I recognize the look."

Her warm gaze smothered his fear, and he longed to put his arms around her. To feel the silkiness of her skin through her scrubs. To put his fingers through that curly mop of hers. To hold her close to him. He groaned and squeezed his eyes shut. His mom was dying, and he was what? Hitting on the nurse?

"What did the doctor say?"

"It's more what my mom said." He opened his eyes, but they burned. "She doesn't want to fight. Doesn't want to try chemo or anything." He couldn't look at Suzy anymore. "What are her chances if she doesn't do anything?"

"Will, you know they're hopeless if she doesn't have treatment." Suzy's phone beeped but she ignored it. "You're sure that's what she said?"

"Yes, I heard her with my own ears. She's tired and doesn't want to fight." He glanced out over the parking lot. He longed to get in his truck and drive far, far away from all this. "Why won't she fight?"

"Forever or just for today?" Suzy took his hand in hers and squeezed it. "She might just be reacting to the news and needs time to let it sink in. She doesn't want to die. If she did, she'd have done it already. But your mom is a fighter. And she's not going to give up."

Words he wanted to hear. Needed to hear. He caressed her hand. It felt good to have someone there for him. Supporting him. "Are you sure?"

"Absolutely."

She gave him a smile, and he longed to join her but he couldn't do it. Didn't feel it. Instead he gave a short nod. "Okay. Will you talk to her?"

She sputtered out a soft laugh. "What makes you think she'll listen to me and not you?"

Because she had the answers that he didn't. "I'm just her son. But you, you're her nurse. You have authority."

Suzy laughed again at that. "Authority. That's a good one." She looked him over. "I tell you what. When I stop in later tonight to see how she's doing, I'll give her my opinion if the subject comes up."

"Thanks."

"Don't be thanking me yet. I haven't convinced her to sign up for chemotherapy."

He tried another smile. "Not yet."

SHE DIDN'T WANT to go in there. Knowing what Mrs. Stone's diagnosis was made it difficult to pretend that everything was going to be okay. Because it might not be. She could fight this, but the end result wasn't guaranteed.

Much like her mother's.

But Suzy forced a bright smile and pushed through the door into Mrs. Stone's room. Both Mrs. Stone and Tori were asleep, the mother in her bed, the daughter in her chair. Suzy walked over to Tori. "Wake up, sleepyhead. Visiting hours are over."

Tori's eyes fluttered open. "What time is it?"

"After nine."

She reached down for her purse. "I can't believe I fell asleep."

"It's been a rough day."

Tori nodded. "I don't think I convinced her of anything. I don't know what to do."

"Just be there for her, no matter what."

"I will." She adjusted the purse strap on her shoulder. "Would you like to go to lunch or something soon? Just the two of us?"

Suzy peered at her. "Why are you asking?"

"It just seems like we could both use a friend." She glanced at her mom. "You've been through this before. I'd like your advice."

Suzy remembered needing someone when she'd been taking care of Mama. Pres had tried, but she hadn't understood. "I think that would be nice. Maybe set something up for next week."

Tori smiled then leaned in to kissed her mother's cheek. "Lovey," she said and left the room.

Suzy rearranged the blankets and switched off the bedside lamp.

"Did she go?"

"How long have you been awake?"

"Long enough. Now you leave too."

Suzy stood at the window and gazed out at the atrium. "It's getting close to that time when all the leaves will be off the trees, and snow will frost the branches instead."

"Good thing you became a nurse and not a poet."

"I do love working with my patients." Suzy turned to face her. "Especially the crabby ones."

Mrs. Stone's frown deepened. "I have a reason to be crabby."

"I heard." She walked forward and took a seat on the side of Mrs. Stone's bed. "So what are you thinking? Feeling?"

"I think I want to go home because what's the point of being here if I'm going to die anyway?" Mrs. Stone crossed her arms over her chest. "And I feel that my children don't understand why I feel that way."

"Because they don't want to think of you as gone." Suzy adjusted her legs so that she could get comfortable. Half of her job was taking care of the physical condition of her patients, but she didn't neglect the emotional side either. "When my mom got diagnosed with cancer, she wanted to give up. She didn't want to do chemo or anything."

"And did she die?"

"Yes, without treatment, she died. For almost a year, I watched my mom waste away to nothing. And I knew things could have been different if she'd just…. I don't know. Tried to do something. Anything."

Mrs. Stone put her hand on Suzy's. "Sweetie, I'm sorry. I didn't know."

"It's not something I share with everyone." Suzy got off the bed and straightened the covers. "But I always wonder what would have happened if she'd fought the cancer. She might still be here. I might have gone to her house next month for Thanksgiving. But I won't know that because she gave up."

Mrs. Stone swallowed with some effort. "I don't know if I have the strength to fight."

"I can understand that. But you won't know if you don't try, right? And you have two wonderful kids who are willing to be there for you. To keep you going when you can't go on. That's got to mean something."

"Did my son put you up to this?" She narrowed her eyes at Suzy.

"No. This is close to the speech I wish I'd given my mom. But I was too afraid."

"It was a good speech."

Suzy knew her words were only as effective as their effect. She sighed. "Did it change your mind about treatment?"

"No." Mrs. Stone gave a short nod. "But it did give me something to think about."

Suzy took a deep breath. "Then I'll leave you to do some thinking."

She headed for the door, but turned around when Mrs. Stone called her name. "How could you watch your mom waste away like that?"

"She asked me to move in and take care of her. Which I did, no problem. I took a leave from work so I could focus all my attention on her. She was my mom, and I loved her. But I wish I could have had more time."

"We all want more time."

Suzy nodded and left the room.

MR. STEPPEY GLARED at Will and planted his feet firmly in the ground. "It's my yard, so it's my business."

"When the condition of the yard causes public concern, it becomes my job." Will glanced beyond the man through the window to the yard where the grass grew over a foot tall. "Tall grass attracts vermin which carry disease."

"Are you implying that I have rats?"

Will took a deep breath and shook his head. Too much of his job involved diplomacy that he'd had to learn quickly in his position. "I'm not implying anything. I'm stating that the condition of the backyard could attract them. I've already given you two warnings. Since this is my third, I'll be sending a crew to mow your lawn. At your expense."

The older man frowned even more if that was possible. "You should be ashamed, trying to squeeze money out of an elderly man. I'm on a fixed income, son."

Will knew that. He also knew that Mr. Steppey was a widower with a son who rarely visited. He also had difficulty walking much less mowing a lawn. Will bit his lip. "Listen. I have two nephews who would be willing to mow your lawn and do any yard work. I can bring them over after school later today."

Mr. Steppey studied him, and Will tried not to shrink back. Had he done the wrong thing? Had showing some mercy only proven him to be weak? It had to be Suzy's influence on him. He would never have done this before. Finally, Mr. Steppey spoke up. "Would they do it for twenty bucks?"

"They can do it for free." Will shook the

man's hand. "I want to work with you, not against you."

Mr. Steppey nodded. "There's more than just me in this situation, son. There're seniors all around this town who need help."

"I know." And that was the problem. Lake Mildred had a growing seniors population that couldn't perform the upkeep of their property nor had the means to do so.

Yet.

What if he could use his office as code inspector to assist them? What if his authority could spur individuals to step up and provide services that the seniors couldn't do on their own? The idea intrigued him.

His office meant more than just getting things up to code. He'd taken the position because he wanted to make a difference. After the Marines, he'd studied engineering at the University of Michigan. Thought he'd change things for the better. But given his time as code inspector, he'd become burned out. Afraid that the only thing he did was push papers from one department to the next. But maybe by providing help to the seniors he could change that and reignite the ambition he'd once had to make a difference.

Will smiled. "I'll bring the boys by this af-

ternoon. Say four?" He'd have to check with
Tori first, of course. But she would probably
love the idea of them blowing off some steam
with him rather than her. "We'd be finished
by dinner time."

Mr. Steppey sneezed which led to several
wracking coughs. He took a handkerchief
from his back pocket and wiped his mouth.
"Thanks, Mr. Stone."

"Will."

"I remember your name. I also remember
your game-winning homerun against Robert Falls High."

"That was many years ago." Too many for
Will to count. High school seemed another
lifetime ago. He'd done and seen a lot since
then. He'd visited parts of the world outside
of Lake Mildred that he'd never dreamed of.
Germany. The Middle East. He'd also seen
battle. Lost friends and a part of himself before he'd found his way home to Michigan
again. "I remember that game as well. Almost made it to the state championships that
year."

"You and Rick were unstoppable." The
older man paused. "Sounds like that's not
the case anymore."

If he meant his and the mayor's ongoing

struggle to limit the town council's harsh budget cuts, Will hoped he wasn't right. Changes needed to be made, but those choices had to make sense and not jeopardize the town. "We still hold our own. Thank you for your time, Mr. Steppey. I'll see you later this afternoon."

Once he was inside his truck, he looked up at Mr. Steppey's house. He pulled his cell phone out and called Tori to make sure that he could borrow the twins then hung up. Next, he phoned Rick. "You busy? Can we meet?"

He could hear the sounds of the diner in the background. "Ernesto called in since his Gracie is having the baby, so I'm working at the diner. As long as you don't mind standing in a hot kitchen and talking, I'm up for it."

"I'll be right there."

THE SMELL OF coffee and fried beef hit his nose as Will stepped inside the diner. His stomach growled in response, but he ignored it and waved to Shirley. "Boss in back?"

"He's been there since this morning without a break." She shook her head but gave a faint smile. "Seems like the old days."

"I heard that." Rick poked his head

through the pass-through window. "Come on back, Will."

Will walked around the counter and through the swinging door to the kitchen. The smells intensified and he added grease to the combination. Rick waved at him with a spatula. "Welcome to my office. Can I get you something?"

"No, I'm good, but thanks." He summarized his meeting with Mr. Steppey then sighed. "He's right, you know. There are a lot of seniors that could use our help."

"So what are you suggesting?" Rick flipped a burger on to a waiting bun. "Keep in mind that our budget is already tight."

"I'm suggesting volunteers can mow lawns and shovel sidewalks for our housebound seniors and others in need." Will leaned against the counter. "Won't cost us a thing but time. And someone would need to oversee and supervise the project."

"Someone like…" Rick added fries to the plate then looked up at Will. "You offering to do the job?"

Will nodded as Rick put the plate in the window and rang the bell. "As code inspector, I'm aware of those households who could use the help. I could also reach out to groups and schools looking for volunteering opportunities." He watched Rick for a moment. This felt important, as if he could change everything with his next words. "Remember when we felt like we could do anything if we just tried? That nothing could stop us?"

"The state championships?" Rick nodded and looked off into the distance. "How could I forget? It seemed like together we could even conquer the world, not just win a baseball game."

"I want to feel that way again."

"And doing this will help you?"

"It will help the community, Rick. Isn't that why you became mayor?"

Rick grinned. "Sounds like you've got a plan. Let me know if you need me to do anything." Rick turned back to the grill. "You're sure you don't want something?"

Will's stomach growled again, but he said, "I've got another appointment. But thanks."

"Anytime."

He regretted that he had to meet with a contractor at a construction site to sign off on some inspection permits. But time was valuable.

Still, he promised himself a meal at the diner very soon.

SUZY SAT IN her car in the parking lot behind the Goodwill donation center and let her car idle for a moment before turning it off. Was she doing the right thing, getting rid of all this stuff? Or would Mama have wanted her to hang on to it all?

She grimaced because she knew the answer to that one. Mama had never wanted to get rid of anything. But she didn't have that option now.

Suzy took her keys out of the ignition, then got out and approached the back door. She rang the doorbell as instructed then waited. A young man with arm muscles larger than her body answered the door. "You dropping off?"

She nodded. "I've got about six bags of clothes and a couple boxes of kitchen items."

He nodded and followed her to her car. She popped open the trunk, and he took out several bags and carried them all to the building. Where was he when she'd been loading up her car with this stuff? She'd had to make a dozen trips at least back and forth. She'd used muscles she didn't know she had.

She took one bag and hugged it to her body as she walked to the building. By the time she made it there, the young man was on his third load. They finished emptying the car in record time. At least to her.

She waited as he wrote her information at the top of a sheet on a clipboard. He glanced at the items and estimated how much she'd brought in. After she signed her name, he tore off her portion and handed it to her. "For your taxes."

"Oh." She glanced at the slip of paper in her hand. "I might have more. Would you take it?"

The young man looked at her. "We always take donations, but this time of year especially. There's a lot of need out there." He nodded with his head towards the swinging doors that led to the store. "Especially if you have any coats, hats, scarves…"

Suzy was sure somewhere in Mama's house there had to be a few dozen of those. She folded the slip of paper and put it in her coat pocket. "I have a lot of stuff to donate, so it could take me several more trips."

"No need. We can send a truck to pick up items when there's a large amount." He walked to the computer and clicked on a calendar. "I have a truck doing pickups next Saturday afternoon. I could add you to the list."

Suzy nodded. "Thanks."

"No. Thank you."

She got back in her car and drove around the building, noticing an empty parking spot close to the front of the store. Deciding that was a sign, she parked the car and walked inside. Maybe if she could see how Mama's things helped others, she could let more of it go. The cashier greeted Suzy and let her know she could help if she needed any assistance. Suzy smiled and continued past her.

Racks of clothes and shelves of items covered every square foot of the store. She spotted a young woman searching through the children's clothes. Recognizing her neighbor, she walked towards her. "Hi, Shelley."

Shelley looked up at her and smiled. "Hi, Miss Suzy. You shopping here?"

She didn't want to make the woman feel bad, so she avoided the question. "I saw that Wesley is growing like a weed."

The young mother gave a sigh and nodded. "That's why I'm here. Can't keep him in jeans and T-shirts long enough before he's outgrown them."

Suzy thought of all the clothes Mama had bought and hoarded. She'd never realized that a family that could use them lived just down the street. Instead, she'd kept it all in piles on the floor where it didn't help anyone.

Suddenly, bringing the donations to the center made her feel like she was doing something good. Like cleaning out the house could help more than just Suzy.

THE DIRECTIONS TO Dr. Layher's office in Robert Falls couldn't have been more complicated. Turn right at the fudge and cheese store then down three streets until you get to the statue of the bear, and the parking lot is to the left of that.

She should have gotten a real map.

Leaving the Bug next to a station wagon that looked like its best days were behind it, she walked into the office building, through the lobby to the row of elevators. Up to the third floor, then it was the fourth office on the left. On the door, it read "Dr. Page Layher, Family Counselor."

Well, Suzy wasn't family. She was her own family now. But she was dealing with issues with her mom, so she guessed that qualified. She opened the door and stepped into a small lobby. A frosted glass window greeted her along with a couple chairs and a square metal and glass coffee table covered in magazines. The note on the window said to ring the bell for service. The small ding of the bell added the only sound besides the soft jazz from an unseen radio.

The frosted window opened, and a young man peeked out. "You're a little early. Pagey, I mean Dr. Layher, isn't back from lunch just yet. But I'll text her so she can hoof it over here."

Suzy waved him off. "She doesn't have to hurry on my account. I'll read a magazine until she returns."

"Are you sure? Cuz those mags have been here a while." The young man smiled. "Dr. Layher inherited those from Dr. Dhondt, and he had them for years too." He glanced at a rack of pamphlets on the counter and pulled out a brochure on bedwetting, then replaced that and pulled another on divorce. He sighed. "I'm writing newer magazines on my list of things to change around here. Right next to better music. It's so dull. Put you right to sleep while you wait."

"Maybe it's meant to be soothing. Calming."

He sighed. "I'd rather have something edgier. Something with a beat."

Suzy leaned on the counter. "You're right.

Something about a woman singing with a hard edge gets me every time."

"You have impeccable music taste." The young man held out his hand. "Henry. Nice to meet you. And if you don't mind me saying, you're a lot more together then some of the noodles we get in here."

"Thanks." She frowned. Noodles? "I think."

He jumped up and straightened his tie. "Dr. Layher will see you in a moment."

Suzy turned and saw a woman about the same age as her rushing in the door. "Sorry, Henry. Give me two minutes."

He waited until Page had left the lobby and gone into a private office. He leaned in towards Suzy. "She's really great, so don't let her being late influence your opinion, okay?"

Suzy glanced at her watch. "She's still got five minutes until my appointment."

"Trust me. She'll be late."

He shut the window, and Suzy took a seat on one of the chairs. Maybe Henry should add more comfortable chairs to his list because the hard bottom would be just that on hers. She chose a magazine and flipped through it. She hadn't even graduated high school when it had been published, so she figured it was like reading a history book. She settled into an article about how to get the feathered hair look.

The door that led into the back opened, and Henry peeked out. "Dr. Layher will see you now." He opened the door wider and let Suzy pass by him. "She must have heard my comment." He closed the door behind her and preceded her down the hall to an office with a large window. Dr. Layher sat behind her desk, and she rose when Henry entered the room. "Your one o'clock." He handed Suzy a clipboard. "This is for your insurance billing info. Toodles."

Suzy took a seat in front of Dr. Layher and glanced at the clipboard. "Do you want me to fill this out first?"

The counselor sighed. "I love Henry, don't get me wrong. But if he wasn't my brother, I would have fired him months ago."

"I don't know. He seems pretty great."

"That's the thing. He is great. Just not at this job." She waved her hand. "But that's not why you're here." She frowned at Suzy. "Why are you here?"

"My friend Presley called you to set this up. I had a panic attack."

Page grinned and nodded. "How is Pres doing? I haven't seen her since we were at State together."

Suzy settled into the chair more. This was going to be a snap if they talked about anyone but her. "Pres will always be Pres. Tall. Gorgeous. And forever single."

"Interesting that you picked those words to describe her. Most are opposites of you." Suzy opened her mouth to protest but Page kept talking. "Don't get me wrong. You're petite. Cute. And something tells me you're not as single as you think."

"That's not why I'm here."

"Right. The panic attack." Page got up from her chair and moved to the sofa that was closer to the window. "Would you be more comfortable sitting over here? We won't be doctor and client, but like two friends."

"I'm not here to find a friend. I'm here to get better."

Page made a note on her pad of paper. "Interesting. Why do you think you need to get better?"

"Because I can't clean out my mother's bedroom without feeling like I can't breathe, and my heart is beating out of my chest." Suzy crossed her legs and stayed firmly where she was. "I can't handle cleaning out the hoard that has taken over my life just as much as it took over my mother's. And I don't need a friend to tell me what to do. I need a professional."

Page stood. "Then you came to the right place." She motioned again to the couch. "Let's just sit and talk. We'll see where we can go."

This was ridiculous. The woman had to be certifiable. But then working with what Henry called noodles all day must do a number on one's psyche. Suzy rose to her feet and walked to the couch. Sat at the far end and crossed her legs. "You're not what I expected."

"You were expecting one of those doctors from TV, maybe?" Page laughed and shook her head. "Sorry. When I get nervous, I make inappropriate jokes. And new patients make me nervous."

"Well there's nothing special about me." Suzy wrung her hands together. Was it too soon to get up and leave? Would it be considered rude?

"Interesting. Why do you say that?"

Suzy shrugged. "Listen. I just need some coping techniques or something to help me clean out my mother's house so I'm not homeless."

Page nodded. "Do you have anyone to help you?"

"Pres volunteered, but I don't know." She looked down at her hands and wished she had some hand cream on her to rub into them and soothe the cracks. "All of it falls on me to deal with. No one else."

"And you don't think you can handle it?"

No. Not at all. She looked up at the counselor. "What would you call hyperventilating and wanting to pass out?"

Page made some more notes on her notepad. She looked up at her then. "What are you afraid will happen if you clean out the house? If you were to clear every little thing out?" Suzy sat and thought about it until Page waved her hand. "Don't answer that. Just close your eyes." Her eyes drifted close. "Now imagine your mom's house completely empty."

Her heart started to race. Her palms began to sweat. She longed to jump off this couch and run out of the office. To get as far away from this as possible. From everything. "Stop."

"What are you feeling, Suzy?"

"She's gone." Suzy opened her eyes. "Mama's gone."

THE SESSION WENT for another half hour and ended with Suzy feeling a lot better about coming to the appointment. Maybe Page wasn't as crazy as she appeared. She might even be brilliant. Suzy certainly felt more calm and in control about the situation. Until Page gave her an assignment. "I'm going to visit you at the house next week. But before I get there, I want you to clean out one room."

"Just one? I'm running out of time here. I have a ton of..."

Page held up her finger. "Just one. We can deal with the rest later. But I need to know if you can handle this."

One room didn't seem so bad. She could do that, right? "And it doesn't matter which room?"

"Your choice." Page got off the couch and led Suzy to the door. "The point is that this is all your choice. How you handle the situation. How you react to it. You've got the power. Always have. Okay?"

Page opened the door and escorted Suzy along the hall where Henry waited at the reception desk. Suzy handed him the clipboard with her insurance information filled in. He glanced at it then at Page. "We'll bill you." When Page opened her mouth, he shrugged. "The computer's on the fritz again."

Page rolled her eyes and started walking down the hall back to her office. She turned before entering. "One room, Suzy. See you next week."

Henry waited until the office door closed. "So how did it go?"

"I didn't know she was your sister."

"One of six. But she's cool." He leaned in closer. "Just don't tell her I said that."

Suzy smiled all the way back to her car.

WILL DROVE DOWN Main in search of some lunch then decided to take his break checking up on Suzy. He pulled down her street and into her driveway. Her little yellow car was there, as sunshiny as she was with her patients. He got out of his car and strode towards the front door. Knocked on it once. Twice. No answer.

He glanced at his watch. Could she still be sleeping after her shift? He tried to remember if he'd seen her come in last night before he'd left Ma's room. He thought he recalled seeing her smile. But then his days blended together lately between going to the home after work every day and again on the weekends.

He knocked again, and this time Suzy answered the door. She had her curls tied back with a bright neon pink bandanna, and she wore a faded T-shirt advertising a band from his college years. "I didn't wake you."

She shook her head and stepped in between the gap of the doorway. "I still have two and a half weeks."

"I know. I thought I'd see if you needed a hand."

"With what?"

Hmm. Grouchy Suzy wasn't very attractive. He frowned. "Are you okay?"

"Why? Am I not allowed to not smile?" She tore the bandanna out of her hair. "Listen. I'm busy. And I don't have time to stand on my porch and chit chat. And do you know why I'm busy? Because of your stupid deadline."

"Deadlines aren't stupid. They're meant to motivate and give a clear goal." He shook his head. "Why are you arguing with me?"

"Because it's easier yelling at you than dealing with my mom's house." She closed her eyes and rubbed them. "What do you really want?"

He looked down at her and thought about things he shouldn't. About pulling her into his arms and kissing that bad mood away. He sighed. "I have a contact that can haul away any old or broken appliances." He reached into his jacket pocket and pulled out a business card. "His number is on there. And he's free."

"Free is good."

"And I want to thank you."

Suzy looked up at him, and he could see the doubt and wariness in her eyes. Had he put those there? If he had, he regretted it because he missed the Suzy he'd come to know. "I appreciate whatever it is that you told my mom. She's decided to go ahead with the chemo."

Suzy gave a soft smile. "That's great."

"At least she'll have a fighting chance of beating this thing now." He shifted his weight to the other foot. "Has the doctor talked to you about her chances?"

"Yes and by her willingness to fight, they've gone up at least fifty percent. But then that's just my experience talking." Suzy bit her lip and looked him over. She seemed as if she wanted to say something else then shook her head. "But just because she's willing to fight doesn't mean this is going to be easy. In fact, it's going to get worse before it gets better."

"Her illness?"

"And her attitude. Her outlook. She'll probably get angry and blame you and your sister for making her miserable." Suzy ran a hand through her curls. "But she's really mad at the cancer. You're just a convenient target."

"Noted. Any other advice?"

"You've brought in some of her things to comfort her, but it's not enough. Bring in more. Anything at home that she adores, like a picture, a memento, anything. It helps her focus when she's in pain or despair." Suzy bit her lip then shrugged. "Visits always help, but then you and your sister have been really good about that."

"I only wish my older sisters would do the same."

"Not everyone deals with cancer the same way."

Will nodded then glanced at the front door that Suzy had closed when she had stepped out on the porch with him. "What's going on in there?"

Suzy glanced behind her and shrugged. "Nothing. Working on one room."

"I meant it when I said I could help."

He took a step forward, but Suzy held up her hand. "I don't need your help. I'm doing fine."

"Then you won't mind if I take a look?"

He tried to edge past her, but Suzy stepped between him and the door, blocking the entrance with her body. "I do mind actually."

"Why are you making this difficult?"

"I'm not the one trying to force myself in."

She put her arms up so that he'd only get in by physically removing her. Will considered it for a moment, but took a step back when it became apparent she didn't want to budge. "What are you trying to hide?"

"Nothing."

"That's not what your body language is saying." He took a step forward until he towered over her. She looked up at him. "You're definitely sending signals to stay out."

"You must not be paying attention to them because you're not giving up."

He looked down into her eyes and smiled. "I'm choosing to ignore them."

She gasped at his smile. "Why?"

Because I want to pay attention to you. I want to kiss you. To hold you. "Because you helped me with my mom. I thought I'd give you a hand as repayment."

"Oh." Her hand reached back and touched the doorknob. And she opened the door, the two of them stumbling into the house. "Don't judge me, okay? I can't handle that today."

The living room looked much the same as the last time he'd seen it. Suzy hustled him out of the room and down the hallway where the piles of books and lines of bags were now gone. There was only a clear pathway. She opened the door to one bedroom, and he grinned at the transformation. He could actually see the floor. Though the carpet would have to be replaced eventually. Still, the mounds of clothes and boxes of stuff were gone. He saw there was furniture in the room though the bed and dresser still had clutter covering their surfaces. Still…. "Oh, Suzy. This looks so much better."

"This used to be my bedroom." She motioned to the crayon markings along the closet door. "Mama measured my growth there." She pointed to the row of stuffed animals on the top shelf of the closet. "They were my friends growing up."

He reached out a hand, tried to touch her shoulder. "Suze…"

"Don't." She stepped away from him. "I picked this room to clean out first because it was the easiest. She filled it with junk when I left for college so that when I came home on breaks, there was nowhere for me to stay. Eventually I had to share a room with her because there wasn't anywhere else for me to sleep." Suzy looked up at him, pain shining in her eyes, the corners of her mouth drooping. "I could clean out this room because most of it was junk that didn't mean anything." She motioned to one of the walls. "But her room is full of my memories of her. How do I throw them away?"

"You don't have to."

She snorted a short laugh. "Really? Because that's not what your deadline means."

He put his arms around her shoulders. "I'm not asking you to get rid of your mom. Only the stuff that is crowding you out." He turned her around so that she could see her bedroom. "Doesn't it make you feel better seeing your room like this? Knowing you could sleep in your own bed?"

"The mattress is lumpy."

Will chuckled. "Still. You'll be able to stretch out and not be cramped on the couch."

She turned and looked at him. "You should do that more often."

"What? Give brilliant advice?"

"Laugh." She reached up and touched his face, and he smiled down at her. "Yes. Like that."

Then he lowered his mouth to hers and kissed her lightly. Testing. Seeing how it felt.

Wow.

He pulled her closer to him, but she pushed him away. "I'm a mess. And I've got to clean. And go to work. And…"

She kept talking as she walked out of the room and down the hall. Will touched his lips and smiled.

SUZY PAUSED IN the hallway and held out a hand to steady herself. What was that? Had he really kissed her? And had she let him? What had she been thinking?

She heard him walking down the hallway, and she hurried into the kitchen. To put stuff between them. Because they couldn't kiss like that again. Not when she had enjoyed it so much. She pulled a box of dishes from the dining room table and put it in his arms when he rounded the corner. "Take that to the garage, okay?"

"We cleaned out the garage."

"I needed a space for things I'm donating to Goodwill. I can take some in within the next few days, but they said they'd send a truck for the rest next weekend. So it's temporarily in the garage."

"I worked hard to get that place cleaned up."

She rolled her eyes. "Would you just take the box out there? You said you'd help."

He grumbled as he left, and she watched from the kitchen window as he walked to the backyard. That's right. Keep him busy and irritated. Because she couldn't allow him to kiss her anymore. It was too confusing, too distracting.

And she needed to stop herself from wishing for more.

SEVERAL DAYS LATER, Suzy had just finished taking the last bag of trash out of her old bedroom when there was a knock on the front door. She took the bag with her and placed it against the old fridge then answered the door. Page stood on the stoop with a notebook in her hand. Suzy gave her a smile. "Just in time."

"Could you record that and send it to Henry? He doesn't seem to think I know how to tell time." She took her coat off then looked around the living room. Seeing an empty spot on the sofa, she tossed her coat and purse there before she opened her notepad and started to take notes.

"Speaking of your brother, how is he doing?"

"We had a staff meeting last night after work about expectations and policies." She took her gaze off the notebook and looked at Suzy. "In other words, he told me his demands. New magazines. Better music. An updated computer." She sighed. "I doubt he heard my speech about professionalism."

"I like your brother."

"I do too. I love him. But he can be…a challenge." She shrugged and glanced again around the living room. "Is this where you do most of your living? I see the pillow and blankets. You seem to have carved out a space for yourself here."

"I used to sleep there."

Page stared at her. "Used to? I like the sound of that. Where do you sleep now?"

Suzy led her down the hallway to her old bedroom. Correction, her new bedroom. The bed had new sheets and a comforter that she'd found as a set still in plastic that Mama must have bought before she got sick. The dresser had been cleared out and now held her underthings, socks, and pajamas. She could actually change into PJs rather than sleep in her scrubs now. She'd try it tomorrow morning after work. Suzy opened the closet door and showed Page how she'd hung her scrubs inside. "This is my new room."

"How does it make you feel?"

Oh boy. Here we go with the psychology stuff. "Fine."

Page took a seat on the bed. "Let's sit and talk for a moment."

"Why?"

"The room looks great. But I'm worried more about you." She indicated the free spot next to her. "How did it feel to get this room cleaned out? What was going on in your head?"

"Nothing." Suzy shifted her weight to the other foot. "It was fine."

"Again with fine. Is that what you used to tell your mother? That things were fine even when they weren't?"

Suzy's heart started to beat faster and her palms were instantly damp. "You don't know what it was like growing up with my mother."

"So tell me."

"This isn't about her."

"Isn't it?" Page looked around the room and sighed. "I'm betting that you chose this room because it would be the simplest. You didn't choose your mother's bedroom because that would bring up some emotions and memories that you don't want to deal with."

That's just what she'd said to Will. But she didn't want to admit that to Page. "I might have been able to handle Mama's room."

"Let's test that." Page got off the bed and walked to Mama's bedroom. Opened the door and peered inside. When Suzy joined her, she picked up the sweatshirt that Suzy had left on the bed after her last disastrous attempt to clean up. "What do you feel when you see this top?"

Suzy shrugged. "It was one of Mama's favorites."

Page unfolded it and glanced at it. "I love the puppies." She looked back at Suzy. "Did your mother?"

"I don't see what that has to do with any-thing."

"You're dealing with the stuff, Suzy, but not what got it here." She held up the sweat-shirt. "This looks well-worn. Well-loved."

"I think she did love it. She wore it often enough."

"So if we threw it out or donated it, how would that make you feel?"

Suzy's racing heart went up another gear. "Fine."

"Find another word. And start with 'it makes me feel' then fill in the blank."

Suzy wiped her sweaty palms on her jeans and took several deep breaths. "It makes me feel…" She paused and closed her eyes. Angry. Anxious. Alone. And those were just the As. She shook her head. "I have a lot to do, and my time is running short. So right now, I feel overwhelmed."

Page nodded and made a note. "Could you donate this top?" She held it up for Suzy to see.

She hesitated. Page must have known be-cause she narrowed her eyes at Suzy who held out her hand. "I think I want to keep that."

"It's stained near the collar." Page held

the sweatshirt closer to her and away from Suzy's reach.

"I know."

"So why keep it?"

"I said. Because it was her favorite." Suzy snatched the top from Page and brought it to her nose. Inhaled deeply. "I'll wear it and think of her."

"It's about three sizes too big for you."

Like that mattered. "So I'll wear it as pajamas. Why do you care?"

Page made another note. "This is just one example of how you're hanging on to your mother's things." She opened the closet and pointed at the contents. "Are you going to keep all these too?"

A stack of T-shirts shifted and started to rain down on Page's head. Suzy rushed over and helped her free herself from them, throwing some back in the closet, which was already packed several layers deep. "Of course not."

"So then let's start weeding some of these out."

"I don't need your help."

Page took a step back at her words. "Why not?"

Suzy stepped away and took a seat on the

bed, shoving some of the boxes aside when they slid towards her. "Because I've never needed anyone's help."

"You sure about that?"

This was driving her crazy. She covered her ears and shook her head. "Stop doing that."

"Doing what?"

"Making me think. Feel." Suzy groaned and buried her face in her hands. "I've survived this long because I've pushed those things down. I had enough to deal with... with Mama's moods and her stuff. There wasn't space to deal with mine too."

Page put her hand on Suzy's shoulder. "There is now."

THEY CONTINUED THROUGH the house, Page categorizing the items that would need to be purged. A checklist of tasks that Suzy would have to complete. They ended in the living room where Page put her coat on. She handed Suzy the checklists they'd made then put the notepad and pen back in her purse. "Have you thought of having a clean out day with your friends?"

Suzy folded the lists and put them in her front jeans pocket. "I did for the backyard, but I don't want to impose on them again. There's a lot more in here than there was out there."

"More reason for you to ask for help." Page pulled her blond hair from beneath her coat then sighed. "I know you have a crazy schedule with working nights and weekends, but I'd like you to schedule it soon, with the deadline coming up."

"Fine." When Page gave her a look, she smiled. "That would be great. How about next Saturday?"

"Perfect. And I'll ask Henry to come with me."

Suzy smiled. Now that would be interesting.

THE NOTES ON Mrs. Stone stated that she'd been quiet most of the day. And that she had sent back her lunch tray. It looked like Harold was carrying a full dinner tray out of her room. Suzy put her tablet down, stormed down the hall and slammed the door open. "What do you think you're doing?"

Mrs. Stone startled. "I'm not hungry."

Suzy left the room and took the tray from the orderly. Returned to Mrs. Stone's room and dropped it on the bedside table. "No one skips meals on my watch."

"I'm. Not. Hungry."

"You want to play games? We can play games." She took the lid off and glanced at the plate. "It's baked chicken night. Mashed potatoes. Corn."

"Don't care."

Suzy picked up the silverware wrapped in a napkin and removed the fork and knife. She cut the chicken into small pieces then pushed the table to the bed. Stabbed a piece of chicken and held it up to Mrs. Stone. "Do I have to feed you?"

"Do what you want. I'm not eating."

"I had to feed my mother to keep her alive, and I loved her. You're just a patient. What do you think I'll do to you?" She wiggled the fork. "Don't try me."

Mrs. Stone scowled at her. "Why do you care if I eat or not?"

"Because I'm your nurse. I've promised to take care of you, and that means making sure you do everything to get better." Suzy put the fork down. "Now why do you really not want to eat?"

"What's the point? I'm going to die anyway."

Suzy took a seat on the bed next to her. "Do you really believe that?"

"That's what the doctor said."

"He said you have to fight. Which means you have to want to live." Suzy paused. "So tell me. Do you?"

There wasn't an answer at first. Mrs. Stone looked down at her hands. Then she looked out the window at the birch tree with the peeling bark. A long moment passed before she finally said, "I don't want to leave my children."

"Okay then. So focus on that." Suzy picked up the fork and held it out to Mrs. Stone. "Eat for their sake."

Mrs. Stone took the fork, and Suzy fixed the table so that the older woman could feed herself. She watched diligently until the first bite was swallowed. Then she got off the bed and tidied the room, giving her space.

She rounded up the extra pillows that had been tossed on the floor and hugged them to her body. She didn't like getting tough with her patients, but sometimes they needed that extra bit of motivation. And though she may look like a cream puff, she was made of steel.

Except when it came to her own situation.

She placed one of the pillows behind Mrs. Stone to give her some support at her back. "Feel a little better?"

"I'm still scared."

"I know." Suzy patted her arm. "And I wish I could say that it will go away, but I can't. Fear doesn't really go away. It's up to us to figure out how to manage it and keep going."

"Is that what you told your mom?"

Suzy shook her head. "She never figured out how to get over the fear of being alone. It lived with her in my father's absence." Mama might as well have been married to it. She went to bed with it at night and woke up with it in the morning. It followed her all day at work. At meals. And especially during the holidays. "It took over her life." She swallowed. "And I've got to stop letting it take over mine."

"Fear is never a good companion. It keeps you from what you want."

"I'm realizing that."

Mrs. Stone observed her. "So what will you do, dearie?"

Clean up the house then sell it. Go back to school and get the degree in veterinary medicine that she'd wanted in the first place. Figure out the rest of her life. She was free from her mother now, no longer tied to Mama's demands. She smiled. "Fear isn't going to keep me back anymore. I'm not my mother, and I won't let it control me like it did her. I'm finally going to live my own life."

WILL PAUSED OUTSIDE of Ma's hospital room before going in. She seemed in foul spirits lately, ever since deciding to go ahead with the treatment. Like Suzy had warned him, Ma blamed him. Another breath and he pushed the door open. Frowned when he saw the empty bed. He checked the bathroom, but that too was empty. What in the world?

He left his mother's room and went to the nurses' station where a young woman directed a patient's family to the dining hall. She turned to him. "Mr. Stone, you're early today."

He gave a short nod. "Where is she?"

The nurse pointed down the hall to the television room. He didn't think his mom had been leaving her room much, but perhaps that had changed. He strode down the hall and paused in the doorway at the sight of Suzy with a large cat in her arms. She tucked her face in his fur then placed the cat in his mother's outstretched arms. "What is going on in here?" he asked.

Suzy's head snapped up, and she gave him a bright smile. "You're just in time for therapy. Do you want to hold Mr. Whiskers next?"

"No. I don't. And neither should my mother." He plucked the cat from Ma's arms. "Do you know how many rules you're breaking by bringing these flea-bitten animals into a sterile environment?"

Suzy plucked the cat from him and gave it back to his mom. "First of all, the community room is already not sterile. Second, no patient in here is at risk. And those flea-bitten critters are therapy for my patients."

Now he'd really heard everything. "Therapy? Really?"

"Could we take this out to the hallway?" A tall woman with long, dark red hair and wearing a white lab coat stepped forward, and Will headed outside. When Suzy started following them, the doctor stopped her. "I'll deal with him. You stay with the patients."

The woman shut the door behind them and folded her arms across her chest. "Suze is right. These animals are important to her patients' healing. Studies show that pets lower blood pressure, relieve stress and promote health and well-being to their owners. Suzy came up with the idea to start this here, and it's brilliant, Mr..."

"Stone."

"So you're Will." The doctor scrutinized him from head to toe then gave a nod. "That explains it."

"And you are..."

She held out her hand. "Dr. Presley Jones. I'm the vet over at the animal rescue." They shook hands, and her smile grew wider. "Firm grip. Nice."

"Excuse me?"

Dr. Jones took a step forward, still hanging on to his hand and pulled him so that he had to bend down, giving her the advantage. "But if you hurt my friend Suzy, it won't be so nice for you anymore." She squeezed his hand hard. "Got it?"

"I'm not doing anything." He let go of her hand and massaged his. The doctor certainly had strength. "It's nice to know she has friends who look out for her."

"I'll do more than that if I have to." She crossed her arms again and glared at him. "So we have an understanding?"

"You bet." He waved his hand to get back some feeling. "You've got some grip."

The door opened, and Suzy popped her head out. "Are we good now?"

Dr. Jones glared at him until he nodded. "The vet explained things."

"Good." She checked her watch. "You're welcome to join us for the last ten minutes, Will. Petting a cat might do wonders for you."

"I don't think..." Another glare from the vet. "I'd like that."

Suzy opened the door for them both. Will soon found himself in an armchair with a small dachshund sitting on his lap and staring up at him with adoring eyes. "This is temporary, pal, so don't get any ideas."

Still, it was nice to run his hand over the sleek pup. To sit back and close his eyes if just for a moment. He could feel his anger and tension disappearing. This was...nice. Unexpected. And darn it if the doctor wasn't right. It was definitely lowering his blood pressure.

He opened his eyes and found Suzy watching him with a look of triumph. He sent a smile back and let his eyes close again. Then she was shaking him awake and taking the dog from him. "He has to go back to the shelter."

Will nodded with a twinge of regret. If his life was more settled, he might consider adopting a pet but there was too much going on. With his mom here at the home, he didn't get to his place until late most evenings. At least taking care of his mom's cats didn't require a lot of attention. A little food in the morning. More at night. A bowl of fresh water. And a litter box. Easy.

Except for the cat hairs that seemed to have invaded every room of his townhouse. And settled on all his clothes.

He stood and kept his gaze on Suzy as she got the animals settled in their crates. She wiped her hands off then rested them on her hips. She glanced at him. "I wouldn't do anything to harm your mom. You get that, right?"

He did, but when he'd seen what was happening, he couldn't control himself. "I overreacted."

"You do that a lot."

Did he ever. He cocked his head to one side. "Do you think we're destined to become like our parents?"

Suzy frowned and checked the lock on one of the crates. "Why do you say that?"

"Because sometimes I hear my dad's voice coming out of my mouth and I don't like it." He rubbed his hand over his face. "I loved my dad, but he was a hard man. I don't want to be like that. Is that how you see me?"

She took too long in answering. Finally, she shrugged. "Maybe at first."

"You're not helping."

"But once I got to know you better, I could see it's just a front. The way you care about your mom and your sister shows a lot more than this gruff exterior. You have a heart, Will. So no, you're not going to become like your father." She gave him a smile, as if she could see right through to his core.

Soon she was going to say he was just a teddy bear deep down inside, and he couldn't allow that. Wouldn't let himself admit that just maybe she was right. Because he was an ex-Marine. Tough. Strong. And not fluffy. Not at all. He was his father's son, after all. "I'm not soft, Suzy. I can't change that."

"If we are doomed to become our parents, then I'm either going to be a hoarder or abandon everyone I love. And I refuse to do that.

We don't have to be who are parents are. We can choose to be who we want to be."

"Easier said than done. It's not only genetics though, it's also how we're brought up."

"Still, it doesn't have to be like that about our parents." She tried to smile, but he could see she wasn't quite successful. "That's why we have therapy, right?"

She scooped up a crate in each hand and walked out of the room.

For a moment, he watched her. He didn't have to be the hard man his father had been or the driven soldier he'd been raised to be. He could be his own man. Someone who was a leader, but who could also show compassion. Wasn't that what his volunteer brigade was about?

He didn't have to follow the path his father had followed. Maybe it was time to find his own.

THE NEXT MORNING, after her shift had ended at the nursing home, Suzy inserted two quarters in the parking meter and turned the dial. She'd probably be in town hall for at least an hour. Longer if it didn't go as she'd planned. She gripped her purse tighter and sprinted up the front steps to town hall. It was an older building, dimly lit and with a musty smell. Suzy stopped in front of the directory and checked for Will's name. William Stone in 227.

She took the stairs to the second floor then counted down the numbers until she stood outside of his office. She noted that the door was open, but the light was off. She poked her head inside. "Hey, you here?"

There was a thump and a muffled curse. His head popped up from under the desk. "What are you doing here?"

"What are you doing hiding under your desk?"

He rubbed the back of his head. "I think a fuse is fried or something because my lights and computer don't work. I was checking the connections to be sure."

Suzy flipped the light switch off and on, but there was no power. "It's probably a circuit breaker or something."

"Perfect." He pointed to the chair in front of his desk. "Stay there. I'll be right back."

Suzy saluted him. "Aye, aye, Captain."

He grimaced. "I meant, would you mind waiting for me here while I take care of this issue?"

"Much better." In his absence, she peeked

at the framed pictures on his desk. Mrs. Stone. Tori and the boys. A gruff looking man in uniform. Must be his dad. She could see the resemblance, especially in those piercing blue eyes. "So you're Mr. Stone."

"Yep, that's my dad."

Suzy almost jumped out of her skin. She turned to face Will. "You shouldn't have snuck up on me like that."

"You shouldn't be snooping." He took the picture from her and glanced down at it then her.

"I wasn't snooping. I was just curious."

He gave her a soft grin, and she was struck again by how good he looked when he smiled. The smile switched to a frown. "Why are you looking at me like there's something on my face?"

"You smiled. You're so hot when you do that." She covered her mouth with her hand. "I meant to say nice looking. You're handsome. Ugh, I'm making it worse."

"I'd say you're making it much better." He approached her but she retreated a few steps until the backs of her legs hit a chair. He stopped. "But you're here on business?"

"Something like that."

"I'm not extending the deadline. Even for you."

Of course he'd jump to that conclusion. "Nothing like that." She took a seat in the chair across from him. "I'm having another clean out day this Saturday, and I wanted to…" He took a seat on his desk so that his feet framed hers on the carpet. She kept her gaze on them "Um…ask you…"

"Ask me…what?"

She looked up at him. "I need help, okay? Pres said she can help for a little. Rick's wedding is coming up, but he said he could stop by for a few hours. But there's so much…and I don't have a lot of time… So I…I'm asking for your help again. But you're not obligated to do anything."

"I'll do it." His answer came quickly. He shrugged. "Maybe I can ask my sister and the boys to give a hand too. More hands make the work light or something like that."

"You'd do that?"

"Why not? You asked so nicely." He dropped the volume of his voice. "Besides, I like you."

She frowned at him. Was he kidding? He loved to make her life miserable with all his lists of what needed to be done and his impossible timelines. "Well, you could have fooled me."

He leaned forward resting his hands on the armrests of her chair. His face was inches away. "Let me assure you. I really like you."

She swallowed hard. Was the room getting warm? She couldn't look away from his blue eyes. "Why?"

He laughed then, and she reached up to cup his face with her hands. She kissed him hard, and he tugged her into his arms. They might have kissed longer if there hadn't been a knock on the office door and the sound of someone clearing his throat. "Sorry to interrupt…"

Suzy hid her face in Will's chest. What had she been thinking? He'd smiled, and she'd acted on impulse like an idiot. No, not an idiot. Desperate and love-starved. She grabbed her purse from where it had fallen beside the chair. She needed to get out of here. Put some distance between her and this crazy idea that she could be falling for Will. That wasn't what this was. It was too soon. Too much. She liked him, and she liked the man she could see him trying to be. But that was it.

Wasn't it?

She glanced at Rick then ran down the hall. She stopped at the top of the stairs when Will called her name. "Suzy, what time on Saturday?"

Saturday? What was happening then? Was he asking her out? Oh, right. The clean out. "Nine a.m."

Will gave a brusque nod. "We'll be there." But then he smiled, and her mouth mirrored his.

She practically flew to her car.

WILL WATCHED SUZY leave the building then turned to find Rick had taken a seat in front of the desk. "I didn't know you two were dating."

Will shook his head. "We're not. Yet." But they would soon if it was up to him. He sat in his chair and laced his fingers behind his head. "What's up?"

Rick looked over his shoulder then rose and shut the office door. "You know that the budget meeting is tomorrow night. And we're looking at some pretty big cuts."

"You're cutting my job?"

"I need you to generate a list of your duties and responsibilities. Things that you've accomplished since taking the position. What you've done, and what you hope to do." Rick took his seat. "The council is talking about outsourcing your position to the county, but I need you to come up with reasons for you to stay here."

Will's feet hit the floor with a loud thud. "I figured they'd cut my hours but not get rid of me completely."

"And they still might."

This couldn't be happening. After the Marines, he'd found himself longing to make a difference in his community. That the fighting he'd done overseas meant something. He'd toyed with the idea of politics, but got disillusioned with the backstabbing and empty promises. He'd studied engineering in college, then taken this job, which he loved. What would he do if he didn't work here? What could he do? His community meant everything to him. He stood and held out his hand to shake Rick's. "Understood. Thanks for the heads up."

Rick paused before leaving. "You're helping at Suzy's on Saturday?"

"She asked me."

"Good. She's been a friend of my family's for years. Her mom worked for my dad, so don't make me have to kick your behind."

He was the second person to warn him off of Suzy. He should listen to them. Keep himself from doing any more damage to either one of them or their hearts. "I don't plan on hurting her."

"Do any of us? Especially those we love?"

Love? Will swallowed but found it difficult with the lump of emotion lodged there. Maybe he liked her a little. Okay, a lot. But love?

That scared him more than anything because if love was like what he'd had growing up with his father, it hurt more than it helped. But with Suzy, love might be something else. Something that built him up rather than tore him down. Something that would add to his life rather than threaten to take something away.

Love?

Will flipped through his note cards one more time. Closed his eyes and mouthed some of the statistics that could save his job. He felt a hand on his back and turned to see Rick. "You ready, man?"

Will adjusted his tie and nodded. "I believe so. I've been going over these numbers so many times that my eyes are starting to cross."

"You don't need numbers to convince them." Rick grimaced. "Well, unless it's how you're saving money. Those numbers they like."

"My role isn't just to save money, but to inspect our community to keep it safe."

"I like that. Make sure you throw that in somewhere."

"Thanks. And if I get an opening, I thought I'd throw in my idea about volunteers helping in the situations where the resident is unable to do the necessary work." Will glanced around the town council chambers and noted the many empty chairs. "Budget meetings don't exactly bring in the crowds, do they?"

"Not exactly." Rick fiddled with his tie. "Man, I hate wearing these things. Do you think they'd notice if I loosened it just a little?"

"Don't you dare. I tied it perfectly." Rick's fiancée Lizzie joined them and swatted Rick's hands away. "And it's important that you present them with a professional, in control demeanor."

"Lizzie likes her big words."

She swatted his shoulder, but smiled at

them both. "You want to win with this budget, and I know how to get you what you want."

Will leaned in. "Then could you give me some tips? Because I really need this job."

"They're looking to cut expenses but maximize services." She seemed to be considering her words. "You ensure the safety and integrity of the community. You're as necessary to them as a police officer or firefighter."

"But if it comes down to one of them or me?" Will shook his head. "I don't stand a chance."

"There's a whole station full of them. There's only one of you. They'd be fools to get rid of someone so essential. Because that's what you are. Important and necessary." She reached up and straightened his tie as well. "I'm going to get a good seat. Good luck, you two."

Rick gave Lizzie a quick peck on the cheek before she walked away. "I'm a lucky man already." He grinned at Will. "I'm putting my support behind you."

"I can't ask you to do that. You don't want to risk your job too."

"My job is to make sure that I do what is

right for the town. You're tough but fair in your inspections. We need someone like you ensuring the safety of our neighborhoods, like Lizzie said."

"Thanks. I appreciate it."

The two men shook hands, and then Rick left to take his seat on the dais. Will meanwhile found an empty seat near the front. He took out his notecards and reviewed them once more. He had to prove to the councilors that they needed him.

The meeting began with a review of the agenda and the minutes from the previous meeting. Will tried to pay attention, but found himself ready to nod off if they didn't get on with things. He reviewed his notes again to keep focused. Soon his name was called. He approached the podium and set his notecards on the lectern.

"I'm Will Stone, the town code inspector." He spoke up, afraid he didn't sound very confident. "Lake Mildred has had forty-eight calls in to the code inspector's office this year regarding violations that threatened public safety. Of those, forty-two were resolved within a thirty day time period." Will looked up from his notes. "And the six that are still outstanding are in the process of being fixed or eliminated as we speak."

He noted several council members write down his figures. A good sign? Maybe. "That's a better than eighty-seven percent success rate."

Mrs. Winkle adjusted her microphone. "You work five days a week, eight hours a day, and you only had forty-eight calls in the last nine months?" She turned to her fellow council members. "That's less than six a month."

"One call leads to several in home visits to resolve the issue. I'm not stuck in my office only answering my phone." He flipped through his note cards. "I'm also approving work permits and inspecting job sites for safety issues. I was on the road for thirty-one of those."

One of the older council members frowned at him. Ol' Mr. Barry looked ready to grill him alive. "What about those six issues still outstanding? When will those get fixed? We need results more than promises."

Suzy's face came to mind. "Soon. I'm working with the home and business owners now to create action plans."

"So by the next full council meeting, we'll have those fixed?"

Will calculated the next meeting to be only three weeks away. With some effort, he could get them mostly resolved. It would take some pressure, but he could do it.

But that meant going back to Suzy. She would need further pressure. And if he was right, more help. Because she couldn't do it on her own. Even with the clean out day, she'd need another dozen hands.

And for some reason, he didn't want her to be alone in this. He wanted to be by her side working together.

He gave a soft smile. "Yes, sir. I will guarantee it."

WILL HURRIED INTO the seniors' home and spotted his favorite nurse. Suzy looked up from her station as he approached. "Uh oh."

He stopped walking and frowned. Glanced behind him. "What?"

"You've got that look."

He tried to pull back his features. "We need to talk."

"I knew it. You get that look, and it means business. And that usually means you have bad news for me."

"Then you should be used to it."

She gave him a smile then, and he was surprised that she could even after everything that had happened. She motioned with her head down the hall and led him to an empty room. She turned to him with her hand on the door. "Is this a talk where the door stays open?"

"Why wouldn't it be?" Will shook his head. She was trying to confuse him. Had to be it. Throw him off his game so that she could get what she wanted. "Leave it open."

"Fine by me." She stepped farther inside the room and grasped her hands in front of her. "So talk."

"The town council has given me three weeks to whip you into shape. I mean, your house."

Suzy nodded. "You already gave me the thirty day notice. I get it."

"I'm serious. I'm not going to have the town council eliminate my job because you bat your eyes at me and smile like everything is okay. And yet nothing gets done. I need results, Suzy."

"You think I'm manipulating you?"

"I think that you're like your mother who gave me every excuse. Who tried many times to get things taken care of, but it was just a smoke screen." He paced back and forth and ran a hand through his hair. "She never intended to clean things up. She was happy with the way things were."

Suzy sighed and looked down at the ground. "Yes, she was. She didn't want things to change."

"But I'm not putting up with that from you."

Her head snapped up, and he saw a glimpse of fire in her eyes. "I am not my mother."

"Really? Because I don't think you want to get that house cleaned up. You're perfectly happy living in the middle of all that stuff."

"You don't know me. I'm not happy at all." Indignation had replaced the anger in her eyes. "I've always hated it."

"Then do something about it."

"I am."

"What are you doing? You've cleared out one room."

She opened her mouth then shut it. She quickly brushed past him as she strode down the hallway. He called her name, but she kept walking.

This wasn't going the way he'd planned. In fact, it seemed to be going nowhere at all.

He rushed after her and stopped her before she reached her station. "I need to know that you're going to do this."

"So you can keep your job?"

Yes and no. "That too. But I want you to be happy. Because even you've admitted that you can't be in that house like that. It's dragging you down."

"I'm working on it." Suzy gave him a bright smile but he wasn't convinced. He knew her secret now. That smile hid a lot of pain. "I've already invited you to the clean out this weekend. What more do you want from me?"

He leaned towards her. "No more kissing. Not until we get this taken care of." He took a step back. "I need to keep a clear head. Stay focused."

"And you can't with me?"

He couldn't find a sane thought in his head with her so close. He took another step back. "We'll get your house cleaned up and then explore what this is between us."

"There's something between us." She broke into a smile, but this time it was genuine. "I promise that once this is all over,

we'll go out to dinner. Or a movie. Or something." She bit her lip. "I haven't exactly been
on a date in a long time, so I'm a little rusty."

"Did you just ask me out?"

A reddish hue colored Suzy's cheeks and
she shrugged. "I told you it's been awhile."

He smiled back at her. "I like that."

"But only after this whole house issue is
over." She walked away then, shaking her
head.

SHE NEEDED ANOTHER three days. Four tops.

Suzy surveyed the progress she'd made in
her mother's house and frowned. Even if she
had a month, she didn't know if she'd have
time to get it all cleared out. The tiny steps
she'd made were good ones, but still small
in comparison to what needed to be done.
There was too much stuff.

Still, tiny steps still got someone to their
destination.

The biggest difference was the clutter inside her. It had shifted and was being cleared
out as well.

A knock at the front door. She abandoned
the bag of trash she'd been collecting in the
hallway and walked to the living room. She
peered out the peephole and found Page

standing on her porch. She opened the door and ushered her inside. "I wasn't expecting you until tomorrow."

"I know. I was in the neighborhood and thought I'd stop by and see how things were going." She looked around the room. "Maybe come up with a strategy for tomorrow."

"I thought we had a plan?" Suzy grimaced. This was getting to be more than she expected. She thought people would come over. She'd sugar them up with donuts and coffee. Then they'd pack things into boxes to put... Where?

She gave a nod. "Okay, so, what are we going to do with all this stuff?"

"Suzy, the question is what are you going to do? You're the one in control of tomorrow." Page handed her a notebook and pen. "So I'd like you to write down some rules that you want us to follow. Who gets final say. Who does what. What stays. What goes."

She looked down at the blank page and felt panic rising in her chest. The room was warm, and her skin prickled in the heat. Her heartbeat started to speed up and her palms were clammy. What was she going to do?

How could she do all this? What was she thinking?

Mama.

She took a deep breath, and it came out in shudders. Page put her hand on her wrist. "Suzy, what are you feeling right now? And don't say fine because I can see you're not."

"I feel…" Overwhelmed. Forced into a corner without an escape. Lost. "So lost."

"It's okay to feel that way."

Suzy shook her head. "No. I'm supposed to know what I'm doing. And the truth is, I have no clue."

"You don't have to have all the answers right now. It's okay."

Suzy held up the notepad and pen. "But you said I'm in control."

"Right. But you're not expected to be perfect or all knowing."

There was another knock on the door. What was this? Grand Central? Suzy went to the door and squinted out the peephole. Why in the world was Will here now? She opened the door. "It's not until tomorrow."

"I wanted to check in with you to see if there was anything you needed." He ducked past her and into the living room. He seemed surprised to see Page there. "Um, hi. I'm the code inspector."

Page held out her hand. "I'm the counselor."

He turned to Suzy, and she could see the questions in his eyes but she wasn't about to explain it. "She's helping me come up with a plan for tomorrow."

"That's exactly why I stopped over. The more organized you are before we start, the more efficient we will be."

Page looked him over. Suzy figured that she was sizing him up and wondered how he'd handle the scrutiny.

Suzy waved her notebook at him. "I'm going to make up some rules and decide who's going to be doing what and where."

"I like it."

"You like things ordered, don't you? All neat and tidy and in their place." Page nodded and smiled. "Ex-military, right?"

"Marines." Will turned to Suzy. "Who is this again?"

"My therapist. So I guess you were right. I am certifiable."

Will shook his head. "I never called you that."

"Might as well have. I've seen how you look at me." She shot him a grin.

Page whistled. "Wow. How long have you two been attracted to each other?"

Suzy laughed while Will frowned. "You can tell that?"

"It's pretty obvious there seems to be something going on between you two."

"You could be wrong."

Suzy blushed and took off with her notebook for the kitchen. Is that what he thought? Hadn't he admitted that they should explore whatever was happening between them after the house was cleaned out? Suzy couldn't figure it out, and honestly she was too tired to. Fine. If that was how he wanted to play it.

She got started on her plan in the kitchen. She wrote down a list of appliances to be removed. Donated to the Goodwill center, if they'd take them. Listed the boxes of china to be taken out. The trash to be disposed of. Maybe Pres could do that with Rick.

Page appeared and scanned the kitchen. "Avoiding the question?"

"No. Avoiding you. Because you don't know what you're talking about." Suzy made more notes. "You heard him. There's nothing happening with Will and me."

"Right."

Will called out to her. "It seems like you've got things taken care of here, so I'm going. I'll see you in the morning."

He sounded a little upset. More than when he'd arrived. Suzy frowned and followed him out the front door, right to his car. "Why are you leaving? Is it because of what I said to Page? *You* said that nothing was happening first."

Will nodded and got into his truck. Turned the key in the ignition and revved the engine. "My mistake."

Suzy watched him back out of her driveway and speed away. She turned and walked back towards the house, only to find Page standing on the porch observing them. "Right. Nothing going on."

"There isn't." But she didn't quite seem to mean the words.

CHAPTER NINE

THE SOUND OF rain on the roof woke Suzy up on the morning of the clean out. She stretched in the bed and lay there for a moment. Looking around her bedroom, she thought if only she could get the rest of the house to look like this room, she'd be set. Happier. Content.

After a quick shower and dressing in a sweatshirt and jeans, she drove to the Sweetheart and picked up the fresh doughnuts and sweet rolls that she'd ordered. She gave Mrs. Sweet an extra tip then practically sang as she drove back to the house. A little rain wasn't going to bring her down. Not today.

When she returned to the house, she saw that Presley had arrived along with Page and Henry. She hugged her friend then turned to her therapist. "You're early."

Henry put his arms around Suzy's shoulders. "Because I drove us here. Now show me what we're working with."

Suzy led them inside and tried to ignore the look of disbelief on Henry's face as they surveyed the living room. The leaning tower of boxes in one corner of the living room was enough to scare anyone off. But he didn't say anything. Instead he glanced at his sister then took the load of pastries from Suzy. "Let's find a place for these."

A few minutes before ten, Rick arrived alone. "Lizzie's swamped with wedding details, but she said she'll give you a hand with anything else you need."

"She didn't happen to hand you a clipboard with a list of things to do, did she?"

Rick chuckled and shook his head. "My Lizzie and her clipboard. It's like she needs it to remember to breathe."

There was a knock at the door, and Will arrived with his sister and nephews. With so many gathered in a tiny, cramped space, Suzy felt her heart starting to pound. Page put a hand on her arm. "Just breathe slowly."

"I'm fine."

"You look like you're going to pass out."

Suzy denied it but then almost jumped when Will walked up behind her. "Everything okay?"

"Everything is fine." She glanced at both of them. "I'm fine. Can we get this started?"

Page nodded and raised her voice. "I'd like to thank everyone for coming out to help Suzy today. A few ground rules before we start. We're doing this to help Suzy keep her house, so she gets the final say on what goes and what stays. If you're not sure, ask before you toss it. And we'll keep this a judgment-free zone for the day. Any questions?"

Suzy looked around her and gave a watery smile. "Thank you, everybody. Mama was all I had for a really long time, so this means a lot to me to have you here."

Everyone split into teams of two. Tori volunteered to help Suzy out in Mama's bedroom. She glanced at Will's sister. "Are you sure you want to do that? It's one of the biggest messes here."

Tori linked her arm through Suzy's. "I love a challenge. Lead the way."

They walked down the hall, and Suzy took a deep breath before opening the door to the bedroom. Tori put a hand on her shoulder. "It's okay. We'll do this together."

Suzy nodded and opened the door. Waited for Tori to mention the books and papers that covered the floor so that you couldn't see the carpeting. Instead, she pointed to a box that held some books. "Do you want me to finish packing those?"

No. She'd do it later. Then Suzy remembered why they were there. "Actually, I thought maybe we could work on Mama's closet. Get the hard stuff done first."

Tori nodded and cleared a spot on the bed. "Why don't we make a pile of keepers and another for donations?"

Sounded good to her. She opened the closet door and held up her hands to catch the stack of T-shirts that wouldn't stay on their shelf. She brought them over to the bed. "I guess we can donate all these."

For the first half hour, she found it easier to donate things than to keep them. Feeling good about it, Suzy reached farther into the closet and pulled out the garment bag that held Mama's wedding dress. She unzipped the bag and pulled out the yellowed lace dress. "I can't believe how damaged this is after all these years."

Tori reached out and fingered the antique lace. "Maybe she hoped to pass it down to you when you got married."

"Maybe." Suzy marveled at all the tiny buttons on the back of the dress. "She should

have taken better care of it then. It's ruined."
She turned and showed Tori where moths
had eaten at the lace edging on the sleeves
and bodice. "I couldn't wear it like this.
What was she thinking?"

Suzy willed the hot tears to leave her
alone. They weren't welcome. Not today.
She threw the wedding gown on the bed.
"Just get rid of it."

Tori nodded and left to get a trash bag.
Alone, Suzy turned back to the closet and
pulled out the red sweatshirt with puppies.
The collar was stained like Page had pointed
out. It was way too big, but she couldn't let
it go. She put it in the keeper pile and by the
time Tori had returned, had emptied most of
the closet into the donation pile.

Tori gave a low whistle. "Wow, you were
busy. How long was I gone?"

Suzy nodded and continued to pull out
more clothes including a bright blue cash-
mere sweater that Mama had worn in her
skinnier days. She put it on the donation pile,
and Tori picked it up. "I love this color, don't
you?"

She considered it for a moment and gave
a shrug. "I prefer yellow actually."

Tori held it up to her chest and measured it

against her body. "Would you mind if I kept this? I love it."

Suzy frowned. "It's been sitting in Mama's closet for who knows how long."

"The classics never go out of style." Tori looked over at Suzy. "I mean, only if it's okay with you."

"Of course."

Tori stepped carefully around the clutter and hugged her. "It's almost like we're sisters sharing clothes." She held the sweater up to her chest. "My sisters were seven and nine years older than me, so we never got to do that."

Suzy almost envied her siblings. For too many years, it had only been her and Mama. No one to share the burden with. "I was an only child."

"That must have been so lonely for you."

It had been, but things were different now. Suzy gave her a smile. "But I have friends that are like family. And I think you're one of those."

The two hugged each other. Then they got back to work.

AN HOUR IN, and it didn't seem as if he and the twins had made much of an impact in the living room. The path to the front door looked wider, but that was as far as they had gotten. Of course, Will had had to break up two fights between Brady and Conner already and threaten them with bodily harm if they didn't put the doughnuts down and get to work. They were young and strong enough to lift the heavy boxes and move them outside under the porch for Suzy to go through later.

Will was determined to clear the room to the corner and remove the wall of boxes and stuff that covered the window. As the twins returned, he put more boxes in their arms and helped them haul them out. He could almost see the outer wall and the ceiling above.

Rick stopped in the living room and motioned Will over. "Can you give me a hand moving the fridge?"

"Sure if you'll help me clear out this corner."

The two of them walked into the kitchen where Suzy's therapist and brother tackled the counters and all the stuff covering them. He gave a short nod then wedged himself between the wall and the fridge. "We've got a bigger path now if you want to take it out the front."

"Good idea. Smits said he'll pick the appliances up later this afternoon."

With effort, they pushed the refrigerator a few feet from the wall then leaned it forward to get the dolly underneath it. On a count of three, they hoisted it and wheeled it through the living room and outside to the curb. Will stretched his arms above his head. "Remember our deal."

Rick grumbled but patted him on the back. "Let's clear that corner."

With his friend's help, the pile of boxes moved outside rather quickly. Two more, and Will would have an empty wall.

With the last one in Rick's arms, he looked around and gave a nod. What was that on the ceiling? He frowned. Was that a crack? And was it just him, or did it look like it was spreading?

Rick asked, "How about a hand with the stove?"

Will pointed towards the ceiling. "Look up there and tell me what you see."

Rick looked up and shrugged. "It's a crack in the ceiling."

"It's more than that." Will found a chair in the dining room and pulled it into the corner of the living room to examine the crack closer. It looked another inch longer in such a short time. A heavy feeling settled in his gut. This was not good. Not at all.

He got down from the chair and walked outside to examine the wall from there. Will couldn't believe it. Almost. The stack of boxes had been giving support to the wall, but with them removed, there was now a problem with the structure of the house. If the cracks in the foundation were any indication, the northern wall could collapse if something wasn't done.

Problem was, it was expensive. And would surely take more time than Suzy had left.

He glanced through the window and saw Suzy's friends. They were all here to help her. To support her. They'd hate him for what he had to do.

So would she.

He groaned and covered his eyes. This was his job. It wasn't personal. With the safety of everyone in the house at stake, he had to act. Had to do something.

He walked into the house and down the hallway to where Suzy and his sister were organizing her mother's bedroom. "Hey, Tor. Can I have a moment alone with Suzy?"

She waggled her eyebrows at him. "Don't

be getting too frisky. We still have the dresser to sort through."

He didn't crack a smile, and hers faded. The teasing left her eyes, and he could see that she wanted to ask him what was wrong. "This won't take long."

He waited until Tori left then turned to Suzy. She looked fragile. As if a puff of air would knock her down. He couldn't do this to her.

But he had to.

"We have a problem."

Suzy followed Will down the hallway to the living room and gasped when she saw the progress Will had made. "I forgot the carpet was blue in here."

"Forget the carpet. Look at the ceiling."

Right. The ceiling. The whole reason he was stopping their work and bringing her out here. "It's a crack. That's always been there."

Will leaned down and brushed his hand on the carpet. "But it's spreading." He showed her the chalky white dust on his hands. "This is a safety concern."

"What? You think the roof is going to collapse?" She smiled but felt it disappear when he didn't smile back. In fact, he looked more serious. "It really could?"

He looked so serious. "Due to the compromised structure of the house, I have to remove all of you from the premises until an engineer can assess the damage."

A hot feeling started in her belly and spread up her chest. "You're getting all technical on me. That's not good."

He shook his head. "It's not."

"So what does that mean?"

She feared the words even before he said them. "It means that for now, you can't live here."

CHAPTER TEN

SUZY STARED AT HIM, her eyebrows tightly knitted together. Not live here anymore? Was this a joke? The whole reason that everyone had helped her was so she could keep the house. And if she didn't live here, where was she supposed to go?

She glanced around the room, listened to her friends' muted conversations nearby. They were here helping her, but to what end? So she could lose the house anyway? "I don't understand. You said if we got this place cleaned up, I could stay. You promised."

He watched her with a hooded expression. She couldn't tell if he was angry or joking or just being himself. He gave an exaggerated sigh. "I was not aware of the structural damage."

"Then you shouldn't make promises you can't keep." This had to be a nightmare. Someone pinch her so she could wake up and realize that it was still morning and she was alone in bed. "So where do I go? What do I do?"

Page walked into the living room and put her hand on her back. "Breathe, Suzy."

She whirled on her counselor. "Don't touch me."

Page looked at Will who pointed to the ceiling. "There's been structural damage to the home which compromises the safety of the house. I need everyone to leave the premises until I can have an engineer assess the situation."

Page nodded. "I'll let everyone know. Thanks, Will."

"You're thanking him for kicking me out of my house?" Was everyone going crazy? None of this made any sense. "I'm homeless." She covered her face with her hands and jerked away from Will when he tried to pat her back. "Don't."

"I need you to pack a bag for the next week or two, but then you have to leave."

"You need me to…" She walked to her new bedroom and opened the closet. She yanked out several pairs of scrubs and tossed them on her bed. She knew there were several luggage sets in the garage that she'd planned to donate, never knowing she'd need to use one herself.

She ignored Pres in the hallway who turned and followed her outside. "Suze, you okay?"

"Perfect." She gave a smile as if to prove it. "I need a suitcase."

Her friend wouldn't let it go. "Why don't you come and stay with me until Will finds out what's going on?"

Tempting. "I don't think so."

Presley blinked at her as if she didn't understand her response. "Why not? Where are you going to go instead?"

Suzy dragged one of the better looking pieces out of the pile of donations. "It's sweet of you to offer, but I honestly don't know what I'm going to do. I need to think."

Pres stopped her mid-stride and put her hand on her shoulder. "So think at my place. It's not big, but I have that extra bedroom."

"Which you're remodeling, right?"

"I can move some things around. Get the bed put back."

"I'll be fine." She rolled the suitcase into the house. Again ignored the sympathetic looks on everyone's faces and concentrated instead on getting packed. She returned to her room and placed the suitcase on the bed. Unzipped it and stared for a moment. This was supposed to be a good day. She was supposed to be living in a better space. Instead, she had nowhere to go.

A knock on the bedroom door, and Tori entered. "Need a hand?"

Suzy started to fold the scrubs and place them in the suitcase. "No. I'm almost finished in here."

Tori sat on the bed next to the suitcase. "Will's worried about you."

Worried about her? Yeah, right. More like worried about his job. But she nodded in what she hoped seemed like understanding. But she didn't understand him. She didn't understand anything. "I know."

Tori got up and walked to the dresser where she retrieved the book that Suzy had fallen asleep reading the night before. She put it in the suitcase. "Do you know where you're going to go?"

Suzy shook her head and left the room to get some things from the bathroom. She reappeared with her toothbrush and toiletries, and tossed them on top of her scrubs. She pulled out socks and underwear from the dresser. Threw those on top of everything and zipped up the suitcase.

Tori helped her set the suitcase on the floor and extend the handle to pull it. "You're welcome to stay with me for a few days."

"I appreciate the offer, but…" She didn't want to be a burden on anyone. She needed time to figure this out, and that meant being alone. "I'll come up with something." She smiled at Will's sister. "But thank you for asking."

Another knock on the door. Will walked in. "I don't mean to rush you, but we need to go."

Suzy pointed to the suitcase on the floor. "I'm ready."

She wheeled the suitcase into the living room. With all the boxes gone, the area looked a lot bigger. Big enough for her to walk through with her suitcase beside her. She pulled it out on to the front yard. Saw her friends standing there still. Watching her. Waiting for her to say she was okay. She smiled. "Didn't exactly end like we expected, huh?"

Pres rushed forward. "My offer is still open. Come home with me. It'll be like our freshman year in college."

"I don't know." She wanted to be alone. To have her pity party in private.

Pres put her hand on the suitcase. "I do. You're going home with me."

Suzy let go of the handle and watched her friend put the suitcase in the back seat of her car. She turned to the rest of them. "Um, thank you for what you did. I only wish we'd had a better finish."

"We'll discuss this on Wednesday." Page nudged Henry who engulfed Suzy in a hug. She didn't have the energy to reciprocate with more than an awkward tap on his back. They left soon after.

Rick approached her. "Real sorry about this, Suze. I'll see what I can do about an engineer, okay?"

Will held up his cell phone. "Already taken care of. Sam'll be here shortly."

"I'd like to hear what he says." Suzy crossed her arms over her chest, daring Will to make her leave. Because that was a fight he wouldn't win.

He agreed then looked at his sister. Tori hugged her. "Let me know if you need anything. Anything at all."

"Thanks for helping me in Mama's room."

"Thank you for the sweater." She turned

to her boys. "You guys hungry?" When they started throwing out lunch suggestions, she groaned. "I should have known."

They left in small groups. Pres promised to get the room ready for her, but to take her time getting there. Then it was only Suzy and Will left, standing on the front lawn looking up at her house.

But not her house. Not anymore.

WILL SAT ON the porch while Suzy, several feet away from him, leaned against the black metal stair railing. He noticed she didn't want to be anywhere near him. He guessed that made sense. She asked, "When's Sam supposed to be here?"

"Soon."

She gave a nod, glanced at the boxes of things. "Might as well be productive while I wait."

He took a step forward. "Suzy—"

"Don't say a word." She walked down the steps and started to rummage through one of the boxes he'd removed from the living room earlier that day. She pulled a couple items out. Examined them. Then tossed them back in. Picked up the box and tossed it in the dumpster.

He winced at her anger as she followed the first box with a second. "I could have helped you with those."

She glanced at him, her eyes dead when they used to sparkle. "Don't you think you've done enough already?"

Good point. He stayed seated and watched her go through another box. She tossed that in the dumpster too. Soon, she was carrying the rest of the boxes and throwing them all away. He got to his feet and went over to her. He gently put his hands on her shoulders. "Stop. What are you doing?"

"What's the point of going through them if I have nowhere to put anything?" She looked up at him, her eyes rimmed in red but no tears stained her cheeks. "Might as well throw everything away."

He'd done this to her. He'd changed her, and he hated himself for it. He reached out to touch her cheek. "This might not be forever. Just until we can get it fixed."

She took a step back out of his reach. "Take your hands off of me."

He dropped his hands to his sides. "I'm only trying to help you."

"You have a funny way of showing it." She squatted down by a box and flipped through the items. "I don't understand why she kept all of this stuff." She pulled out a book on container gardening. "We never planted flowers much less a vegetable garden. But this is the fourth book I've found." She tossed it back into the box and leaned down to pick the box up. She struggled with the weight of it.

Will hoisted it up for her and took it to the dumpster. "You don't have to do all of this yourself, you know."

She gave a bitter chuckle. "I had help. Much good it did me today."

She continued through another couple boxes as he watched her. Finally, he hung his head. "I'm sorry."

"You were only doing your job."

The words sounded nice, but the way she had said job made it sound like a dirty word. Yes, he'd done his job but he hadn't taken any joy in it. In fact, he regretted it at the moment.

A white pickup truck with Etchason Construction on the panel pulled up to the curb, and Sam got out. He wasn't tall but he was built, probably a result of his job. Will came forward and extended his hand. "I appreciate you coming out on a Saturday like this."

They shook hands. "No problem." Sam turned to Suzy. "Let's take a look and see what we have."

The three of them walked into the living room, and Sam pulled out a flashlight. He ran the light across the crack and frowned. He walked outside to view the foundation then went to his truck. From the back, he pulled out a ladder. Suzy stepped aside as he set it up to get a closer view of the crack and the wall by the front window.

Will hoped he was wrong. He was hardly an expert on home construction, but he knew a problem when he saw it. Maybe Sam would tell him that he'd been mistaken and it wasn't as serious as Will suspected. He'd gladly take the blame for being wrong and give the house back to Suzy. But the other man's frown didn't assure him.

Sam got down from the ladder. "It's like you thought, Will. The weight of the stuff that had been piled in front of the window shifted the support beams. The roof was then resting on the items rather than the beams. Removing all that means we don't have the support, and the roof and front wall could collapse."

Shoot. He'd been hoping for better news.

By the lost look in Suzy's eyes, so had she. "Can it be fixed?"

"Well, that's the good news. I could fix it." Sam glanced up and squinted at the ceiling. "Adding materials and labor, I'd say between five to ten thousand dollars and at least a few weeks. More if we find other damage in the rest of the house. That's the bad news."

Suzy groaned and turned away. Without looking back, she walked outside. Will shook the contractor's hand. "Thanks. That's what I'd feared. How quickly can you start?"

Sam pulled out his phone and moved his finger along the surface. "I'm starting a job down state next week, but after that I'm available."

"I'll call you. And thanks again."

"No problem." Sam glanced outside where Suzy sat on the porch. "She going to be okay?"

"I hope so." But he really wasn't sure how high those hopes were.

Sam walked by her and stood on the sidewalk. "I wish my news had been better, ma'am."

"Me too. Thank you for coming out so soon."

Sam nodded, then got in his truck and gave a short wave before leaving. Will reappeared on the porch and looked down at her. "Let's lock up."

She rose to her feet and once inside, checked to be sure that lights were turned off and everything was okay. She remembered her purse on the dining room table and removed her keys. She glanced around, wondered when or if she'd ever be able to return. Walked out and closed the door behind her. Locked it tight. "Don't you have to post a sign or something saying the house isn't safe to enter?"

He winced. "I have some in my car."

Of course he did. He was Mr. Efficient. "So just do it. Post the sign."

"Suzy, I never meant for this to happen."

But that was the problem, wasn't it? Her dad had never meant to leave her. Mama had never meant to die. To leave her with this mess to deal with. She was used to people letting her down. She'd grown up with it. She had hoped that Will would be different. But he had turned out to be precisely like them. She was so naive. "I know. Just put the sign up."

He walked to his car and returned with

a bright yellow sign. Used a black marker to date it and put her address on it. Then he taped it to the front door.

No entry.

He sighed as he placed the last piece of scotch tape on the sign and stepped back. "Are you going to be okay?"

"Why do you care?"

"Because you matter to me. You mean more to me than some job."

"But the job came first today, didn't it?" Suzy shook her head. "Forget it."

"Your safety came first. But that meant making a hard choice, and I won't apologize for that." He put his hands on her upper arms and pulled her to him so that she had to look up at him. "If something had happened to you because I didn't…I don't want to think about finding you buried under a ton of rubble."

"I would have been fine. I've lived here all my life without any problems. Then you show up with your orders to clean up. And look what happened when we did." She stepped away from him and started walking to her car. "Goodbye, Will."

"Are you working tonight?"

She didn't answer but got in her car. Once

the engine was running, she turned the volume of the radio up so she wouldn't have to hear him calling to her. She had to leave. To get out of there. Nothing would ever be the same after she drove away.

And maybe that was for the best.

THE ATMOSPHERE AT the seniors' home was hushed as Will approached his mother's room. He could hear the faint sounds of people talking, televisions playing and the persistent beeps of machines monitoring residents. He paused outside her door then pushed inside. His mom lay on her side, her back to him. "Hey, Ma." He stepped around the bed so she could see him and placed a hand on her foot. "How you feeling today?"

She stopped reading and smiled at him. "Will, what are you doing here? I thought you were helping a friend this afternoon."

He claimed the chair next to the bed. "Seems like the more I try to help, the more I mess things up. I tried to save Tori's marriage." He ran a hand over his face. "You remember how that turned out? The buddy I tried to help when he got back from Iraq? Even trying to reach out to Carol and Joanie. But I really made a disaster of this one."

Ma set her book to the side and smiled warmly. "Now I know that's not true. You're a good man who always does your best."

"Well, my best is hurting my friend right now. Ma, I don't know how to come back from this. I really don't. I did what was right, but that means she's homeless."

"She?"

He knew he shouldn't have gone there. Should have kept it gender neutral, otherwise she would focus on Suzy and not the situation. "Ma, the point is that I did my best and that hurt my friend. I fix things. That's who I am. I don't make them worse."

"Maybe this isn't for you to fix." She shifted in the bed, wincing slightly then adjusted her blanket. "Maybe it's up to you to simply be there for her. And help when she asks."

He sighed, then stood and walked to the window. "She probably won't even be my friend anymore. So I guess I won't have to wait for her to ask."

He closed his eyes. That's what hurt the most.

He turned back to Ma. "Sorry. I didn't mean to come here and lay all this on you. You've got enough to deal with."

"I didn't know the cancer made me stop being your mom."

"That's not what I meant." He took a few steps toward the bed. "I know you have a lot of stuff going on with you. I don't want to add to your stress."

Ma shook her head and pulled on the blanket to cover her leg. "That's something your father would say. He seemed to think that he had to protect me from everything. But instead, it made me feel alone."

Will stared at the floor and counted the tiles for a moment. He glanced back up. "Dad was a hard man to love. Am I like that too?"

"No."

Her answer came quick, but he wasn't sure if he believed it. "Because sometimes I feel that way. Why else am I alone?"

"You've been concentrating on bettering yourself." Will was skeptical and it must have shown on his face because she grinned knowingly. "Yes, that's what I've been telling myself. That you can't exactly provide for a family until you have a stable job and are happy with yourself. I think that's commendable, and so would your father."

"Oh, sure. He'd actually be telling me that

I haven't been living up to what he expected from me."

His mom didn't say anything at first, and his heart sank much like it had when he'd brought home his report card with all A's and one B. Didn't matter that everything else was perfect. It was the B that would get commented on. Scolded for. And eventually held over his head until he felt as if he'd failed everything. He shook his head in an attempt to shake loose those memories, those feelings.

He again took a seat in the chair next to the bed. Will thought his mom might as well know the rest. "I'll find out soon if the council is keeping my job."

His mom exclaimed, "Oh, honey. Why didn't you say anything?"

"Because we were dealing with enough things around here." He looked down at his hands. "So I'm not the man my father wanted me to be."

"You're wrong. You're exactly what he hoped for."

He gave her a look that he hoped showed that he didn't believe her. "Ma..."

"He wanted you to help others. To be strong for your family. And to be a man of integrity. And that's exactly what you are. You're a good man."

How much his mother's words meant to him surprised him. "Thanks, Ma. That means a lot. Especially after today."

"You did what you had to do. I know that. And your friend probably does too."

"I hope you're right."

WILL SHOULD NEVER have kicked her out of her house. He'd been wrong, so wrong. It wasn't a danger. It wouldn't have collapsed. Right?

It was the uncertainty that hurt the most. Uncertain if he'd done the right thing. If she could have stayed. If things could have been different.

Suzy pulled her car to the curb in front of Presley's townhouse and turned off the engine. She rested her head on the steering wheel and took a deep breath. It felt worse than before and she hadn't thought that was possible. A few breaths later, she got out of the car and approached the house.

Pres met her at the front door. "How are you doing?"

"Fine." She walked past her friend and

into the living room. "I went for a drive to clear my head."

"Did it help?"

Suzy shrugged. Not really, but it hadn't hurt either. She glanced around the room and spied her suitcase sitting at the bottom of the stairs. She reached for it and turned to Pres. "Where would you like me?"

They took the stairs and turned right. Pres held the door open for Suzy who pulled her suitcase in and placed it at the end of the unmade bed. At least there was a bed in here. Last time she'd been over, it'd been a room full of painting supplies. Pres left then returned with a set of sheets. "Sorry I didn't get the bed made before you got here."

"It's fine. I wasn't expecting you to play my maid." She took the sheets and started to unfold them. She struggled with the fitted sheet until Pres gave her a hand. Within minutes, the bed was made and had four pillows that invited Suzy to lie down and enjoy them. "This is great. Thanks for letting me stay."

Presley put a hand on her shoulder. "Are you really okay?"

"Fine." She gave an exaggerated yawn. "I think I'll turn in."

"It's nine o'clock."

"It's been a long day." She held the bedroom door open for Pres. "Good night. I'll see you in the morning."

Presley took a few steps, but stopped. "So that's it? You're shutting me out?"

"I can't talk about this."

"Why not?"

"Because I don't know what to say." Suzy refused to let the tears fall. "I thought I'd be sleeping in my own bed in a clean house tonight. I thought I'd have all this weight off my shoulders. That cleaning the house was going to solve my problems." She sighed. "Instead, it gives me a whole new set of issues that I don't know what to do with."

Pres sat on the bed. "What did the engineer say?"

"That it's going to cost money that I don't have. My credit is shot. I forgot to pay the insurance on the house, and it's lapsed. My credit cards can't handle another purchase. Could I even qualify for a loan?" Suzy sighed again and sat on the edge of the bed so that she didn't have to face Pres. "I might as well let the town take it."

"You can't. You sound like you've given up before you've even tried."

Oh yes, she could. Hand the keys over and

wave goodbye. "Why not? Maybe it would be better."

"For who? You'll regret it if you don't do something."

Suzy didn't have the energy. "Maybe at first."

"I know you. You love that house more than you want to admit. Otherwise, you would have let it go before now."

Suzy considered her words but couldn't agree. But she couldn't disagree either. "It's taking up more of my life than I want to give. I saw what it did to my mom, and I don't want to end up letting the house and the things own me." She shifted from her spot on the bed and looked at Pres. "Let's say I found the money and fixed it up. What then?" She pulled at the neckline of her T-shirt. "It feels like a chain that I can't get rid of."

"So sell it."

Suzy gave a laugh. "Mama would haunt me if I did that."

"So let her." Pres put her arm around her shoulders. "What do you want to do? Deep down inside, what is it that you want?"

That was the big question. What did she want? "For now? Sleep." She pulled her knees up to her chest. "I'll be Scarlett O'Hara for the night and deal with this tomorrow."

Pres nodded and got up from the bed. She walked to the door then turned. "The kittens are ready to come home."

Suzy frowned. What did the kittens have to do with any of this? All it reminded her of was that she didn't have somewhere to bring them home to. "That's great."

"What do you want me to do about them?"

She thought of their little furry faces and sighed. She couldn't offer them anything, not even a home. Especially right now when they needed her. "Find them families, I guess. They deserve them. And it's not like I can take them in."

"Maybe not right now. But soon you could bring them home." Pres looked so hopeful, as if she was giving Suzy all the answers she needed.

Instead, it felt like one more burden. "No, I can't."

Pres frowned on her. "You want to sit in here and feel sorry for yourself, go ahead. Have that pity party, but eventually you have to do something." She put her hand on the doorknob and stared at Suzy. "When you're ready to deal with this, I'm here. Always."

She shut the door softly behind her. Suzy noted the closed door. She'd seen enough of those in her life. Seemed like as soon as she got somewhere that she wanted to be, something else would happen and close the door on her.

She got off the bed and opened her suitcase, searching for her pajamas. She found a pair of navy polka dot yoga pants and a light blue T-shirt and put them on. She flipped off the lights then slipped between the sheets. They still smelled of fabric softener, and she took in a deep breath.

This is just temporary. I don't belong here.

She laid back and stared at the ceiling then pulled the covers over her head. Beneath the sheets, it was quiet. Peaceful. She could stay here awhile.

Maybe she was more like her mom than she wanted to think.

Suzy thumbed through the women's magazine while she waited for Page to return from lunch. She dropped it back on the table and tapped on the receptionist's window. Henry looked up from his cell phone. "I told you she needs newer mags."

"Maybe I'll give her a gift subscription for Christmas."

Henry nodded then cocked his head to one side. "You doing okay, sunshine? You don't seem your perky self."

"I just lost my home. How should I be?"

Henry flinched. "Yikes. Bitter much?"

"I'm fine." And as if to prove it, she pasted on a smile until her cheeks hurt.

"You do that a lot? Pretend to smile?"

So maybe he wasn't easy to convince. "Fake it till you make it. Isn't that what they say?"

"Sweetie, you shouldn't have to fake anything. You're too good for that."

The office door swung open, and Page breezed in. "I'm not late, you're early." She quickstepped back to her office then reappeared a moment later without her purse and coat. She held the door open. "I'm ready for you."

Suzy nodded and joined the counselor on her walk down the hall. She hoped, prayed, that Page wouldn't bring up the house. They could deal with plenty of other issues, after all, Mama's place was only one of many that she needed to deal with.

"So...." Page took a seat on the sofa and

looked her over. "How have you been doing since Saturday?"

Crud. "Fine."

Page glanced at her as she uncapped her pen. "We've talked about that word. Find another one."

"I'm staying with my friend Pres for now. Just until I decide what to do."

"That's what you're doing. But what are you feeling?"

She didn't want to deal with feelings. She wanted to be doing something. Moving forward. Making decisions. Problem was that she didn't know what to do. Fix the house? Sell it? And could she sell it as it was? Or should she just walk away and let the whole thing disappear. "I feel overwhelmed."

"That's nothing new, right?" Page wound her hair behind her ear and cocked her head sideways, much like her brother had earlier. "What does feeling overwhelmed do for you?"

"I don't need a session with some quack today. In fact, I'm thinking that I don't need you anymore. I haven't had a panic attack. And without the house and all the stuff, I won't have those anymore."

"So you're cured?"

"I wasn't sick to begin with. Isn't that what you told me?" Suzy got off the sofa and started towards the door. "I'll pay Henry on the way out."

Page got off the sofa and stood. She walked to her desk and picked up the phone. "I'll call him and tell him to keep you here."

Suzy turned and stared at her. "That's unlawful imprisonment. You can't do that."

Page put the phone down and took a step towards her. "What are you feeling right now? Overwhelmed?"

"No. I'm angry." Suzy whirled and stared at the counselor who looked so calm standing there, looking at her. Calm! How could she act like nothing had changed? Her whole life had been turned upside down since Mama died, and now she was homeless. She had lost it all even though she'd tried so hard to hang on to it. "How dare he kick me out of my home. He had no right."

"Actually he did. It's his job."

"Don't stick up for him. He promised if I got everything cleaned up, I could keep the house. I was doing my part. And cleaning it all up ruined everything."

Page returned to the sofa and picked up

her notepad and pen, made a few notes. "Are you angry with anyone else?"

Suzy frowned. She considered the possibilities. "Myself?"

"No. Who are you really angry with, Suzy? Deep down, white hot angry? Ready to pop them in the nose angry?" Page got off the sofa again and walked towards her. "Who do you want to yell at?"

"Nobody."

Page stepped closer and scrutinized her. "Come on. Besides the code inspector, there has to be one person you'd like to get in their face and shout at? Just one."

A face popped into her head, but she shook away the image. No. Not going there.

"I can see you thinking about it. Just say a name."

"But it's not her fault."

Page leaned forward. "Really? She left you, left the mess and ruined your house. Aren't you the tiniest bit angry with her?"

Oh, Mama. Why?

Again, Suzy shook her head. "But she's dead. How can I be angry with her after she's gone?"

"Why not? Because she died that means you can't feel anything towards her?"

"I feel sad." The easy answer.

"What else?"

"Lonely because she's gone." Another easy one.

"And…."

The hot feeling in her stomach wasn't going away. In fact, it felt like it churned and burned even more. "She did the best she could."

Page watched her and frowned. "You like to offer a lot of excuses for her."

"She could have used your help, but no one saw it. No one but me. I had to live with the mess. With the stuff. I had to take care of her when she got so sad that she couldn't get out of bed. It was me who bathed her in the end. Fed her. Gave her the meds I hoped would keep her alive." Suzy couldn't stop now. "I had to close her eyes after she took that last breath. It was me. I did it all."

The words hung in the air for a silent moment. Suzy rubbed her face and Page took a seat on the sofa. "I'm sure you took great care of her."

She didn't know. No one did. "I gave up my life for her. My dreams. My plans. I did it all so I could help her, but it wasn't enough.

She wanted to own me just like she held on to all her stuff. And I hated her for that."

Suzy covered her mouth with her hand. "I don't mean I hated her. I didn't. I don't."

Page leaned forward on the sofa. "But you hated what she did to you."

She nodded. "It was like I was the mother while she could stay the kid." She felt her hands clutch into fists. "And I'm angry at her."

Page got off the sofa and approached her. She put her hand on Suzy's shoulder. "I know. Why don't you sit down and we can talk about it."

THE DAY FOR Mrs. Stone's first chemo treatment had arrived, and Suzy knew that she'd be feeling anxious. She peeked her head into Mrs. Stone's room. "Wakey wakey."

"Go away."

Suzy walked to the windows and opened the curtains. "I'm afraid that you're stuck with me." She turned and saw Mrs. Stone with the covers over her head. "I hate to tell you but hiding in bed won't change things. I've recently discovered that myself because of some things I'm going through."

Mrs. Stone peered over the edge of the blanket. "You mean because of the house."

Suzy frowned. "He told you?"

"I'm his mother."

Right. Blood thicker than water. "What did he say?"

Mrs. Stone's shoulders moved up and down in an exaggerated motion. "That he's sorry but he had to do it."

She resisted the urge to roll her eyes. "For my safety. I know."

"If I know my son, he'll fix it. He's good at that."

"I'm sure he is." Suzy glanced at her tablet. "The ambulance will come and get you about nine this morning. The first treatment will last approximately four hours, and then they'll observe you for a few more to make sure there are no issues. Then bring you back here."

Mrs. Stone scoffed, "I'd rather go home."

"Let's go through the treatment and see how that goes first."

Mrs. Stone picked at her blanket, avoiding Suzy's eyes. "Will it hurt?"

"Patients say that the worst part isn't the chemo itself, but the side effects. Mrs. Lemuel complained that her mouth tasted funny, like metal. And of course, the nausea."

Mrs. Stone reached up and fluffed up her hair. "Am I going to lose my hair?"

"Probably. But the good news is that once chemo is over, your hair will grow back. I've known patients whose hair turned curly once it grew back."

Mrs. Stone looked at Suzy's hair. "I've always wanted curls."

Suzy reached up and touched her own. "It's not all that it's cracked up to be. Believe me."

There was a pause then a small voice. "I'm scared."

Suzy held her hand and squeezed it. "I know. Me too."

WILL ARRIVED AT the home and noticed that an ambulance waited by the front doors, but the lights weren't flashing. His first thoughts were for his mother. They hadn't come for her, had they? He hurried his gait and whipped down the hall towards her room. When he saw the gurney outside her room, he froze on the spot.

No. She had to be okay.

He pushed open the door. Suzy was helping his mother put on a coat. She smoothed the lapel and gave his mom a smile. "It's gotten cooler so you'll probably need this. Plus they keep the treatment room pretty cool."

Ma reached up and patted the nurse's hand. "I wish you could go with me."

"I promised to stay until they came and got you, but I tell you what. You and me have a date at your next one, okay?" She gave a wink.

Will cleared his throat. "Is everything okay?"

They turned to see him in the doorway. Ma smiled and nodded. "They hired a special car to get me to the hospital today."

"Because when I saw…I thought that…" He swallowed hard. She was okay. He closed his eyes and tried to slow his breathing.

One of the EMTs brushed past him. "We'll need you to move, sir."

Will stepped aside while they got Ma onto the gurney then out the door. He turned to Suzy who averted her gaze and tidied the room. She looked worse than he'd seen her a few days ago. The dark smudges under her eyes. Her curls even seemed to have lost some of their spunk and lay in controlled waves on top of her head. "How are you?"

She answered him without looking at him. "You'll want to meet the ambulance at the hospital. Your mother will need to see a familiar face."

He took a step towards Suzy. "I asked how you were doing."

"I heard." She walked around him and left the room. Removed the stethoscope from the pocket of her scrubs and swung it back and forth as she returned to the nurses' station. She plugged her tablet into an outlet then started gathering her things. She looked up and saw him watching her.

He reached out. "Are you going to be okay?"

She flinched and moved out of his touch. "Worry about your mother instead. She needs you."

"You look like you need someone too."

"I'm fine."

But she wasn't. He could tell. She didn't even try to put on a smile for him or anyone else. At least not that he'd seen since he'd arrived. "About the house…"

Her eyes flashed the first emotion he'd seen since Saturday. "We are not talking about that. Not here."

He leaned in and dropped the volume of his voice. "What do you plan on doing?"

"That's none of your concern."

"Actually it is. I have to report to the town whether you're going to fix it." He paused. "Or bulldoze it."

"Bulldoze? You'd like that wouldn't you?" She glanced at the other nurse who started to eavesdrop on their conversation. "Sorry, Carly. I'll see you tonight." She removed her purse from beneath the desk then grabbed her jacket and walked past Will, not even looking in his direction.

He flashed an apologetic look at the other nurse then ran to keep up with Suzy's short quick steps. "Suzy, wait."

She turned so quickly that he almost ran her over. "If you're not going to meet your mother before treatment, then I will."

"I'll see her. Don't worry. But I need to talk to you."

She shook her head and glanced in the direction that the ambulance had taken. "No, you don't. You need to take care of your mother because I'll be fine."

"You don't think the chemo is going to work."

"Don't put words in my mouth." Suzy

clenched her jaw, and he was surprised how it changed her appearance. Gone was the flighty nurse who had taken such good care of his mother. In her place was an angry woman who had built up walls around her. "I think you'll find out for yourself if you stop bothering me and go see your mother. Goodbye, Mr. Stone."

He watched her leave. She was right. He needed to get to the hospital. But first he needed to fix this new Suzy. Because he missed the old one. He brought out his cell phone and dialed the contractor's number.

He could fix the house, and then he'd see about fixing her.

AFTER A LONG day at the hospital with his mom, Will drove back to the nursing home to wait to greet his mother when she returned to her room. As he entered it, glad that he'd made it before she had, he discovered her room wasn't empty.

His sister Carol sat in the chair near the window instead.

He stopped short. She looked so much older than the last time he'd seen her. It had been at least six years, and those years had not been kind to her. There was one streak of gray through her dark hair that she had pulled back tight. Her blue eyes now looked gray as well. She'd grown old in her absence.

"Carol."

His sister nodded. "Will. How you been?"

"What are you doing here?"

"You called."

"Over a month ago." He glared at her. "You should have come before now. She's been waiting for you. And Joan." He glanced around the room. "Did she come with you?"

"Joanie vowed never to set foot back here in this town after Daddy died."

Will bristled and tried to calm the churn of emotions in his chest. Ma was due back from the hospital any moment, and she didn't need any extra drama. "I remember. So what made you decide to change your mind and come?"

Carol swallowed several times. Her fingers twitched in her lap as if holding a cigarette. "George thought it best."

Will didn't care much for his brother-in-law, but for this he was grateful. "Where you staying?"

She glanced at him. "I've been waiting here for a while. I was hoping to stay at Ma's."

Not if he had a say in that. She'd probably pack Ma's good jewelry in her suitcase before leaving again. "She's getting her first chemo."

Carol paled even more than she already was. "How bad is it?"

"Bad enough." Will took a seat in a chair across from his sister. "But you know Ma. She's a Stone."

They sat in silence for a while. Carol's fingers twitching. Will tapping his foot. They heard a pop and squeak of wheels coming closer down the hall. A moment later, an EMT wheeled in Ma sitting in a wheelchair. The EMT locked the wheels then scooped his mom into his arms and back into bed. She groaned on impact then fussed with the blankets to cover her.

Carol stood and rushed to Ma's side. "Oh, Ma. It's Carol."

Ma's face split into a grin and opened her arms to the prodigal daughter. They hugged while Will looked on. "My Carey baby. You're home. You're home."

Disgusted with how easily his sister could wheedle herself back into the family fold, Will stood and walked out of the room. "I'll be back."

He doubted they heard him.

He walked past the nurses' station and to the dining hall where several tables of seniors played cards. He wondered if he would end up doing the same one day. Locked in a home, away from his family. Playing cards with other inmates.

And yet, this nursing home was different. They welcomed the seniors as part of an extended family. They held activities for the seniors and their children. It felt less like a prison hospital and more like…

Home.

Will turned and headed for the lobby and out to his truck. He checked the messages on his phone and frowned when he saw Tori's car pull into the parking lot. He'd hoped to have time alone with Ma to find out how the treatment went, but now needed to deal with not one, but two sisters. He went over to her car and leaned down to speak to her. Tori jumped at the sight of him. "Don't scare ten years off of me like that."

"Carol's here."

Tori rolled her window up and exited her car. She hit the button on the remote to lock it. "About time she showed up."

As she walked towards the seniors' home,

he took long strides to keep up with her. "That's it? That's all you're going to say?"

She shrugged. "What? She's Ma's daughter too."

"But where's she been? We're the ones who have been here every day. Carol suddenly shows up, and Ma blubbers over her like she's been the favorite all this time." He held the door open for Tori.

She glanced up at him as she passed him. "It's not like that."

"Really? You're missing the love fest in Ma's room then."

"It's because Ma hasn't seen her in years." Tori started for Ma's room. "Let her have her moment. She'll be gone again before you know it."

Probably with Ma's silver. Will frowned and stalked after his sister. It was easier to channel his emotions to their sister's return rather than Ma's from the hospital. And yet, he hadn't seen Ma this happy in a while. Maybe Carol being there wasn't the worst thing.

Back in Ma's room, Carol sat on the bed beside her, holding her hand. Tori ran around the bed and hugged their sister. "I can't believe you're here."

He couldn't believe how blind they were being. Or forgetful. Did the last six years of silence mean nothing? He stared at the three women crying and hugging. "How did it go, Ma?"

Ma raised her head to look at him. She looked so frail. So weak. "Okay, I guess. The doctor says it will feel worse tomorrow."

Tori placed a hand on the arm that now looked bruised from the IV. "Did it hurt?"

"Burned a little." She rubbed the bruise. "And my mouth tastes funny, just like Suzy told me it would."

Will nodded. "I can get you something to drink."

"You know what I'd like? Remember that one summer night when Daddy took us to the beach, and we watched the fireworks and drank tart lemonade?" Ma closed her eyes and sighed. "I sure could use some more of that."

"I'll get it." Will was out the door before anyone could stop him. His mother wanted lemonade, so he would get it for her. This was something he could do.

Finally.

CHAPTER ELEVEN

WILL STRETCHED HIS legs out and tried to massage the kink out of his calf while not falling off the chair. He looked over at his mom, relieved that she still slept. The chemo treatment had taken a lot out of her, so she needed to sleep. He stood and stretched. Sleep sounded good, but he wanted… No, needed to be sure that everything was going to be okay. That his mom would recover. That this treatment would mean that the cancer would go away, and Ma return to normal. The waiting for answers was killing him.

He checked on her again, then left the room, shutting the door softly. The nurses' station was vacant, so he leaned against the counter and waited for Suzy's return. He looked at the monitors and wondered what each of the numbers meant. They were all green, so that must be good, he assumed.

"Why are you holding up my counter?"

He turned and caught sight of Suzy. Her

light blue scrubs would seem subdued for her if she didn't have her hair pulled back by a neon green bandana. "You like bright colors, don't you?"

She shrugged. "Why not? Let me guess. You're a black and white kind of guy."

"There's nothing wrong with those colors." He reached up and loosened the silver tie he'd put on that morning. "They're straightforward. Honest."

The humor in her eyes faded. "What do you want?"

So they were back to that? He already missed the Suzy who would tease him. "I wanted to talk to you."

"Well, I'm still not in the mood to talk to you." She tightened the ties of her bandana. "And I have patients waiting for me."

"Could I have a moment after you're done with rounds?"

She shook her head and started to walk down the hall. He followed her. "Suzy, we need to talk."

She kept her pace quick, and he hurried to keep up with her even with his long strides. "What else is there to say? It's inevitable, right? It's over."

"You really think that?"

"Listen, what happened has happened. We can't come back from that. And I can't forget. Better to just let it all go."

"So you think she's going to die?"

Suzy stopped walking and turned to face him. "I meant that my house is ruined. What are you talking about?"

"My mom."

"Oh." She took a deep breath. Closed her eyes for a moment. "Sorry. I need to switch gears."

He waited and watched her. He could almost see her pack the emotions that had been building up back inside their compartments to be dealt with later. He knew how to do that pretty well. He'd done it enough himself. Pack away the emotions and handle them at a more convenient time.

He ran a hand through his hair and grimaced at how long it was. He really needed to get a haircut. And soon. But he had other priorities. His mom's health. His job security.

And if he wanted to admit it, the woman in front of him had started to become important to him too.

He sighed. "She seems sicker than she was when she was brought in here."

"Probably because her attitude has

changed. What was your mom like before she got here? Was she a go-getter? Unstoppable? Active?"

"Yes. All those."

"I figured. She seems the type." Suzy took a deep breath. "But since coming here, I've seen her attitude change, and because of that, her overall well-being. She's taken this diagnosis pretty hard."

Who wouldn't? "We all have."

"That's the thing, Will. She needs to be in a fighting mood to beat this. If not, I don't know if she'll make it."

He swallowed and found it hard to do with the lump there. "So what do we do? How do we change it?"

"I know that you want to swoop in and fix things. I get that. But it's not up to you."

"Then who? Ma? I can't watch her fade away a little every day." He started to blink fast, trying to keep the tears from forming there. "She needs to fight. Why won't she fight?" He felt a hand on his back and knew that it was Suzy's. "Maybe that's something you need to talk about with her."

He shook his head and let it fall forward. "I can't."

"Why not?
"Because that's not what Stones do."

SUZY LONGED TO reach up and touch his face. To give him comfort with a simple hand on his cheek.

But he was her nemesis. He'd kicked her out of her home. It was because of him that she was sleeping in Presley's guest room. He was the enemy.

And yet he needed comfort. She could almost see the little boy in him crying out for a hug.

And it was that image that moved her.

She put her arms around his shoulders and pulled him into a tight hug. He wasn't made of ice. Or stone. He was human and needed to be held.

Be loved.

She closed her eyes and breathed slower. Pretended that she didn't hear his breathing get labored and heavy. That the sighs weren't cries. She brought her left hand up to the base of his neck and ran her fingers through the hair there that was starting to grow out and curl up.

He smelled like coffee and peppermint.

She breathed it in, surprised at how homey he smelled. And how inviting it seemed.

She held on to him and let him cling to her. Until he found the strength in himself to let go.

She regretted the moment his arms left her waist. They'd felt natural there. As if they'd belonged there all this time.

She looked up into his eyes and saw the steel growing behind them. He was a Stone again.

And that might be just what his mom needed.

She nodded. "Better?"

He glanced down. "I didn't mean to do that."

"It's okay." More than okay. "I find myself comforting a lot of my patients' families." But not quite like that.

And she had never found it hard to let go. But with Will....

She cleared her throat. "I need to check on my patients."

"I need to see my mom."

They looked at each other for another moment, and Suzy wondered what he was thinking. Was he thinking of holding her again?

Because despite everything that had happened, she was. It didn't matter that he'd ruined her life. He'd only wanted to help her. She could see that now. But helping her had meant hurting her at the same time. She opened her mouth to say something then sighed and shook her head.

And then he turned and walked in the other direction down the hall.

SUZY FOUND HERSELF staring out a window of the seniors' home one morning after sunrise. The weather had turned colder which left the vegetation starting to shrivel and die. The large stalks that had once held blooming pink elephant hibiscus were now empty and barren. She knew how they felt. Because that's what was inside her.

Nothing.

Someone called her name, and she turned to face her supervisor Rita. "I was daydreaming."

"At least that hasn't changed."

Rita handed her a piece of paper. Next week's schedule. Suzy scanned it and frowned. "I didn't request any vacation time."

"I need you to be on top of your game,

Bylin." Rita leaned on the counter. "Go home. Get your head straight. See a shrink. Whatever you need to do to get over this because I need you at a hundred percent. All your patients do."

Suzy gave a nod, but didn't feel it. "I love my patients. And working with them makes me feel better."

"Take these next couple of weeks to get healthier." Rita put her arm around her shoulders. "We'll reassess the situation, and you'll return even better. This isn't forever."

Maybe. Maybe not. Maybe this was her sign to start all over somewhere else. No home, no job. Maybe it was time to move on. Run away when things got too scary or uncertain.

Maybe she was more like her father than she'd thought. He'd run when things got too uncertain. And he'd never looked back.

She thought about saying something to her patients. Telling them goodbye or... She stopped in Mrs. Henderson's room first and noticed that the older woman's eyes focused even less these days. "How are you today? Breakfast will be coming soon."

Mrs. Henderson nodded. "Did Mr. Selznick get my script to you yet? I need to learn my lines."

Suzy patted her shoulder. "I'll make sure to bring it to you as soon as it arrives."

"I'm playing Scarlett O'Hara, you know."

"I've heard." Suzy gave her a smile. "I'll be gone a couple days." Or weeks. "And I wanted to be sure to tell you goodbye."

Mrs. Henderson nodded. "I'll see you at the movies."

"You bet."

Mrs. Stone's room was next. The older woman was sitting up in bed, reading a book. When she noticed Suzy standing in the doorway, she put her bookmark in place and closed the book. "Good morning, dearie."

"I wanted to check and see how you were feeling."

"Better than yesterday." She patted the bed. "But you're looking horrible. What's wrong?"

Suzy sighed and took a seat on the bed. "I'm going on administrative leave for a few days or so."

Mrs. Stone gasped. "Suspended? For what?"

"I'm going through a lot right now, and my supervisor thought I needed some time to take care of things." She gave a soft shrug. "I have some vacation time I haven't used anyway, so why not?"

"Because of the house?"

"That's part of it." She pulled her ankle higher on to her leg. "I need to figure out what I'm going to do about that. And now my job. And…"

"And my son?"

"Your son is definitely something I'm not sure what to do about." Suzy almost laughed at the look of expectation on Mrs. Stone's face. "But right now, that means staying far, far away."

"He loves you."

"If he does, he has a funny way of showing it." She got off the bed and walked to the door. "I might not be working here, but I'll check in on you. And we have a date for your next chemo. Don't forget."

Mrs. Stone held out her hand, and Suzy walked to her and grasped it in hers. "I've come to think of you like a daughter, so I hope you'll forgive me if I'm too forward." She gave her hand a squeeze. "Don't let your situation ruin the beautiful person you are. You are stronger than that."

"Thanks, Mrs. Stone." She leaned forward and kissed the woman's cheek.

The older woman in turn patted Suzy's cheek. "Lovey."

PRES MOVED THE hangers from left to right as they perused the dresses at the mall in Traverse City. Rick and Lizzie's wedding was the following afternoon, and neither Pres nor Suzy had something to wear. Pres pulled out a red strapless cocktail dress and held it against her body. "What about this one?"

Suzy gave her a thumbs up. "I'm sure it will look great on you. You've got the body for it." She looked down at her own. "I'm short and stubby. That would make me look like a cherry."

Pres laughed and placed the dress back on the rack. "No, it wouldn't. It would give you color."

Suzy shook her head and kept looking. "I don't understand why Will wouldn't let me into the house just to get that one dress in my closet. Would it have killed him?"

"I think he was more worried that it could kill you." Pres flipped through more dresses then looked up at her. "Have you decided what you're going to do with the house?"

Uncertainty still reigned. Should she try to find the money to fix it or let it go? Maybe bulldoze it like Will had suggested. "I don't know yet. I haven't wanted to deal with it." She put one dress down and picked up another. "Are you asking me to leave?"

Pres put her hand on Suzy's arm. "Not at all. I'm enjoying our time together. Like tonight. When's the last time we had a girls' night out?"

True, but Suzy didn't want to overstay her welcome. "If that changes, you'll tell me, right?"

"I will always be honest with you." Pres chose another dress then walked close to Suzy and held the royal blue dress up to her. "So I need you to listen to me. Until you decide what you want to do, you're not going to be okay."

"You sound like Page."

Pres put the dress back. "Then she's a brilliant therapist because I'm right. You're stuck under this black cloud until you decide what you're going to do. And putting off the decision is only hurting you."

"I'm fine." Suzy left the rack and circled around to another one. Maybe there would be a better selection on this one.

Pres soon joined her. "You're not sleeping. Barely eating." Pres crossed her arms. "That doesn't sound fine to me."

"You don't know what it's like."

"So explain it to me."

Suzy kept her head down, focused on the silky blouse in her hands. "It feels like I've lost Mama all over again. That she's gone, and I'm alone, and I don't know what to do." Suzy covered her face and started to sob. "I'm barely hanging on here, Pres. I've been trying to stay positive, telling myself that it's all going to be okay. That it's all going to work out. But I honestly don't know if it will. I'm so lost."

Presley put her arms around her and rubbed her back. "This is the first time I've seen you cry since your mom got sick. It's okay to let this out."

Suzy shook her head. "Mama didn't like my tears. She only wanted my smiles, so I made sure to give them to her."

"That's not healthy, Suze. That means you've been denying your emotions for years."

"And now it feels like they're all coming out." Suzy wiped her face. For years, she'd been ignoring them, but she couldn't keep doing that anymore. She didn't want to. She needed to get to where she could take control of her own life. Figure out what she wanted and make the right choices for her future. "You're right, though. I need to make a decision soon."

"If you want to move, why don't we go looking at places on my next day off? Now that you have all this free time, we can get an idea of what's out there. See if it would be worth letting your mom's house go."

That actually was a great idea. At this point, she could commit to considering the idea of moving. She couldn't live in Mama's house as it was, and she didn't have the money handy to get it fixed. But she couldn't live in limbo for long because Presley was right—she wasn't fine.

Suzy agreed. "On your next day off then. I'll call a real estate agent to set up some showings. And I should go to the bank and discuss my options. I can't put this off anymore."

Pres rubbed her arm. "I know it feels like you're lost right now, but you'll find your way."

Suzy hoped so. She held up a light green

top with matching linen skirt. "What about these?"

Pres wrinkled her nose. "I think we can find something better."

HIS MOTHER HAD decided it was time to start thinking about her funeral. "I want to be buried next to your father."

The harmless conversation between Will, Carol and Tori about the weather ended with those words. Will stared at her. "Ma, you're not going to die."

"You don't know that."

"And you do?" He glanced at Tori who was blinking back tears. "Why are you bringing this up now?"

"Because your father never had a chance to talk about it. I did what I wanted even though I knew he'd hate the service and all those long-winded speeches by people who didn't really know him." She put her tea cup down on the table next to her bed. "I want my funeral to go my way. And I want to be buried next to your father. We already paid for the plot."

Tori got up from the chair and hurried to their mother's side. Sat on the bed next to her and held her hand. "Ma, you're not going to die. You can't."

"I wish it was up to you, baby." She placed a hand on Tori's cheek. "But no one knows when something like that will happen. And I want to be prepared."

Carol glanced at Will, who shrugged. What had brought this on? And why? "It sounds like you're giving up."

"Not giving up. Just being prepared." She gave him the eye. "And I figured you of all people would understand that. Isn't that what you would do?"

She had him there. He'd already written a will and had purchased his own plot in the cemetery where his father was buried. He had written out instructions for how he wanted his funeral to be and had even suggested songs to be sung and scripture to be read.

So he could see her point. Almost.

"Then this isn't a way of giving up?" He leaned in towards his mom. "You're not doing this as a way of surrendering?"

She shook her head, but didn't look him in the eye either. Shoot. He'd hoped they'd gotten past that. She glanced at him then at his sisters. "It wouldn't hurt to be prepared."

"But talking about funerals and caskets and stuff is depressing," Tori blurted. "I don't want to think about it. So I don't want to talk about it."

It was the Stone way. Will took a seat on the bed opposite Tori and asked, "Would it make you feel better to talk about it, Ma?"

She didn't answer for a moment then shook her head. "Not really. But I think we should."

Will nodded and got off the bed. He found an empty envelope and a marker. It would have to do. He took his seat at the chair next to the bedside table. "Okay then. We'll do this. Who do you want to hold your service?"

Carol jumped up. "What? No. We're not doing this. Ma isn't going to die and I refuse to sit here and listen to this."

"This is what Ma wants."

"You're forcing her to deal with this because you're too weak to deal with the details yourself." Carol picked up her purse and walked to the door. "Sorry, Ma, but I gotta go."

After his sister left, Will sighed and glanced at Ma. "We don't have to do this if you don't want to."

"Carol's wrong. I need to do this." She

thought for several minutes. "I've always liked that Rick fellow. You know, the mayor? Do you think he'd agree to do the service?"

"Doesn't it have to be a pastor or something?" Will wrote Rick's name down anyway. If anyone could manage to get around the rules, it would be him. "I'm writing his name, but we'll have to check to see if he can officiate."

"I don't need a fancy party either. Just get me in the ground. Sing a few songs. Then done."

"That's what you want?" Tori looked at her as if she had really lost it. "When you said you wanted the funeral your way, I was expecting something...I don't know. More elaborate." She grimaced. "This talk is depressing me. Will can help you plan." She kissed their mother on the cheek. "I'll check in on you tomorrow night. Lovey."

"Lovey." Ma kissed her back and waved as Tori departed. She looked at Will. "You planning on leaving me to this too?"

"I gave my word. Besides, I'm tough." He poised the marker on the envelope. "Now, be honest. Is a few songs all you want?"

"Do you remember Great Grandma Heller's funeral? You must have been about nine at the time." His mother closed her eyes and smiled. "Now that was some funeral. People drove for days to come and pay their respects. My ma and I must have cooked enough to feed a hundred people. It was tiring, but it was so nice to see everyone." She opened her eyes. "Weddings and funerals. They're the only occasions when you get to see the whole family."

Will put the marker down. "So why don't we plan something now while you're still alive and kicking? Like a family reunion so you can see everyone too? Why should you have to miss out on the party?"

Ma smiled. "I'd like that. But I'm going to lose my hair and become skin and bones with that chemo."

"So we'll plan it for when you're better. A celebration of beating this thing."

She looked at him sharply. "Do you really think I can beat this?"

"With the right attitude, yes."

Ma swallowed and closed her eyes. "I don't want you to get your hopes up, son."

"My hopes or yours?" Will stood and stalked to the window. "We need you to fight this, Ma. Don't give up and give in to the cancer. Do what you have to do to survive."

He turned and looked at her, his eyes burning. He approached her bed and sat next to her. "I need you to fight. I can't do this without you."

She reached up and touched his cheek. Looked deep into his eyes. "You've always been the strong one. Tough. On your own. I didn't think you needed anyone."

"You're wrong. We all need you, Ma. Especially me." He looked up at her and shrugged. "There's this woman."

His mom nodded. "Suzy."

"I don't know what to do about her."

"What do you want to do?"

Kiss her. Hold her. Love her.

But he pushed those feelings down to examine later. "I want to help her."

She eyed him over the top of her glasses. "Has she asked for your help?"

"She needs it whether she wants it or not."

"She's a tough woman. Dealt with things you may not know about. And you need to let her decide what she wants on her own."

He pictured Suzy standing in the living room surrounded by all the stuff. "But I know I can help her. I've already started to fix it for her."

"After we told you not to?"

"I thought I knew what was best."

"And now?"

He still thought he knew best, but it didn't bring him any comfort. What if fixing it himself only made it worse?

Ma glanced down at her hands. "I don't know if I should tell you this, but management asked her to take some time off from here." She looked up at him, and he wanted to squirm in his seat. "Because of the house and everything she needs to do, she can't work here." She took a deep breath. "It's been two days, and I miss her already."

He did too.

But Ma wouldn't let it go. "You want my advice? Wait until she asks for help."

Too late. To cover that up, he gave a crooked grin. "If you didn't notice, she has a hard time asking. She can be stubborn."

"She can also be an amazingly loving and patient nurse." She smiled. "Believe me. I've put her through enough."

Will shared her grin. "Me too. She's tough enough to take it though."

"You are too." Ma grabbed his hands in hers and clutched them tightly. "No matter what happens, you're strong enough to cope with whatever comes. You did it after Daddy died. And if I die…"

"Ma. No."

"Hear me, son. If I die, the others will certainly be looking to you for direction. You need to be prepared to help them through this." She reached up and touched his cheek. "I know you can do it."

He blinked away the tears. "I don't want to do this without you."

"I don't either." She pulled him into her arms and put his head on her shoulder. "But whatever comes up, we can face it. We're Stones."

Will nodded and made himself stop the tears. He sat back and put his hands on her shoulders. "We're tough."

"When your dad said that he meant to ignore how you felt and do whatever it was anyways. But I'm telling you that it means we don't give up. We get scared but we do it because our family is worth it."

She took another deep breath, her expression calm. "So can we talk about my funeral now?"

Will nodded and got off the bed. Found the envelope and marker he'd discarded.

He was poised, ready for her instructions. "It's whatever you want."

IT SEEMED LIKE the entire town of Lake Mildred was on the guest list for Rick and Lizzie's wedding. The church's parking lot was full, so they had started to park in the empty space next door and walk the half block. Suzy was glad that Pres had volunteered to drive. It was one less thing for her to worry about.

But she did have to manage in high heels all the way to the church. Maybe she should have planned her outfit better. She had eventually found a dark pink dress that hit her just above the knee. It was lacy and flirty, and Pres said it made her skin glow. She'd put her hair up into a knot on top of her head and borrowed an ivory crocheted shawl from Pres to complete the ensemble. So maybe it wasn't the outfit that was the issue but the heels. She took them off and walked barefoot on the cold concrete.

Pres looked down at her feet and shook her head. Suzy shrugged. "What? I don't want to get blisters before we even get to the reception."

"And you wore heels why?"

"We shorties need something to get us attention."

Pres leaned in close and gestured ahead of them. "I think you're getting plenty of that without them."

Suzy squinted and saw Will standing outside the church watching them approach. He wore a grey tailored suit that brought out the hard lines of his body. He cleaned up really nicely. "Just the person I don't want to see today."

"Be nice."

"I'm always nice." She pasted a smile on her face as they reached the church and Will strode towards them. "Mr. Stone, good to see you."

She glanced at Pres as if to prove her point. Her friend rolled her eyes.

"Suzy. Presley. I think the entire town is here," he said.

"We should probably get inside and find our seats. Bye, Mr. Stone."

He took a fast step towards her. "Will you save a dance for me later?"

"Why?" Okay, so she lost points for the question. But why in the world would he want to dance with her? And why would he think she'd agree? "I mean, I don't plan on doing any dancing."

"That would be a waste of a great dress."

Suzy looked down and fingered the silky material then turned to Pres. "Should we go inside?"

They entered the church, and Suzy was awed by the decorations. It had been transformed from a typical church into something magical with hundreds of lit candles giving it an ethereal glow. Pretty satin bows decorated the end of each pew, and a red carpet runner ran from the back of the church down the center aisle to the front where the ceremony would take place. Pres nudged Suzy, and they entered a pew that was already filling quickly.

Suzy whispered to Pres, "When I get married, I want to do this."

"Might be nice to find the guy first."

As if on cue, Will entered the pew in front of them and turned around to face Suzy. "You really look fantastic."

Suzy bit her lip to keep from answering him, but Pres nodded. "I knew Lizzie could make this something special. She's got the touch."

Will glanced at Suzy then switched his

attention to the altar when the organ started to play Canon in D. The ushers seated the mother of the groom and of the bride, and then took their places at the front. Rick, his brother Dan and the pastor arrived via the side door and stood near the front of the church as the flower girl started her march down the aisle, strewing pale pink rose petals on the red carpet. Two bridesmaids came next then the maid of honor, Dawn, who winked at her husband Dan. The organist went on to play a selection from Lohengrin, then Lizzie appeared. A hush fell on the crowd as she began her journey up the aisle. When she almost reached Rick, he left his position by the pastor and dashed towards his bride. He took both her hands in his and smiled at her. Then he walked with her, the rest of the aisle, to the front of the church.

Suzy dabbed at the corners of her eyes as the ceremony happened. Rick and Lizzie loved each other, and everyone in the packed church could feel it as well as see it. When the pastor announced them as husband and wife, people shot to their feet and applauded.

Suzy sighed. Yep, she had to do this. But like Pres said. Maybe she should find the guy first.

WILL SCANNED THE seating chart and snickered when he found his name. Rick and Lizzie had placed him at the same table as Suzy. Thank you, Rick.

He placed his wedding card in the mailbox standing to the side then entered the VFW hall. He had played charity poker games in the room, but it didn't look like the same place. Lizzie had apparently been hard at work because white lights twinkled behind see through fabric woven around the room and at each table. There was a photo booth in one corner next to a large dance floor where a band was setting up.

At table forty-two, he pulled out a seat then switched a few names around so that Suzy would sit next to him. Then he checked to see if she'd arrived yet.

He'd never been one for weddings, but even he wouldn't mind having one like this. When Rick had kissed his wife for the first time, Will had fought the urge to find someone to do the same. The fact that an image of Suzy had popped into his head wasn't lost on him. He already knew he cared about her. What would a marriage to her be like?

Before he could go down that path, several guests joined him at the table. He knew

Suzy had arrived even before he heard her voice. It was like a tingling at the back of his neck that made him turn. And there she was. Beautiful. Intriguing. Caring. He held up a hand and waved.

She frowned at him. Okay, so he knew she was still angry with him. But he'd hoped after she'd comforted him the other night... He pulled out her chair for her when she got to the table. "Seems Lizzie sat you next to me."

Suzy glanced at the place cards then plucked Presley's to switch them. Her friend shook her head. "I'm fine where I'm at."

"But don't you want to sit closer to the buffet?"

"I think I can handle the six inch difference." Pres took her seat.

Suzy glanced at the chair that Will still held for her then sat with a frown. "Fine."

"You say that a lot, you know." Will took the seat next to her. "But somehow I don't think you quite mean it."

She turned at him, her eyes shooting daggers into his. "You arranged this seating, didn't you?"

He held up his hand. "We were assigned to the same table. I swear."

She talked with Presley non-stop until the bride and groom arrived at the hall. The band leader came to the microphone. "Everyone, please join me in welcoming for the first time, Mr. and Mrs. Rick Allyn."

Everyone stood and applauded as the bride and groom took their places at the head table. Soon the band started playing music, and a hostess began circulating around the room, letting tables go up to the buffet. Will leaned towards Suzy. "I still want that dance later."

It wasn't long before their table's turn at the buffet came. Will pulled out Suzy's chair for her and tried to ignore the disappointment when she walked away from him without a word. He followed her but was stopped by town councilor Mrs. Winkle. "Beautiful wedding."

Somehow he didn't think she'd held him up to merely comment on the ceremony. "They'll have a great life together."

Mrs. Winkle nodded. "The budget vote is coming up soon."

Ahh, so that's what this was about. "I know. I'm hoping I'll have your support."

"My good friend George Steppey told me that you discussed volunteers mowing his lawn and helping him care for his house."

"I think we could make a difference. Not just for Mr. Steppey, but for the other seniors who could use a helping hand."

She peered at him. "I know you could use that. The community needs more people like you, people who see a problem and offer solutions, not complaints. Not to speak ill of my fellow council members, but they're short-sighted and focused on numbers. We should be looking at results."

That sounded ominous. Was this a warning? Will held out his hand. "That's what I want too, Mrs. Winkle. Thank you."

"No, thank you, young man. Have you thought about running for council yourself if your position gets cut?"

He'd rather keep his job. Instead, he smiled. "I'll consider it."

WITH DINNER THEN the cutting of the cake, Will didn't get a chance to dance with Suzy until much later. But he took advantage of her feeling sentimental to pull her out on to the dance floor. A fast song had just ended, and a slow ballad replaced it. He held Suzy tight to him. "How are you really doing, Suzy?"

She kept her gaze on everyone but him as she shrugged. "Okay, I guess."

"You're staying with Presley?"

"Since you kicked me out of my home, yes."

"Your safety was more important than…" He swallowed hard. "More important than our friendship or my feelings toward you."

She opened her mouth then tried to walk away. Instead, he gripped her hand and kept her close to him. She looked up at him. "Your feelings? You want to talk about those? Because I can tell you what it felt like to be ripped away from everything I knew."

"Only temporarily."

She glanced down at her feet. "I can't afford to fix it. So it could be more permanent than you think."

He wanted to tell her what he'd done. But it wasn't the right time. She had to learn to trust him first. "So what will you do?"

"I don't know."

"We can fix this. I know we can."

She let go of his hand and stopped moving despite his efforts to keep dancing. "I'm not something you can fix, Will."

She stepped back but he caught her hand in his. "I know, Suzy. But I do want to make things better. As for making real changes, I've realized only you can do that. Though, I can be there for you. I can help."

"I don't need your help, Will. Good night."

Then she was walking off the dance floor, leaving him alone. And that wasn't something he wanted to be.

CHAPTER TWELVE

STANDING BEFORE THE MIRROR, Suzy carefully pushed the gold hoop through her earlobe. Except for Rick and Lizzie's wedding, she couldn't remember the last time she'd worn earrings or had an occasion to wear them. Mama's funeral maybe? And now she'd worn them twice in one week. She turned her head in the other direction and put in the matching hoop. She checked her reflection. Ruffled her curls a little then added a touch of hairspray.

A knock on the bedroom door, and Pres asked, "Almost ready?" She entered the room and did a spin, showing off her look.

Suzy dabbed some clear lip gloss on then pursed her lips. "We're not putting too much into this one night, are we?"

"Nah, not us." Pres chuckled. "Besides it's just dinner at your favorite restaurant."

"My favorite? You mean, yours." Suzy turned and pressed a hand against her abdomen. She'd put on her skinny jeans but they felt a little tight. "Maybe I should change."

"Again? This is your third outfit."

"Fourth." She opened the suitcase and glanced inside. She hated living out of it, but her current housing situation was temporary. Wasn't it? "Didn't I pack my stretchy jeans?"

"Suze, relax. We're just having some dinner. Totally low key."

Suzy looked over at her and nodded. "I know. I'm just not in the mood."

"What? To eat? Please." Pres put her arm around her. "Let's just go now so we can get a good table." She nudged Suzy with her hip. "And a cute waiter."

"Maybe we could order in. Watch a movie or something."

"Nice try. We're going out, so get your purse and let's go." Pres walked across the room towards the door. "I'll meet you downstairs in five minutes. And if you're not there, I will come up here and drag you out myself."

"Empty threats." Suzy grinned. "I'll be down there. I promise."

"Good. Because you need this."

Suzy rechecked her look. This would have to be good enough. She bent to reach for her purse then coughed. But first things first, she'd have to change out of these tight jeans.

THE DRIVE TO the Mexican restaurant took only twenty minutes. As she and Pres were about to go in, her friend said, "Looks like we're not the only ones to find this place." Through the glass door, they could see the place was packed.

Suzy frowned. Not only wasn't she in the mood to go out, she really didn't want to have to deal with a crowd of people. She wanted to be in bed with the covers over her. "Maybe we could find somewhere more quiet."

"I've been looking forward to this margarita all week."

Pres strode into the restaurant. Suzy waited a moment then took a deep breath and opened the door. She could do this.

Pres was already walking back towards her, shaking her head. "Well, you win. They're closed for a private party."

"So now what? We go home?"

Pres shook her head even more. "I didn't get all dressed up just to go home and sit in front of the television. We'll find another place. I'm getting my margarita."

They drove towards Traverse City where they would have more choices. Suzy fiddled with the radio stations, trying to find a song to pull her out of this funk. She settled on a current hit and shifted back in her seat. "We could get some Chinese takeout."

"No way." Pres glanced at her then back to the road. "We are going out and enjoying ourselves. Don't you think it's time?"

They fell silent, listening to the radio which had changed to a song that had been popular when they'd been in college. Pres turned up the volume. "Now this is what I'm talking about."

Suzy leaned back into the headrest. "Do you remember the night we snuck up onto the dorm roof and made our wish list for the perfect life?" Pres, Suzy and another roommate had lay on the roof and watched the stars while dreaming of their futures. It had been wonderful. But now it felt so long ago to Suzy. Another lifetime. "Mama called the next month and asked me to come home. To go to school near her. And that was the end of it."

"You talk like your life is over."

"The problem is that it never started." Suzy looked out the window at the passing landscape. "She ended my dreams of a career like yours. Of us opening a veterinary office together." She blinked back tears. "I never wanted something so bad. I still think of it."

"Our lives turned out different. That's all." Pres reached out and patted Suzy's hand. "But we can still dream. You have a job that you love, right?"

"Do I? I don't know anymore." She got out a tissue to dry her eyes. "She didn't want me to leave her like my dad did. Didn't matter if I had dreams of my own. It was all about her." She gave a low laugh. "She's dead, and it still is. All about her. Her stuff. And her house."

"It doesn't have to be." Pres glanced behind her then pulled over on to the shoulder. She faced Suzy. "You don't have to let her decide your future anymore. You're the one in control."

Pres was a good friend, but she couldn't understand. "She still has a hold on me."

"Only if you let her." Pres took her hand. "I know she was your mom, and you love her. But you can live your own life now. Make your own choices."

"What if I don't know how?"

"Then you'll learn."

WILL FROWNED AT the empty nurses' station. Suzy still wasn't back from her leave, and it made the seniors' home seem less warm. Less complete.

He knocked on Ma's door before opening it and sticking his head inside. "You decent, Ma?"

"Do you think I'm entertaining gentlemen callers?" Ma laughed and shook her head. "Carol and I were just talking about my next chemo."

"Tomorrow, right?" Was it time already for another? Would this be the one that cured his mom? Or killed her? No, he had to think positively. Focus on the healing. "The sooner the better. Then you can come home."

Ma smiled. "Home."

Carol stood and kissed their mother's cheek. "I'll head out. Think I need a long bubble bath and a glass of wine before I drive back home tomorrow."

"Sounds heavenly." They kissed again. "Lovey."

Carol gave Will a nod then left them. He turned to Ma. "She's still ticked off at me."

"She's angry with the world, not just you." Ma patted the bed beside her. "Tell me about your day."

"Nothing to tell. I shuffled paperwork and scheduled a site inspection." He shrugged. "Typical day."

"Yet you love it."

He did. He'd always enjoyed taking things apart and putting them back together. And with this job, he loved looking at problems and finding solutions. Who knows what would happen if he lost the job to budget cuts? And then he understood what Suzy had felt when he'd kicked her out of her home. Despite the mess and chaos, it was home. Comfortable and familiar. And having it taken from her had pushed her into an unknown. One caused by him.

He closed his eyes, felt a hand on his cheek and opened them again. "What is it, son?"

"I love her." He shook his head. "How? When did that happen?"

Ma grinned. "It's been happening for some time now. I'm just glad you finally realized it."

He groaned and rubbed his face with his hands. Loved her. What was he supposed to do now? He'd ruined her life, but tried to fix it. Only to discover that she needed to fix it herself. So he couldn't exactly go to her and offer her his heart? She'd crush it and hand it back.

Wouldn't she?

"I don't know what to do."

"Did I ever tell you about how I knew I loved your father?" Ma's face softened. "He was a Marine. All tough and emotionless. And strong. So strong. But he had a soft spot for animals." She laughed at Will's expression. "He'd tell you that we had our cats because I wanted them, but the truth was that he chose them. Named them. Fed and watered them. They slept on his side of the bed, not mine."

She waved her hands. "But I'm getting ahead of myself. It was our third date, and we had walked to the movies. When it ended, it was pouring rain. We stayed under the marquee, waiting for it to stop, when your father heard a soft mewling." She chuckled and seemed to see the scene playing again just outside her window. "A cat was caught in a sewer drain, and your father was afraid that it would drown if he didn't get it out quickly. So he removed the sewer grate and pulled her free. Took off his coat and wrapped her in it to get her warm."

She looked at him. "That was when I knew that I loved him. This gruff man with a huge heart. He brought her over to where I stood and handed her to me. Told me to keep her. That I'd know what to do next."

"And did you?"

"I kissed him and told him I'd love him until the day I died." She touched her chest. "And I've kept that promise all these years."

"When did he tell you he loved you?"

"The day he proposed. Your father wasn't romantic by any means, but I knew he'd take care of me."

"That's not the man I remember. He was never sentimental around me."

Ma nodded. "I wish you could have had the father I knew he could have been. For whatever reason, he was afraid to show how much he cared." She touched his hand, squeezed it tightly. "You don't have to be like him."

"I know." But he wasn't sure if he could completely escape from the genetic pull to become his father.

"If you love her, tell her. Don't let something like that pass you by."

He agreed. He couldn't let her go. She may not love him the same way. At least not yet. But he could prove it. Would show her how much she meant to him.

THE BAKERY SMELLED delicious as Suzy stepped inside the Sweetheart. Pres had done so much for her, so she thought she'd reward her friend with a special treat. She walked to the glass case and searched the rows of cookies. Mrs. Sweet came over and smiled at her. "Finding what you want?"

Suzy looked up at the older woman who could have played Mrs. Claus at any time of year. She sighed. "It all looks so good."

"What's the occasion?"

"Thank you for a friend." Suzy bit her lip and considered the baklava. "She's more a dark chocolate kind of girl. What would you recommend?"

Mrs. Sweet motioned for Suzy to join her at another case. The baker took out a small chocolate cake decorated with fresh raspberries and set it on the counter. "This would be my first choice. Thin layers of chocolate cake with raspberry mousse sandwiched between them. Dark chocolate ganache over it."

"Sold." Suzy pulled out her wallet. "You had me at cake."

Mrs. Sweet laughed as she placed the cake into a box then tied it with string. She took the package with her to the cash register. "I hope your friend likes it."

"Oh she will." Suzy handed her a credit card. She leaned against the counter. "Where's Megs? I haven't seen her lately."

"In the back, she's experimenting with a new recipe." Mrs. Sweet smiled, the pride showing in her face. "She's about ready to take over the business from me."

"Are you retiring? I can't imagine the Sweetheart without you."

Mrs. Sweet scoffed. "Not retiring, just stepping down so that Megan can take over. It's time."

"She's certainly learned from the best. And Kelly?"

Mrs. Sweet lit up. "Still in Nashville, trying to become a star. She only needs some time and then we'll be hearing her sing on the radio."

Suzy smiled and took her credit card back and tucked it into her wallet. "Well, some dreams take longer to find." She accepted the bakery box. "Thanks, Mrs. Sweet."

"How's the house coming?"

Suzy fought to keep the smile on her face. "It's at a standstill for the moment. A work in progress."

"Good luck. And if you need any help…"

Suzy held up the box. "This is a good start. Thanks."

She left the bakery and started down Main Street where she'd parked her car. A woman passed her, and Suzy recognized the familiar red jacket, the long wavy blond hair and large form.

Mama.

She veered from the direction of her car and followed the woman. It couldn't be, but there was something recognizable about the woman. She had to hurry to keep up with her. When the woman paused at the corner before crossing Main, Suzy kept her distance and watched her. She felt her body warm and her face flush, the prickling heat making her skin tingle. Mama was dead, but here she was walking in downtown Lake Mildred and waiting at a street corner.

The light changed, and the woman crossed the street. Suzy continued to follow her as she headed for Roxy's department store. She pushed through the front door, and Suzy rushed to touch the woman's arm. She turned to look at Suzy.

Oh. Not Mama.

Of course, not Mama. Because her mother was dead. She wasn't coming back. The joy she'd been feeling crumbled. "Sorry. I thought you were someone else."

The woman shook her head and continued into the department store. Suzy stared after her. She'd looked like Mama. Wore her red jacket. For a few seconds, she wanted to believe her mother had returned.

She stared down at the bakery box and saw that the string had cut into her hand. Breathe in, breathe out. Time to return to reality. She began to walk back to her car, but heard someone calling her name. She turned and spotted Tori.

Will's sister smiled and pushed a strand of hair behind her ear. "Hey, Suzy. How are you doing?"

Suzy opened her mouth, but didn't know how to answer. I thought I saw my dead mother. Your brother ruined my life. I think I'm going crazy? Nah, none of those worked. Instead, she shrugged. "Fine. I'm heading over to the hospital later to see your mom."

"Yes. Her chemo." Tori crossed her arms

just below where her name tag advertised
her place of employment. She glanced back
at the department store. "I saw you through
the front window and thought I'd come and
say hi. I haven't seen you since…"

Since that horrible day when she'd lost
Mama's house. "Right." She gestured at the
cake box in her hand. "Well, I gotta go."

Tori nodded, as if this meeting wasn't
more awkward than it was. "Yeah, I have to
get back." She took a few steps then turned
around. "If you need anything, I can always
help."

Everyone seemed to want to help, but what
use was it when you didn't know what you
wanted in the first place? She gave a faint
smile. "Thanks, Tori. I'll keep that in mind."

Tori smiled then walked back into Roxy's.

Suzy walked back to the corner then to
her car. She'd drop off the cake at Presley's
then go to the hospital. She had a date with
Mrs. Stone.

Suzy pulled the edges of her cardigan together as she walked down one corridor
then another to the chemotherapy treatment
room at the hospital. She signed in and indicated who she was there to visit with. A

few minutes later, a nurse in bright pink
scrubs showed her to where Mrs. Stone sat
in a lounge chair, already hooked up to an
IV. She smiled from ear to ear when she noticed her. "I wondered if you'd come see me
today."

"We had a date, right?" Suzy brought a
stool on wheels closer to her chair and placed
the orange gift bag she'd been carrying on
the floor at her feet before giving the older
woman a hug. "Nervous?"

Mrs. Stone shook her head, but her eyes
told a different story. "I'm a Stone. Didn't
you hear we don't get nervous?"

Right. Suzy glanced around the room. "Is
your daughter Carol still in town?"

"She's leaving today." Mrs. Stone frowned
and picked at the blanket that covered her
lap. "I wish she'd stay, but she's got to go
back to work."

"We all do what we have to." Suzy held up
the bag of supplies she'd brought with her. "I
brought us some surprises to pass the time."

Mrs. Stone leaned over to get a look, so
Suzy handed it to her. She pulled out puzzle
books, a romance novel, a big bottle of body
lotion and a fleece tie blanket in hot pinks

and purples. Mrs. Stone ran a hand along the fleece. "It's so soft."

Suzy stood and helped her drape the blanket over her legs. "I had someone at the fabric store teach me how to make it myself."

"I love it." She put the books back into the bag and held up the lotion. "But I'm curious why you think I need this."

"The toxins in the chemo can dry out your skin, so I thought it might help you." She took the bottle from Mrs. Stone. "If you'd like, I can put some on your legs and feet while we wait."

"I don't know."

Suzy put a hand on Mrs. Stone's arm. "I'd like to do this for you. It's something that I did for Mama, and to be honest I kind of miss it."

When Mrs. Stone nodded, Suzy pushed the blanket up from one leg then rolled up the leg of her pants. She squirted some lotion into one hand then rubbed both of them together before applying the cream to the older woman's legs. Mrs. Stone sighed and closed her eyes as she continued to moisturize first one leg then the other.

Once finished, Suzy pushed the blanket back down over her legs then rolled up a sleeve of Mrs. Stone's shirt before applying the lotion to her arm. Tears leaked from the woman's eyes, and Suzy stopped massaging her arm. "What's wrong?"

Mrs. Stone opened her eyes. "You are an angel. I don't know how to thank you."

"You don't have to. It's only lotion."

The older woman shook her head. "It's more than that." She wiped away the tears that continued to stream down her face. "So much more. Your touch means more."

Suzy waited until Mrs. Stone calmed down then applied the lotion to the other arm. "I used to think that I was supposed to be a veterinarian. That I was meant to care for the animals I love so much. But I must admit that doing this for you means a lot more to me than anything I've done since I've been out on leave." She looked at the older woman then moved to massage the lotion into her hands. "I've missed my patients. Especially you."

"You have a gift."

"No more than most in my profession." Once she finished with Mrs. Stone, Suzy used the lotion on her own arms and hands. "I've been rethinking everything lately, wondering if I was supposed to be doing something else. But maybe I'm right where I was supposed to be all this time. I've blamed Mama for my choices during these years. That she made me become a nurse. And move back to Lake Mildred. But I chose all that. And if it's brought me here, then they weren't the wrong decisions."

"You were thinking of quitting the seniors' home?" Mrs. Stone shook her head and grabbed Suzy's arm. "But you can't. We need you, dearie. We've missed you. I've missed you. You can't leave."

Suzy smiled. "Well if that isn't a reason to stay, then I don't know what is." She plucked up the gift bag from the floor where it had fallen. "I also put a deck of cards in there if you're interested in a game."

Mrs. Stone returned her grin. "Game on."

THE PAPERWORK NEVER STOPPED. Will initialed the section detailing the improvements the homeowner would need to make to bring the electrical system up to code. A shadow fell across his desk, and he looked up to find Rick standing in the door way. "Come on in, but should I be worried?"

Rick stepped inside and shut the office

door. Okay, so it was going to be that kind of a talk. "I wish I had better news."

Will's world tilted, and he took a deep breath. "The council?"

"They've decided to reduce your hours by half for now." Rick slumped into the chair across from Will. "We'll review the situation again in six months' time and make further recommendations then."

Oh. Will placed his pen on the desk and sat back in his chair. "In half."

"I'm sorry, Will. I fought for you, but I was outvoted."

"I know." He glanced at the paperwork waiting for his review. He was supposed to complete all of this in half the time? Plus make site inspections? "Well, at least I still have a job." He stood and held his hand out to Rick. "Thanks, man."

Rick frowned at him. "For what? Being the messenger of bad news?"

"For being upfront with me."

The two men shook hands, and an awkward silence took over the office. "When do they cut my hours?"

"Next week." Rick motioned to the stack of paperwork. "And I better not find out that you brought that home and did it on your own time. They want to cut you, fine. But the town council can figure out a way to handle things when you're not here."

"Sure." All this free time. He could only handle so much sitting in his mother's room at the seniors' home. And the four walls of his townhouse tended to close in on him the more hours he spent there. He needed a new focus.

Could he quit this job and find something else? He could start over at thirty-four. There were plenty of people who had. Changed their career path and found fulfillment on a different road. People out there needed his skills. This wasn't the end. Just a new beginning.

Will claimed his seat again behind the desk. "Hey, this could have been worse."

"I'll keep fighting to get you back to full time. I don't think they realize everything you did for the community."

"I guess they're about to find out."

Rick shifted in the chair and glanced around the office. "And if you decide to move on, I understand. I hope you don't, but I'd be happy to give you a letter of recommendation should you need one."

Leave a job that he loved? He couldn't,

but he did have bills to pay. "To be honest, I don't know what I'm going to do. I probably need to let this sink in some more."

"Seriously. If you need anything."

Will stood, and they shook hands again. Rick sighed then opened the office door. "And if you want to play hooky the rest of the day, I wouldn't blame you."

Now that's something he hadn't done in a long time. And once Rick had suggested the idea, the better it sounded. He turned back to his desk. That paperwork could wait until tomorrow. He grabbed his coat and keys then locked the door behind him. He walked down the stairs to the parking lot and his truck, unlocked the door and got in. Sat staring out the windshield and tried to come up with a plan. What would his dad say if he were here?

No. He wasn't going to play that self-defeating game again. He considered his options, a different future. He could almost hear his dad's voice. "Loser. Can't even hold on to his job."

Will shook his head. He loved it here, and if they only wanted him part time than that's what he'd give them. At least for now.

With careful planning, he wouldn't hurt

for money. He'd be fine. Get a second job, or third if he had to.

Or create an opportunity that had been just waiting for him. Someone still needed to head up the volunteers. To take on community projects that no one else wanted to do.

And the council would see that they needed him more. Some day.

He started the engine and turned up the radio, but didn't know where to go. Home? Nah, too quiet. See Ma? Later. He could think of only one place he'd like to see.

Within a few minutes, he pulled into the driveway at Suzy's house. Sam's truck was parked by the curb. Will walked up to the porch and knocked on the open door. The whine of a sander stopped, and Sam appeared from the hallway. "I'm not ready for inspection."

Will waved off his worries. "Not why I'm here." He glanced up at the ceiling where the crack had once been. He could almost reach it. "It looks great, man. You can't even tell where it was."

Sam nodded. "This hasn't taken as long as I expected. I should be done by the end of the week. Tuesday at the latest."

"I can't wait for Suzy to see this."

"She still doesn't know?"

Will shook his head. "Haven't found the right way to tell her. And I'm not sure she's going to be as happy as I'd hoped. I thought that I could fix it for her, but what if I've taken away the chance for her to fix it herself?"

"Could be there's no right way except to just say it." Sam motioned to the bedrooms. "Want to see what I've done down here?"

He gave Will the tour, and he could see how things would be once everything was repaired and painted. It would be better than new. He could see Suzy living here again. He only hoped he hadn't fixed himself out of the picture.

THE TINY COTTAGE was cute, but just that: tiny. It was little more than a glorified one room with a small bathroom. Still, it fit her equally tiny budget. Suzy looked at Pres then at her real estate agent, Dawn. "I don't know."

"Yes, it's small but there's potential." Dawn pointed at the open floor plan. "You're single without kids, so living here would keep things simple."

They'd have to be simple because there was no room for complicated. Suzy strolled to the kitchen area. It was a two foot square section of counter and a single sink. A refrigerator with a cupboard above. She looked around some more. "There's no stove?"

Dawn blanched. "But think of the great location. You're only steps from the beach." She led them outside where they could see a glimpse of the lake down a path of trees. "Picture yourself on this great deck, drinking margaritas and watching sunsets."

Pres glanced at Suzy. "She's getting me with the margaritas."

Suzy sighed. It would be nice to be able to wake up and go running on the beach. Or walking the shore at night with the moon shining down.

She turned and glanced back at the cottage. She could put a recliner near the big front window and let the kittens sleep there. A sofa bed or futon would give her comfort. Still, she shook her head. "I'm sorry, but I really can't see myself here. I think I need some place that has…"

"A bedroom?" Pres finished the sentence for her. "This doesn't scream Suzy."

"Then that answers that question." Dawn held up a sheet of paper. "There's another listing down the road. A little farther from the beach, but it might have the space you need."

She directed them back to the driveway where the agent's car waited. Suzy leaned against the car before getting in and tapped Pres on the shoulder. "What do you think? Am I making the right decision looking at houses?" She held up the spec sheet for the cottage. "And I can't even afford this."

Pres opened her arms as if to say the world was Suzy's oyster. "If it doesn't feel like you, then don't force it. It might be nice to come out here on the weekends and hang with you at the beach, but where would I sleep?"

"I can't stay with you forever either."

Pres reached out and touched her hand. "You can if you want. I really wouldn't mind."

But she couldn't. Wouldn't. She needed to find her own place, her own way. She might be lost but she couldn't depend on anyone else to find her. She had to do it herself.

Until then, it wouldn't hurt to look at other possibilities. Suzy opened the car door. "Let's go take a look at the one down the road."

THE HOUSE SEARCH resulted in a big zero, so they headed to the grocery store for supplies.

Suzy perused the fresh produce section trying to find a pumpkin that would be perfect to carve for Halloween which was only a week away. Hard to believe that after that, it would soon be Thanksgiving then Christmas and a new year. Where did the time go?

She picked up one pumpkin, but didn't like how light it felt. She wanted one that had plenty of seeds to roast and snack on. Another was squished in on one side, making it look lopsided. She tried a third but deemed it too small. Pres groaned behind her. "It's just a pumpkin."

"It's going to decorate your front porch, so it has to be perfect."

"I'm not asking for perfection." She leaned on the cart. "Um, Suze, I have to tell you something and I don't want to freak you out."

Suzy put the pumpkin back on the pile and picked up another. It felt right. She gazed at it from different angles. Looked round and except for a dent near the stem, it was near perfection. She looked up at Pres. "So tell me."

"It's about the kittens."

Suzy placed the pumpkin in the cart and pushed it towards the fruit section. She'd been craving bananas lately, and she'd eaten the last one that morning. She chose a bunch and put them in a plastic bag. "What about the kittens? Are they okay?" She glanced up at her friend. "They looked great the last time I stopped in."

Pres seemed anxious, yet nodded. "Some-one adopted them."

Oh. Suzy held on to the cart to steady her-self. Despite being homeless and not know-ing where she was going, she really had hoped to take them with her one day. "Did they at least go to a good family?"

"I think so."

"You think so? Didn't you check their ap-plication? Call their references?" Suzy tried to stop the panic from getting its claws into her. She took a deep breath. "I know you do a good job of finding the right homes, but are you sure this was the right one for them?"

Pres nodded again. "I was waiting for you to adopt them once you were ready for them, but I think they're going to be happy in their new home."

She hoped so. With all her heart, Suzy wanted them to find a family who loved them as much as she did. Another loss. "That's all I wanted for them."

Pres smiled at her. "Once you decide

where you're going to settle down, you can have the pick of my animals. I promise."

Suzy nodded, but she didn't feel it. She'd wanted those three cuddly kittens.

CHAPTER THIRTEEN

WILL SIGNED THE check and kept staring at it. He'd thought that fixing the house for Suzy would solve all their problems, but the closer it got to completion, the more he doubted it. She hadn't asked him to fix this, but he'd stepped in and done it like he always did. Tori and Ma had warned him, but he insisted he knew what was best. With reluctance, he handed the check to Sam. "I appreciate your speed on this project. It will mean the world to Suzy."

Sam nodded as he folded the check and placed it into his back pocket. "Thanks for this. It's one more step to expanding my business. Finding my dream."

"Mine too." Will shook Sam's hand. "If I hear of anyone needing a contractor, I'll recommend you."

"Thanks, man."

After Sam left the house, Will used his phone and dialed Suzy's cell. It went straight to voicemail, so he waited for the beep. Tried for a casual tone. "Hi Suzy, Will here. It's important that I speak to you as soon as I can in regards to your house. There's been a... development." He hung up before he could say too much.

The ball was in her court now.

He went from room to room, imagining all the little things that made a house a home. Towels. Pillows. Dishes. But then if he bought all that he'd be fixing things again, and he imagined that Suzy would be much better at making those decisions. She had a warmth and style about her that he didn't know how to reach within himself.

He was tired of his sterile townhouse. He wanted something with character and love.

He wanted Suzy decorating this home with just her presence. And bringing that into his life too.

THERE'S BEEN A DEVELOPMENT? Suzy played Will's voicemail for the fourth time. Okay, so she had to make a decision. Needed to figure out what she was going to do.

The thing was she knew what she wanted to do. Had known it all along. Losing Mama's house only showed her how much she wanted to keep it.

A few days ago, she'd contacted the bank manager. She had a little equity in the house, and he had confidence that she would qualify for a home improvement loan or mortgage refinancing. She'd hear something in a few days. It gave her options. Hope.

She dialed Will's number, and he answered it on the first ring. "Hey, thanks for calling me back. You busy?"

She glanced around at the stack of magazines that surrounded her. "Nothing that can't wait. What do you want?"

He cleared his throat. "I want to see you."

She didn't really want to see him though. "If you're asking what I want to do about the house, I've made my decision. But there's some things I need to take care of first."

"I know. But I was hoping we could get together and discuss some possibilities."

Possibilities? The only one that mattered to her was doing what she needed to do to get it back. To make it livable. And pretty.

And her own home.

"You want to meet right now?" It wasn't as if she had anything more important to do.

"Actually, there are some items that I need

to take care of before we get together. How's tomorrow morning?"

She still wasn't working, although Rita had called to tell her she was on the schedule for next week. Suzy told her that she'd love to come back. She missed her patients. And Page felt like it was time. "I'm free."

"Good. Me too."

She frowned. That didn't sound right. Not for Will. He was the nine to five kind of guy. "But it's a Wednesday. Don't you have to work?"

"Long story." He paused on the other end. Then his voice dropped to a whisper. "I miss you, Suze. Why don't we meet at the house?"

He wanted to go back to the house. But why? "Fine. Ten o'clock."

THE NEXT MORNING, Suzy searched through her few outfits and settled on a pair of jeans and a yellow sweater that reminded her of the color of sunflowers. She glanced in the mirror before she left. She looked almost normal.

She still had dark circles under her eyes. And she'd lost seven pounds since this had all started. Her curls actually lay in controlled waves, as if they'd lost their life when she'd lost the house. She sighed. But she wasn't losing anything. Not anymore. She'd made some choices, and it was time to act on them.

She jacked up the volume of the radio as she drove to the house. The familiar route lodged an ache in her chest. She'd longed to say good morning to Mr. Fletcher's cat and set out a plate of food for her. She'd missed her neighbor Shelley and her kids who always waved to her as they left for school and she came home from finishing a shift. She wondered what fundraiser she'd missed out on while she was at Presley's house. The kids in the neighborhood seemed to know when to hit her up for donations for their school.

When she got to the house, she saw that Will was already there, and the front door was ajar. She parked in the driveway behind his truck then took a few deep breaths before getting out and walking up the front walk. She poked her head in and frowned. Stepped back outside and checked the address.

Yep, it was Mama's house.

She stepped inside. But it wasn't Mama's house. Gone were the boxes of things. The stained carpet. The cobwebs in every corner of the living room. The crack on the ceiling had disappeared. As had the old sofa and coffee tables.

She shook her head. It was fixed.

Clean.

Beautiful.

The walls had been freshly painted pale yellow, and the carpet had been replaced with gleaming maple wood floors. Although there was no furniture, it still looked charming. Inviting.

Only one man could be responsible. She turned and found him standing in the front doorway behind her. "Surprise."

"Mama's things…"

"In storage until you can sort through them."

"The foundation?"

"Repaired."

She nodded and glanced around. Walked into the kitchen and ran a hand on the new butcher block counter. The appliances had disappeared as had the clutter. She looked at him before walking down the hall to Mama's bedroom. The door was closed, and she took a deep breath before opening it. The bed had a new comforter and sheets. The dresser cleared off except for a picture of Mama and herself on her graduation from nursing school. In the corner, three familiar fur balls slept on a large pillow. She smiled and scooped the smallest into her arms. She rubbed her face into his side. "Oh, how I've missed you."

She took the kitten with her and sat on the bed and looked up at Will. He braced his hands on either side of the door frame. "What do you think?"

She stroked the kitten's head and was rewarded with a rumbly purr. "I don't know what to say."

"Thank you is a start."

That was only the beginning of what she wanted, needed to say. "Thank you."

He stepped forward and opened the closet door. Inside hung Mama's clothes. Suzy placed the kitten on the bed and joined him at the closet, pulled out the red puppy sweatshirt. "You know I thought I would need this to remember her. But even when I was at Presley's, I could still feel her. Like she was watching over me."

He turned and gazed down at her. "I'm sure she was."

She clutched the sweatshirt to her chest. "No one can take away my memories of her."

"Right."

"You fixed this."

"I had help."

Suzy couldn't get over the room. The new bed. The kittens. "I don't know how long it will take for me to repay you for this. I mean, I don't have a lot. But whatever I have, I'll pay you back one day."

"There's only one thing you have that I want."

She looked up at him then placed her hand on his chest. "Then ask me for it."

"Before I do, you need to understand something." He stepped away and gestured to the room. "I didn't fix you. Yes, I hired someone to fix the house. I packed boxes and rented a storage unit." He paused for a beat, yet didn't look away. "But I can't fix you."

"I know."

He looked down into her eyes. "I am willing to help you find your way again though."

She took a few steps towards him. "You understand that I can't fix you either. But I'll stand by your side and help you through it."

They both took a few steps closer. He shook his head. "I can be too structured and serious."

"That means you'll make sure I'm safe and secure."

He smiled and reached out to touch one of her curls. She stepped back. "And I can be flighty and spontaneous."

"Which will bring joy to my life." He pulled her to him, tenderly, gently. "I love you so much it makes me want to smile."

She reached up and touched his cheek. "My favorite thing you do."

He smiled at her then lowered his mouth to hers. Tentatively at first then with certainty. She kissed him back, knowing she'd be doing that for years to come.

He broke away and rested his forehead against hers. She kissed his cheek. "Oh, how I've missed you too."

He pulled her tighter in his arms. "I'm thinking we should get married."

"Right now?"

Will laughed. "I'm not as impetuous as you. I need to take things slow."

"Slow." Suzy gave him a peck. "Will a month be enough?"

"I was thinking more like two weeks."

EPILOGUE

S_UZY_ TOOK THE plastic wrap off the bowl of potato salad and placed it on the kitchen counter next to the other potluck items. She smiled at her sister-in-law Carol, who chatted with Tori, then turned back to add a serving spoon next to her salad.

Connor, who'd been perching near the front door, stood and cupped his mouth. "They're here," he shouted.

Family and friends moved to gather around the front door as Eva walked in. They all held their breath until Eva raised her arms. "I'm clear! The cancer is gone."

Joyous claps and hoots filled the living room as Will followed Eva through the crowd. He helped her settle on the sofa then sought out Suzy. She gave him a smile, which he returned. He did that more often these days, a fact that she wouldn't take for granted. She needed those smiles as much as he needed her.

Her heart full, she wiped her first tears away, but then gave in to the emotion and let them flow freely. An arm came around her shoulders. She looked up at her husband. "The doctor was very encouraged by her test results. She's going to be okay."

"Did you tell her about our test results?"

Will shook his head. "This is her celebration." He slipped his arms around Suzy's waist and brought her closer to him. "We'll have plenty of time to tell her our news."

"Only thirty-four more weeks." She touched her still flat belly. "But plenty of time."

He kissed the top of her head, and left her to talk to Rick about the volunteer brigade's last successful project. Now that Will was back to work full-time with the town and she was going back to school to get her Master's degree in nursing, their lives felt very busy, but they always had plenty of room for each other. And now a baby.

Suzy glanced up at the ceiling. She still felt Mama's presence in her life even though her stuff had been cleared. And now this new family meant she'd never be alone again.

Yes, life was full of blessings.

* * * * *